"You haven't mentioned your birth mother in a while, Nicki."

Nicki's heart started to beat fast. "You said you'd let me know when you found out something, and I didn't want to nag you." Whenever she thought about never seeing her mom and dad again, she felt as if she was just going to curl up and die. Then she'd think about finding her other mother, and the scared feeling would go away a little bit.

"So, have you found out anything?" Nicki hoped it wasn't nagging to ask, since he'd brought up the subject.

"Not yet, but they're narrowing it down." He grinned at her. For an uncle, he was really handsome.

Nicki just had to know why her birth mother had given her away. She was afraid, sometimes, that Uncle Bryan thought it wasn't fair that he *had* to keep her, when even the woman who'd actually had her didn't want her.

She *knew* that he had to think it wasn't fair, 'cause Uncle Bryan had told Grandma he wasn't the marrying kind and he wouldn't make a good father.

Nicki thought he'd make the best dad ever, next to her own. She just wished he felt differently about wanting kids.

ABOUT THE AUTHOR

Tara Taylor Quinn first thought about writing *The Birth Mother* when she saw a commercial on television depicting a pregnant teenager advertising for a local adoption agency. According to Tara, "The teenager looked like Donna Reed's daughter, i.e., she was a very nice girl, and I thought, 'What if...?' I then went onto America On-Line and visited the adoption bulletin boards, which are public boards where people with a common interest can talk to each other anonymously. When I found myself sympathizing with all three parts of the adoption triangle—the child, the birth mother and the adoptive family—I *knew* I had a story to write."

Tara loves to hear from her readers. You can reach her at P.O. Box 15065, Scottsdale, Arizona 85267-5065.

Books by Tara Taylor Quinn

HARLEQUIN SUPERROMANCE

Tara Taylor Quinn
THE BIRTH MOTHER

Harlequin Books

TORONTO • NEW YORK • LONDON
AMSTERDAM • PARIS • SYDNEY • HAMBURG
STOCKHOLM • ATHENS • TOKYO • MILAN
MADRID • WARSAW • BUDAPEST • AUCKLAND

For Walter Wright Gumser, Sr.
I'll look at your wallet anytime, Dad...
I love you.

ISBN 0-373-70696-0

THE BIRTH MOTHER

Copyright © 1996 by Tara Lee Reames.

Printed in U.S.A.

ACKNOWLEDGMENT

Thanks to Kevin S. Reames for his technical support.
I'd buy my cars from you even if we weren't married.

SHE WITH A PAST

PROLOGUE

SHE WAS ALONE when she went into labor. But sixteen-year-old Jennifer Teal expected nothing else. In the ways that mattered she'd been alone since the day she was born, which was why she'd been so ripe for Tommy Mason's pickings. All he'd had to do was say he loved her...

The pain came again, gripping her lower body so tightly it squeezed the breath out of her. She pushed back into the couch, fighting the panic that wasn't far from the surface.

Her stomach muscles relaxed, and she tried to concentrate on the book she'd been reading. The pains were still almost ten minutes apart. She didn't want to call her parents home from work until it was time to go to the hospital.

The hospital. Tears sprang to Jennifer's eyes as she thought about the cold sterile place. Oh, please, little darling, please don't come yet. She rubbed at the huge mound of her belly, comforting the baby girl who'd stolen her heart the second she'd seen the barely discernible outline on the ultrasound film. She couldn't bear to think about what was going to happen.

The next pain froze Jennifer's tears as she concentrated completely on riding it out. She let the pain come, let it rip into her lower body. She wished desperately for someplace she could go to escape what had to happen, someplace where she didn't have to be afraid. She knew better than to wish she didn't have to face it all alone.

The pain faded and she thought again about calling the dealership to tell her parents it was almost time. But she didn't reach for the receiver. No. She was going to savor these last hours she had with the baby she loved more than she'd ever loved anything in her life. She was the only person in the world who wanted this baby—other than the couple who were out there somewhere, waiting, with a nursery set up, a whole wardrobe of tiny newborn clothes ready. Jennifer had never met them, didn't even know their names.

Worried that her water might break and soil her parents' couch, Jennifer took advantage of her reprieve from pain and hoisted her heavy body up. She didn't want to mess up the carpet, either, so grabbing her book and a pillow from her bed, she went into the bathroom. Using the wall as a brace, she slid down to the floor. If her water broke she could have it cleaned up before her mother got home. Not that Eloise Teal would be angry about the mess, but Jennifer didn't like to be any more of a hassle to her elderly parents than necessary.

The next twenty-one hours became something of a blur to Jennifer, remembered only in pieces of mind-robbing pain intermingled with snatches of blessed peace. The peace she took from her baby. For sometime during her pain-induced delirium she'd realized she wasn't the only one sharing the incredible experience. Her baby was with her one hundred percent of the way, through the phone call she finally made to her parents, the agonizing trip to the hospital sitting in the back seat of her father's used Coronado while her parents sat silently in front, the disappointment when, in the emergency room, her mother opted to stay with her father out in the waiting room.

Through the long hours of pain, the brief moments of relief, the times when medical personnel prepared her body for childbirth, and even during the minutes she attempted, unsuccessfully, to push the baby from her body, Jennifer's daughter was with her all the way. She wasn't alone, after all.

And then they injected her with something to knock her out. It was nighttime when Jennifer finally came to, when she learned the baby had been delivered by cesarean section, when she realized she'd been denied the few seconds after the birth to meet the tiny being she'd brought to life. She was no longer the mother. Another woman, a grown woman, was waiting for that right.

Jennifer wasn't even sure how much time had passed, what day it was. She wasn't sure it mattered. She didn't try to stem the tears that ran silently down her cheeks. There was no one there to see them. She hadn't known it was possible to feel so empty and still be alive.

She turned her head away as the door to her private room opened. She didn't want to see anybody.

"You having troubles sleeping, honey?" The soft words fell into the darkness.

Jennifer looked toward the nurse's shadowy figure walking toward her. She remembered her from the labor room. She was young for a nurse, and pretty, too. She'd been nice to Jennifer through those long agonizing hours.

"I can give you something to help you sleep or help with the pain if you need it, sweetie. You just say the word." The nurse lifted Jennifer's wrist, feeling for her pulse.

"Is my baby gone yet?" Jennifer asked. She was afraid to fall back to sleep. Afraid they were going to take her baby away while she was unconscious. Not that her being awake would make any difference; she just couldn't bear to think of sleeping through it.

The nurse's eyes filled with pity as she smoothed Jennifer's hair away from her forehead. She hesitated, as if she wasn't going to answer Jennifer, and then she shook her head.

"She's still here."

"Is she pretty?"

The nurse smiled, her knuckles rubbing Jennifer's shoulder. "She's beautiful, honey. And healthy as a horse. You did a great job. Now—" she stepped back and tucked the covers around Jennifer "—why don't you try to get some sleep, huh? The doctor said you get to go home tomorrow."

The thought panicked Jennifer. Not that she liked the hospital, but when she left, she'd never be near her baby again. She watched desperately as the nurse walked to the door of her room.

"Can I see her?"

The nurse stopped just inside the door. "You know it's against regulations, honey."

She didn't say no. "I haven't signed any papers yet. Doesn't that mean that technically she's still mine?"

The nurse moved quickly back to the bed, frowning. "You aren't thinking of changing your mind, are you? You're so young, honey, barely sixteen. What are you, a senior this year?"

"I'll be a junior when school starts, and no, I'm not going to change my mind. I just need to see her."

"It's not a good idea, honey, believe me. It'll be so much harder to give her up if you see her."

"Have you ever given a baby away?"

The nurse looked shocked. "No."

"Then how can you know it'll be harder? I'll tell you what's hard—lying here knowing my baby is only a few feet away and I can't tell her how much I love her. Doesn't she deserve that, at least? To know that even though her own mother is giving her away, she still loves her?"

"I'll tell her you love her."

Jennifer sat up, mature beyond her years, not only because of the past nine months but from a lifetime of trying to make life easier for her elderly parents. She'd never really been a kid. And especially not now.

"I need to tell her myself. I promise I won't change my mind. I just need to tell her goodbye. Is that too much to ask?" Jennifer's words dissolved into tears.

The young nurse hesitated, tears in her own eyes as she looked at Jennifer, and then she turned away. "I'll see what I can do, but you change your mind and it'll cost me my job."

She left the room, not giving Jennifer a chance to reply.

Jennifer tensed when her door opened fifteen minutes later and the young nurse crossed the shadowy room carrying a blanket-wrapped bundle. Jennifer's heart swelled till she thought it would burst.

Giving no thought to tomorrow, to an hour from then, she reached up to take her daughter in her arms. She was beautiful! And so soft and warm and sweet-smelling. Jennifer's arms trembled as she held her baby against her breast, where she belonged.

She was barely aware of the nurse hovering at the end of the bed as she studied the precious little face, soaking up a lifetime's worth of loving in those few brief moments. She wanted to unwrap the baby, see her tiny fingers and toes, actually touch the little feet that had been kicking her for so many months. But she was afraid to, afraid she'd make the baby cry.

So she just continued to hold her, smiling as she watched the sleeping infant. Suddenly, the baby stiffened, stretching her tiny legs and arms, and opened her eyes, those big blue eyes, to stare up at Jennifer. And then, just when she thought the baby was going to fall back to sleep, she stiffened again, and one tiny hand popped out of the baby blanket, flailing in the air until it caught Jennifer under the chin.

Jennifer reached for the little fist instinctively, raising it to her lips, kissing the soft, sweet skin. Then her daughter's mouth opened, and she turned her head toward Jennifer's breast.

The nurse came forward. "I need to take her back now, honey. It's time for her to eat."

Jennifer nodded, her eyes never leaving the child in her arms. "I love you, baby girl, I love you so much," she said, her whisper thick with tears. She lifted the infant, burying her face against the baby's warm neck—and kissed her daughter for the last time.

Please, God, just give her a happy, loving home, and I promise I'll never bother her again or go looking for her or anything. And I'll never have another baby to replace her or ever make love with a boy again, either. Not if you'll keep her happy for me. Please, God.

She sobbed as the nurse took her baby away from her, sobbed and hated herself for not being strong enough to fight them all and insist on keeping her child. Logically she knew she'd made the right decision, the only decision, by giving her baby to a loving couple who could provide a much better life for her than Jennifer could ever hope to.

But as she cried long into the night, Jennifer couldn't silence the part of her that said there were places she could go, places that would help, places designed to make it possible for unwed mothers to provide for their babies. If only she was strong enough.

A part of Jennifer died that night. The tender, vulnerable, young mother in her was slowly suffocated until all she had left to tell of its existence was the hospital birth picture the young nurse slipped to her just before she went off duty.

CHAPTER ONE

BRYAN CHAMBERS hadn't had sex in eight months. His chair, which he'd had tilted back on two legs, came down to the floor with a bang. Damn. Maybe that's what was bothering him. He stared at the little calendar lying on the side of his drafting table as if it would prove he was mistaken, as if he actually made a notation when he took a woman to bed.

He didn't collect notches on his bedpost, never had. Hell, until eight months ago, he'd never even owned a bedpost. But he'd always had his share of women.

Bryan pushed himself away from the sketches he'd been working on all morning, a campaign for one of his newest clients, a national soup company. He was too restless to be creative. He started to run his fingers through the hair at the back of his head, but stopped. It had gotten so long he was wearing it in a ponytail.

"Jacci!" he hollered, ignoring the intercom on his desk.

His secretary poked her head inside his door. "Yeah?"

"I'm outta here. If Wonderly calls, put him through on my mobile."

"Did you get the sketches done for tomorrow's meeting?"

He tidied the morning's clutter, shoving the Wonderly client folder into his sketchbook. "Nope."

"You want me to see if Calvin can give them a shot? The meeting's tomorrow at nine."

"I'll get them done." Bryan didn't need his partner pinch-hitting for him. And if Jacci wasn't such a damn good secretary, he'd fire her. She had a tendency to forget who was boss here. But he had to hand it to her. She'd lasted longer than any other secretary he'd ever had. What was it now? Six months? Seven?

"How long you been here, Jacci?" he asked, crossing to his supply cupboard to put away his charcoals.

"Since eight," she said, frowning as she watched him.

He frowned back at her. "Not today. How long you been with the company?"

"Going on two years. Why? Is it time for my raise?"

She had a point there. She probably deserved a raise after putting up with his moods these past months. She kept the office running like clockwork, too.

"Maybe. How much of a raise we talking about?"

She shrugged, naming an outrageous sum.

Bryan pulled his aviator sunglasses out of his shirt pocket and put them on. He shoved his calendar into the back pocket of his jeans. "If you'll settle for half that, you got it," he said, heading for the door with his sketchbook under his arm.

"What happens if I don't settle?" Jacci asked, following him out to her office.

"Then you're fired."

She sat down behind her desk and started typing on her computer keyboard as if she'd never been interrupted. "You really should carry a briefcase, you know," was all she said.

"Forget it," Bryan mumbled, heading outside into the bright Atlanta sunshine. Jacci's nagging irritated him almost as much as the thought of carrying a briefcase. He hated the trappings of conventionality, hated being tied down, even to a briefcase.

Which was why it was so strange that he was eager to get home. He'd never bought himself a real home, either, until eight months ago, always preferring to live in generic, though elegantly furnished, condominiums rather than tie himself down to a bunch of belongings that would make mobility difficult. But all that changed in the split second it took for a tornado to touch down in Shallowbrook. All that changed the minute he got Nicki.

"HEY, BOBBY, how's it going?"

"Just fine, Ms. Teal." The young mechanic smiled at her from beneath the Tempo hoisted up in his bay.

"And how about your boy? Is he completely recovered?"

"Yes, ma'am, he's back in school this week and bragging about the accident like he's a hero or something. My wife and I sure appreciate you being so understanding with me missing so much work this past month."

"I'm glad we could make things a little easier for you, Bobby. Now, how's Mr. Corales's car coming along?"

"Almost done. He won't find another thing wrong with this car, ma'am. Not unless he breaks it himself."

"Good. He's been more than patient with us. I want him happy."

"I can guarantee it, Ms. Teal," Bobby said, grinning at her as he stepped back beneath the car.

Jennifer continued on through the mechanic's bays behind Teal Ford, one of a half-dozen big sparkling dealerships in the Teal Automotive chain, taking in every last pristine detail as she exchanged pleasantries with her employees. She ran a good ship, an unusual ship, an honest ship. She was proud of that.

Reaching the last of the sixteen bays, she stopped. "Okay, Sam, what's wrong with her?" Jennifer's gaze was focused on the Caspian Blue Mustang convertible up on the mechanic's rack.

"I think it's the rear axle, Jen." The gray-haired man had his head buried underneath the car.

As soon as she'd noticed the clunking sound when she'd switched gears that morning, Jennifer had suspected that the internal gears in the rear axle were stripped, but she'd hoped she was wrong. "What about the U-joint?" She had to ask the question, though it was a waste of time. If Sam thought it was the rear axle, it was the rear axle. In the twenty-odd years she'd watched Sam Whitfield work, he'd never been wrong about a car. Which was why he was the only one she trusted near her Mustang.

Shrugging out of the jacket of her suit, she stepped beneath the car, as familiar with its underside as she was with the driver's seat.

"See this?" Sam grunted, tapping a length of U-shaped piping with his wrench.

Jennifer slid her fingers around the casing that connected the rear axle to the transmission, finding it as solid as it should be. "We're going to have to drain the transmission fluid, aren't we?" she asked. It was Friday, and she'd hoped to have her car over the weekend. She didn't like being without it.

"Yep. Be a sin to drive it like this."

Jennifer nodded, taking another cursory look before stepping back from under the car. She pulled a towel out of the dispenser on the wall of the bay and wiped the grease off her hands. She had an important lunch in less than an hour, and it wouldn't do to have dirt under her fingernails when she shook hands with the mayor. She needed the rezoning if she was going to get that lot next to Teal Chevrolet for her trucks.

Slipping into her jacket, she said to Sam, "Would you mind doing it tonight? I'll bring dinner just like—"

"I'll be here, Jen. Ain't I always?" he interrupted.

"Six o'clock okay?"

"Yep. And don't bring none of that Chinese crap, you here? A man's gotta have something more substantial than that if he's gonna keep going."

"How about a T-bone steak?" Jennifer asked, grinning at the old man encased in greasy overalls. No Teal Automotive uniform for Sam. He was still wearing the striped denim overalls he'd worn when he'd been the only mechanic here, back when her parents had started Teal Motors with only one small lot of used cars.

Sam cursed as his wrench slipped. "Burgers'd do."

"See ya at six," Jennifer said, making a mental note to call her secretary and ask her to arrange for a steak dinner with all the trimmings to be here at six o'clock sharp. Rachel knew just how Sam liked his steaks.

Jennifer was already looking forward to getting into the jeans and sweatshirt she had stashed in the trunk of the Lincoln she was driving today and joining Sam beneath her baby—the 1964 ½ Ford Mustang convertible she'd rescued eleven years ago. She couldn't think of a better way to spend a Friday night.

But first she had to convince the mayor that the deserted plot of land next to Teal Chevrolet would be much better suited to a truck lot than to the garbage- and graffiti-strewn crumbling foundation that resided there now.

"HEY, KID, YOU WANNA go up with me for a while? See the sunset? Go to Florida for some ice cream?" Bryan leaned against the doorjamb of Nicki's bedroom, trying not to worry that his niece was right where he'd left her that morning, lying on top of her bed. He knew she'd been to school. Not only because they were under strict orders to call him if she didn't show up, but because her book bag had been moved from the kitchen table where he'd left it after packing her lunch that morning. But she needed to be up out of bed for more than six hours a day.

"You don't have to take me. I'm big enough to stay home alone," she said, scooting up to a sitting position. Bryan watched her, frustration eating away at him. He knew she'd only made the effort to sit up for his sake. The minute he left the room, she'd lie right back down. Dammit, would she ever again have traces of the impetuous imp who'd stolen his heart more than eleven years ago? Did that child even exist in Nicki anymore? Or had she died right along with the rest of his family?

He wandered into her room, noticing how neat everything was. At least *that* was Nicky. "I don't want to go alone, sprite. What fun is ice cream if you don't get to share flavors?"

"But it's Friday night, Uncle Bryan, and you always said a Friday night without a date was like pizza without the cheese."

"I don't want a date, Nick. I want you. Won't you come?"

She sent him a look that said she was certain he was humoring her and she didn't need to be humored. But she slid off the bed.

"Okay. But if you really want to invite a date, instead, I won't care."

She wouldn't. And that was what worried Bryan the most. Nicky didn't care about much of anything these days. Not since the tornado had hit Shallowbrook eight months ago, wiping out half the town and an entire family, as well. Nicky's family. Nicky's and Bryan's. His parents, Nicki's grandparents, his sister and brother-in-law—Nicki's parents—and a mass of cousins and aunts and uncles. They'd all been having a cookout, celebrating Nicki's eleventh birthday. God knows why Nicki had chosen that moment to run inside to use the bathroom, the one room in the house without a window. Bryan only knew that when he'd rolled into the mass of rubble that had been his hometown, two hours late for the party, he'd found his niece, speechless and trembling, in the arms of the preacher's wife. That good woman had been the one to tell Bryan that Nicki was the only family he had left.

"YOU WANT TO TAKE HER for a while?" Bryan said into his headset an hour later, glancing at the child in the copilot's seat.

Nicki shrugged. "Nah." Her voice, coming to him through his earphones, was as lifeless as her eyes. There wasn't a hint of the glow he used to see when he took her up with him.

Bryan despaired as he looked out from the cockpit of his four-seater Cessna. Even flying didn't excite Nicki anymore. He was running out of ideas. Keeping a close watch on the myriad gages in front of him, he set a course for his favorite airport just inside the Florida border, remembering the first time he'd seen Nicki, the only child of his only sibling.

Though he'd been well liked in Shallowbrook, the son of the town doctor, he'd never found the small community to be the nirvana everyone claimed it was. To him, during the long years of his growing up, it had seemed like a prison. He'd always yearned for whatever was in the next meadow or over the next hill. Within Shallowbrook's slow-paced, if loving confines, he'd never been able to find the peace, the serenity that his parents and older sister had thrived on. He hadn't been content just to live his life; he'd wanted to shape it, to make it happen. By the time he'd graduated from high school, he'd felt like an explosion waiting to happen, and had hightailed it out of town as fast as his old Jeep could carry him.

But he'd never forgotten the family he'd left behind, never abandoned them. No matter how claustrophobic he got, he made a point to visit them several times a year. And always, after a few days in town, he was more than ready to return to his condo in Atlanta, to a city full of opportunities, instead of one so predictable it made him want to run naked in the streets just to see something different happen.

But he'd been in Shallowbrook the day Lori had brought Nicki home. He wouldn't have missed that day for anything. Half the town had turned out at his mother's house to welcome home the much-awaited newest addition to the Chambers-Hubbard clan. Just as they'd all grieved with Lori when she'd learned she couldn't conceive, they'd rejoiced with her as she'd walked up the front steps with her newly adopted daughter in her arms and happy tears streaming down her face.

And for once, as he'd taken his turn to peer down into the curious blue eyes of his infant niece, Bryan had felt magic, right there in Shallowbrook.

Recognizing the terrain below him, Bryan banked the plane, waiting for landing clearance from the control tower.

"What flavor you gonna have?" he asked the silent girl beside him.

Nicki continued to stare sightlessly out at the lush green Florida landscape, her earphones seeming to swallow up most of her head. "I'm not very hungry."

"Chocolate, huh? I thought so."

That brought her eyes to him, if not a smile. "I really don't need any, Uncle Bryan."

"No one *needs* ice cream, Nick. It's a treat. So, you want two scoops or three?"

He received clearance from the tower and headed in.

"One," Nicki said wearily, closing her eyes on his spectacular landing. Bryan felt completely helpless as he glimpsed the tear that slid slowly down her pale young cheek.

"IT'S RISKY, Jennifer."

"Yeah."

"So why mess with a good thing? We're not in high school anymore. You don't have anything more to prove."

"You think that's what this is? Me proving something? To whom?"

"I don't know, Jen. Your parents maybe."

"They're dead, Dennis."

"Okay, maybe to yourself. But you don't have to do this. You're an incredible success. The business could run itself you have it so well established. Why would you want to screw that up?"

"I don't happen to think One Price Selling will screw that up, but if it does, that's a risk I'll have to take. As soon as I find the right agency to help me, I'm launching One Price Selling."

Dennis Bradford looked hurt as he fell back into the padded leather chair behind his desk. "What am I, vice president in name only? My opinion doesn't count?"

Leaning her hands on the front of his desk, Jennifer looked him straight in the eye, imploring him to understand, just as he always had. "Your opinion matters more to me than anyone's. I wouldn't be here, or probably anywhere else for that matter, if not for you. I need your support on this, Dennis."

He watched her silently for several long moments. "I need to know why, Jen."

"Because it's right." She sat down in the rich blue armchair in front of his desk. "We run an honest business here, which has a lot to do with our success. But One Price Selling is the step beyond that could make Teal Automotive more than just a successful business. It could make us great."

"It'll give your competitors a golden opportunity to eat you alive."

"Which is why we need the best ad agency this city has to head them off."

"It won't matter, Jen. Either way, we stand to lose. You may sell the idea to the public—hell, I'm sure you will—but as soon as some of the shysters in this business start doing the same, or *say* they're doing the same, it'll tarnish the whole thing. You'll begin to look like all the others, just peddling some new gimmick."

"But that's just it! It's not a gimmick. We'll have price tags on every car showing the factory list price and the lower Teal Automotive price right next to it. No haggling, no hard selling, just a fair honest price, take it or leave it. It's just what the automotive industry needs."

"In theory, I agree with you one hundred percent. But what happens when everyone else starts saying they're doing the same thing, but instead of following through in good faith, they jack down a trade, or make the 'fair' price a different price for each customer who walks in the door? We're right back to the same old way of doing business, and we've cheapened ourselves by gimmick-selling."

"The difference will be that every customer who walks onto a Teal lot will get the same fair price for his trade and for his purchase. No exceptions. Period. If I've built the reputation you say I have, people will give me a chance to show them *I* mean what I say."

"You're not going to budge on this, are you?"

"I can't, Dennis."

"Still paying for past mistakes?"

Jennifer smiled. "Nothing so melodramatic as that, my friend. I just want to do things right."

"This doesn't have anything to do with a certain birthday coming up, does it? You always push a little harder this time of year."

"I resent that, Dennis. I'm not going to make a business decision as important as this one on the basis of past pain."

Dennis studied her silently for a moment, then nodded. "Okay, Jen, but we better hope there's a damn good advertising man willing to take this on."

"We'll find one. But I need you behind me, too. Not only for the support, but for a lot of the decision-making, as well. We're going to have to retrain our entire management and sales team, come up with a pay-plan alternative to the straight-commission policy we now run under, choose new incentive programs..." She grinned at him.

Dennis came around his desk and pulled Jennifer up out of her chair. "You know I'm behind you, Jennifer. I always have been. If this ship goes down, we'll be swimming for shore together."

Jennifer squeezed his hands, telling him with a look all the things she couldn't say, before heading toward the door of his office.

"Oh, Jen, I almost forgot. Tanya wanted me to ask you to come for dinner tomorrow night before the city-council meeting. She needs your opinion on her newest creation."

Jennifer turned with her hand on the door and smiled at him. "Her paintings are selling for thousands and she needs *my* opinion? Your wife has a screw loose, Den."

"So you'll come? She's already phoned twice today, nagging me to ask you."

Jennifer thought of the pixie-faced four-foot-nine-inch woman she'd brought home from college one summer several years ago with the express purpose of fixing her up with Dennis. "Yeah, I'll be there."

She was still smiling as she walked down the hall of executive suites to the door marked President. She was lucky to have such good friends.

CHAPTER TWO

"CAN I TALK TO YOU, Uncle Bryan?"

Bryan's heart hammered as he spun away from the layout he'd been mulling over for most of the evening. Nicki was instigating a conversation?

"Sure, sprite, whatcha need?" *Anything. I'll give you anything. Just tell me what.* In the week since their impromptu trip to Florida, he'd barely been able to coerce her out of her room for dinner.

"My mother."

He stared at his niece. Had she gone over the edge? Had she forgotten Lori was dead? Blocked the whole tragedy from her mind? The doctor had mentioned the remote possibility of such an extreme reaction, but Bryan had thought they'd passed that point months ago. *Come on, Nick, hang in there,* he silently implored her. *We'll get through this together if only you'll let me help.*

"We can head to Shallowbrook first thing in the morning, hon. But we just visited the cemetery two weeks ago. You sure you wouldn't like to go shopping or something, instead?"

Nicki slid into an armchair, her skinny body barely filling half the seat. "I mean my *real* mother."

"Lori *was* your real mother." Bryan's words came out more sharply than he'd intended. He felt as if he was soaring over the Rockies in a plane whose engine had just died.

Nicki didn't budge. Her long auburn hair lay around her bony shoulders like a cloak as she stared at her fingers, fidgeting with them in her lap. "I want to find the woman who had me," she whispered.

He froze, on his way to a crash and burn. He wasn't prepared.

"I don't think you can do that, Nick. They have laws against stuff like that." *Why, Nicki? You're Lori's baby. And now mine.*

She looked up at him, her hazel eyes pleading. "I think you can do it now sometimes. They have places you can go to find out."

Her look tore at Bryan, making him wish he were Superman. There was nothing he wouldn't do for this child. But find her biological mother? The woman whose blood ties made Nicki more hers than his? The woman who'd given her away? He kneeled down beside her, sandwiching her thin cold hands between his own.

"I don't think it's that easy, honey. Adoption records are sealed. What you're talking about is when someone *wants* to be found, there's a place where they can register their names and give pertinent information."

Nicki's eyes were almost determined as she looked at him. "We have to go to that register, Uncle Bryan. Maybe she's there. Maybe she's been looking for me and we don't even know it."

"And maybe she isn't, Nick. Why set yourself up for disappointment? I know how much you miss your mother. Hell, I miss her, too. But she's still your mother in here—" he tapped her rib cage "—and she always will be. That's the way the woman who gave birth to you wanted it, honey.''

Nicki looked down at their clasped hands. "She coulda changed her mind.''

"That's not the way adoption works, honey. It's for keeps. She would've known that when she gave you up.''

"But what if she *did* change her mind? What if she wants me?''

"*I* want you, Nick. We're doing okay together, don't you think?''

Nicki looked at him again, her eyes swimming with tears as she nodded. "I just gotta know who I am,'' she whispered, her young body tense as if begging him to give her this, to move mountains if need be to find her missing link.

It was just another of life's ironies that the one thing in which Nicki expressed interest in the eight months since she'd come to Atlanta was the one thing he didn't want to give her. But, looking into her eyes, Bryan knew he had no choice.

"I'll see what I can do.''

Nicki smiled at him through her tears. The first real smile he'd seen in eight long months. He hoped to God he was doing the right thing.

JENNIFER SMILED her goodbyes to Ralph Goodwin, the general manager of Teal Pontiac, and his wife at the door of the Teal Automotive suite in Hawk's Stadium. She felt good. The Hawks had won in overtime. It had been a great game. And she'd just gained Ralph's support for One Price. He hadn't been nearly as hard to convince as Dennis two weeks before. He hadn't even asked why. But then, he didn't know her as well as Dennis did.

She was still smiling when she pulled her Mustang into the parking garage below her luxury apartment building an hour later. It felt good to be home. She'd been out every night that week, and as much as she loved the socializing that went with her job, she was looking forward to a long soak in the Jacuzzi she'd had installed in her master bathroom. Taking a moment to exchange a few words with the doorman about the Hawks' victory, she entered the elevator, inserted her key and pushed the button for the penthouse apartment.

Yeah, Ralph had been a much easier sell than Dennis. And tomorrow night she'd tackle Frank Dorian, the GM of Teal Ford. She was going with him and his wife to the Peachtree Celebrity Cook-off where they were going to prepare pots and pots of Celia Dorian's chili in an attempt to raise money for the city's homeless. Celia was a quiet woman, kind of reminding Jennifer of herself in an earlier day, back before she'd figured out that more people liked her if she reached out to them. She'd discovered a whole new side to herself, a happier side, when she'd learned to be a little more outgoing. She'd also found out that a talkative gregarious teenager had much less chance of hearing the voice in her head than a quiet introspective one.

But that time in her life was long behind her. There was only so much grieving a body could do, only so much self-loathing. The past was sealed as tightly as the records that gave proof to it.

Soft lights were glowing in the foyer as she let herself in, and Jennifer took a moment to soak in the calm cool atmosphere of her spotlessly clean, professionally decorated home. She'd surrounded herself with the same blue-and-white color scheme that was found in all the Teal Automotive offices and showrooms.

Leaving the lights on, she headed across the plush white carpet to the master suite. She'd check messages in the morning. Right now she just wanted that soak.

And some music. The house was too quiet. Backtracking, she slipped her original recording of Rogers' and Hammerstein's *Sound of Music* into her compact-disc player. And then ejected it. Not that one. Too many children. She glanced down the rack. *Oklahoma* was too much of a love story, *Carousel* too noisy, and *The King and I* too surreal. Irritated by her indecision, she grabbed the double CD set of *Phantom of the Opera*, dropped the discs into the player and jabbed the play button. *Phantom* suited her mood. The phantom was in control. He lived alone. He didn't fall in love and live happily ever after. And he was fiction.

Taking one more detour, Jennifer poured herself a glass of chilled white wine before finally heading for the bedroom. She hadn't been so restless in ages. She assured herself that it meant nothing, that with the deliberate fullness of her calendar over the next few weeks, the feeling would pass.

She'd make sure of it. She didn't have time to be sidetracked. Not even for a second. Because the byroads she traveled were all the same—they led to the same deserted place. She'd spent years learning how to stay on course; she was not going to let The Day, which was looming, send her hurtling back, not like it had last year.

But she took her wallet with her when she went into the bathroom. She laid it on the marble vanity as she brushed her teeth and removed her makeup. Routine. Control. They served her well. Detours did not.

She meant to undress, to take her wine and step into the tub. But Christine's hauntingly beautiful voice floated to her from her built-in sound system. Christine. The Phantom's one true love. *Think of me... Remember me...*

Jennifer froze, her eyes glued on her wallet. Slowly, as if of its own accord, her hand reached for the wallet, unfastened it, her fingers searching unerringly beneath her health-insurance card. She slid the battered hospital photo out of hiding and gazed at it. *Remember me...* It never got easier. It never got better. Never.

THE WOMAN hadn't signed up with any register. At least none in the state of Georgia. Bryan didn't know whether to be glad about that or not. He only knew he had a knot in his stomach that wouldn't go away.

He couldn't leave it like that. He couldn't just tell Nicki that her biological mother hadn't even thought of her enough to register in the slim chance Nicki might be looking. But he also knew, considering the fact that the woman was making no effort to be found in these times of open adoption, that chances were good she wasn't going to be receptive to having her eleven-year-old castoff suddenly show up in her life— if and when he did find her. Nicki wasn't strong enough to handle that. And maybe the woman had a right to her privacy. Not sure what he was going to say, he walked slowly toward his niece's room.

She was sitting on her bed, brushing her hair. Just brushing it. Over and over. The new fashion magazine he'd brought home for her lay unopened beside her. At least she'd carried it that far. He was pretty sure the last one had never made it off her desk.

"Hey, Nick, can we talk?"

She looked up, her hazel eyes filled with alarm. "What?"

For the life of him Bryan couldn't understand that look. He'd been seeing it more and more often lately. He understood Nicki's grief, but what in hell did she have to be afraid of? He stayed in her doorway.

"I did what I promised. I looked for your biological mother in the registries."

"Did you find her?" Nicki's face lit up; the knot in his stomach grew tighter.

"She wasn't listed, Nick."

She looked away and went back to brushing her hair. "Oh."

Bryan entered her room and sat down beside her. It was tearing him up to see her hurting. "Maybe it's best this way, honey."

She shrugged—and then sniffled. *Hell.*

"She loved you enough to give you a good life, Nicki, but in doing so, she had to say goodbye to you. That had to have been a really hard thing, going on with her life without you. But if she hadn't, you wouldn't have had your mom and dad, or your grandma or grandpa, or me. We need to be really thankful to her for giving you to us. And maybe the best way to thank her is to leave her alone. If she's gone on with her life, made her peace with the past, said her goodbyes, then she has the right to continue as she is. That's the right *she* got when we got you."

Nicki started turning the pages of the fashion magazine.

Lori, help me out here. What in the hell do I do now?

"You said you needed to know who you are, but you don't need to find some stranger to know that, sweetheart. You're Nicki Hubbard, the little imp who stole my heart the first time I ever laid eyes on you."

Her lips twitched, almost smiling, but she still wasn't looking at him.

"We're a team, Nick, you and I. You're all the family I have left in the world. You just stick with me and we'll come through this. I promise."

She glanced up at him, but didn't look convinced.

"Have I ever let you down before?"

She shook her head.

"Remember the time you wanted to go on that roller coaster that went upside down and your mother wouldn't hear of it?"

She nodded.

"Who came through for you? Who explained the physics that convinced her to let you go? And then held your hair back when you threw up afterward?"

Nicki did grin then. "You did."

"That's right. And who helped you out that year you wanted to surprise your mom and dad with a new puppy for Christmas?"

"You did."

"And what about that birthday party when Miss Debra What's-her-name was inviting all your friends to her party at the same time you were having yours— and was promising them a magician if they'd come. Didn't I come through for you then? Taking all those little girls up in my plane so they'd come to your party?''

She nodded, but her eyes were getting cloudy again. *Damn. I'm losing her.*

He took her brush and turned her back to him, pulling the bristles through the thick chestnut locks. "Have I ever lied to you, Nick?''

"Uh-uh." Her voice was so soft he could barely hear it.

"So trust me, honey. I said we'll make it just fine, you and me, and we will. I know I can't take Lori's place, or your dad's, either, but I love you with everything I've got." And they *would* make it, no matter how penned in he might someday feel, because he'd die before he let Nicki down.

She sniffled again. "I love you, too, Uncle Bryan..."

He continued brushing. "But?"

Her thin shoulders lifted in a shrug. "But who gave me my hazel eyes? Mom's were brown like yours, and so were Dad's. And what about my hair? No one in the family has red hair."

"Neither do you. It's auburn." *Great answer, Chambers. Way to come through.*

"And what about how tall I am? Mom and Grandma were both short."

"And what about your ability to see the good in people? Even when old Debra What's-her-name tried to steal your party, you still invited her. You said she'd only done it because she was lonely and wanted friends. Remember? You used to do stuff like that all the time, Nick, and you know why? 'Cause that's how your grandma was. It used to drive me and Lori crazy when we were growing up 'cause anytime we complained about anything she'd find something good about it. You know how hard it is to get riled up when everything's so rosy?''

Nicki turned around, nodding, a sad little smile flitting across her lips.

Bryan tapped the brush against the fashion magazine in her lap. ''You've always been interested in dressing well, and that came straight from your mother. As long as I can remember Lori claimed that just because she lived in a small town didn't mean she couldn't look as good as the girls on TV. And your love of science? That came from your grandfather. I can remember when you were about a year old, barely walking, and he had you up on the kitchen counter, showing you how he could mix things together and make them fizz. You used to make him do it over and over, until Lori finally complained about him wasting all her cooking ingredients.''

''Did he stop?''

''Of course not.''

''Did Mom get mad?''

''What do you think?''

''Uh-uh.''

''You're right, she just stood there and watched right along with you. And look at this room, Nick. You've always kept things neat. Just like your dad. He made a game out of picking up your toys with you when you were still a baby. When he played with you he'd race you to see who could put away one toy first before getting out another. By the time you were three, you were driving your mother crazy insisting she put the lid back on the shampoo *before* you'd let her wash your hair.''

Bryan thought of his sister, how happy she'd been every day of her life after she got Nicki, what a great mother she'd been. He felt that familiar pang, the crushing weight he got every time he thought of his family. God, he missed them.

"But...but what about other things?" Nicki's tentative question interrupted his thoughts. She was crying again. "You know, like medical stuff you can get? Diseases and things. And maybe..."

"Maybe what?" He was brushing for all he was worth.

"Maybe other stuff, too. What if my mother was crazy or something and that's why they gave me away? What if I take after her?"

Bryan was beginning to get the picture and he didn't like it one bit.

"You're not crazy, Nick. And I'll find her if I have to, just to prove it to you."

IT TOOK SIX WEEKS and a professional search consultant, but Bryan finally had Nicki's answer. Or at least he thought he did. He sat in his office after hours on Thursday, Nicki's packet in front of him, and knew he could no longer put off opening it. It was stupid to feel threatened by a few pieces of paper. Knowing the name of Nicki's biological mother wasn't going to change anything. Nicki was his legally, and every other way that counted. He wasn't going to lose her. He couldn't. She was his family.

He opened the packet, read for a few minutes, then stared. He couldn't believe it. According to these reports, Nicki's mother was Jennifer Teal. *The* Jennifer Teal. Of Teal Automotive.

Everyone in Atlanta who watched television or listened to radio had heard of Jennifer Teal. Her ads were memorable if for no other reason than Ms. Teal claimed to be an honest car dealer. And judging by her success, Bryan figured she might just be.

Or else she had one hell of a sales staff.

Balancing on the back two legs of his chair, Bryan shuffled through the forms until he found Nicki's original birth certificate, listing Jennifer Marie Teal as the mother. No name was listed for the father. Nicki had been born at one in the afternoon. Her mother's birthdate was...Bryan read the date, then looked again, doing some quick calculations. Good God, she'd been barely sixteen when she'd had Nicki, which would have made her barely fifteen when she'd conceived. That was just four years older than Nicki was now.

His chair came down with a crash and he reached for the phone.

"Sandra, Bryan Chambers here. Sorry to bother you at home, but I was just going over these papers."

"Yes, Mr. Chambers." The search consultant's tone was as sympathetic as it had been for the entire six weeks she'd been working for him.

"How sure are you that these records are referring to *my* Nicki?"

"Quite sure, Mr. Chambers. As you can see, the original birth certificate matches Nicole's modified one exactly, with your sister and her husband's names inserted for Ms. Teal's as the parents. And the other documents support the same findings. Ms. Teal signed the adoption papers that were on file with the state, giving custody of Nicole to Lori and Tom Hubbard."

Bryan nodded. "Thank you, Sandra. You did a great job."

"I'm glad I could help. Have you thought of how you're going to approach Ms. Teal? Assuming that you are, of course. I'd suggest a letter of introduction to begin with. That usually works best, giving everyone a little time to get used to the idea before actually meeting face-to-face."

"Thanks for the advice. I'll think about it." Bryan rang off.

He didn't want to write to Ms. Teal. He didn't even want to accept her existence. But Nicki did. His niece was showing no signs of picking up her life. Bryan had called the counselor he and Nicki had seen right after the tornado, and she'd been concerned enough to speak with Nicki again. Nicki had gone because he'd asked her to, but the session had done no good. It was up to Nicki now. Nicki and him. And hadn't he promised her, promised himself, as he'd seen his family's caskets laid in their graves, that he'd do whatever it took to take care of Nicki?

But he couldn't just introduce Nicki to her birth mother. Not yet. Not until he'd met the woman, assured himself he wasn't setting Nicki up for another blow. Until he was certain Ms. Teal wasn't going to reject Nicki, he was going to keep the fact that he'd found the woman to himself.

And until he was ready to let Nicki know about Ms. Teal, he couldn't tell Ms. Teal about Nicki, either. Not until he was certain he could trust her with the information. Which meant he was going to have to orchestrate a meeting between himself and Ms. Jennifer Teal. He reached for the phone again. He needed all the information on Jennifer Teal he could get.

DENNIS POPPED his head around the door of Jennifer's office late one Tuesday afternoon. "Tanya wants to know who you're bringing to her opening a week from Friday, because if you don't have a date yet, she knows someone who would love to take you. And before you even suggest it, she says she absolutely won't allow you to come alone because then you'll leave early, and she hates it when you do that."

Jennifer looked up from the customer letter she was reading and smiled at him. "So who does she have picked out for me this time? Let's see, we've done a stockbroker, two doctors, an accountant, three attorneys, and wasn't there a professor of something in there once? What's left?"

Dennis shrugged. "Who knows? But you can bet he's cover-model material and ready to settle down. You know as well as I do Tanya's not going to rest until someone is sharing that 'big lonely penthouse you go home to every night,'" he said, mimicking Tanya.

"Yeah, well, tell your wife to quit her matchmaking or I'll bring Sam, and the closest thing he has to a suit is a semiclean pair of overalls."

Dennis raised both hands in the air. "Hey, she was your friend before she was my wife. You deal with her," he said.

"She never listens to me," Jennifer replied, hoping that one of the men she dated occasionally would be free to escort her to the opening. Because the men Tanya chose for her all had one major flaw. They were ready to get married. And she wasn't—not yet.

JENNIFER CONGRATULATED herself on her choice of dates. He was charming, intelligent—and no readier to settle down than she was. The fact that he'd left early to attend to a problem at his plastics plant, a problem that could probably have waited until morning, was his only drawback. Having promised Tanya she wouldn't leave early, Jennifer was left without an escort for the rest of the evening.

"Interesting painting."

Jennifer glanced over her shoulder at the man standing just behind her and nodded politely before turning back to the painting she'd been considering.

"Tanya said you were an expert on her work. She thought you might be willing to show me around."

Damn. Apparently she'd underestimated Tanya's determination. Because if Tanya had sent this man over to her, it could only mean one thing—he was her newest marriage candidate. Trust Tanya to have him around tonight just in case.

Jennifer wondered where she'd found this one.

He was gorgeous, with his deep brown eyes and strong chin that jutted just enough to give him character without being obnoxious. And the clothes he was wearing definitely fit his body to perfection. While they weren't as formal, even with the tie, as the occasion demanded, they were courtesy of one of Atlanta's more expensive tailors, according to the label on his pocket. And he had a ponytail. She looked back at the painting she'd been studying, ignoring him. She was going to get Tanya for this.

"Kind of thought-provoking isn't it?"

His voice did things to her he should be ashamed of. "It's supposed to be."

He stepped forward, just as Dennis's senile old aunt came wandering around the corner.

"Oomph!" Aunt Abigail exclaimed as she careered into Jennifer's handsome companion, dumping the contents of her purse all over the floor in the process.

The man was on his haunches before Jennifer was even sure what was happening, helping the flustered old woman gather her belongings. Jennifer bent down, as well, retrieving a lipstick that had rolled to the wall.

"Where you headed, Auntie?" Jennifer asked, concerned that the woman was on her own. The members of the Bradford family took turns keeping Aunt Abigail in their homes and included her in everything they did. They also never let her out of their sight.

"Oh, Jennifer, it's you," the old woman said, patting her breast as she smiled at Jennifer, obviously relieved. "Dear me, where did all this stuff come from?" She was kneeling down beside the man, holding her purse open while he deposited the various notes and hankies that Aunt Abigail always carried back inside.

"I think that's it," he said, the tenderness in his voice doing strange things to Jennifer.

"I dropped my purse, you know," the old woman said, as if he hadn't been there to see the whole thing. "I came around the corner looking at one of dear Tara's pictures. Such a sweet girl Dennis married. Dennis is my nephew. The son of my only sister's daughter, Abigail the second. She was named after me, you know. He's quite a fine lad, don't you think?" she asked, turning to Jennifer.

"He's the best friend I've ever had," Jennifer said, as if it was the first time she'd told the old woman that. Truth was they had this same conversation every time they saw each other. Aunt Abigail's memory was almost nonexistent, but she always remembered that Jennifer was somehow associated with the family through Dennis.

Tanya's marriage prospect glanced at Jennifer over Aunt Abigail's head, his dark eyes full of understanding. Jennifer looked back at the old woman, willing her heart to settle back to its normal pace.

"I think that's everything, Auntie," she said, rising. The man helped the old woman to her feet, holding her gently by the shoulders until she steadied herself.

"Thank you, young man. You're a true gentleman. I must say." Aunt Abigail held up her wallet, opening it with slightly unsteady hands. "I'll bet you've never seen this before, have you."

"I don't believe I have," the man replied.

Jennifer watched him, impressed with his patience. Aunt Abigail went through phases where she had her wallet out every few minutes, looking through it and trying to show its contents to whichever family member was closest.

She pulled out a plastic card. "See this? It says Abigail Swenson. That's me."

The man nodded. "That's your health-insurance card. A good thing to have."

The old woman preened under his praise, pulling out a driver's license that was no longer valid.

"That's me, too," she said, pointing to the name printed there. "Abigail Swenson, it says. But what's this?" she asked, frowning at the little plastic card.

"It's your driver's license, Auntie," Jennifer said.

"Oh, yes, yes it is. My driver's license. Issued by the state of Georgia, see? Did you know they won't let me drive anymore?" she asked, looking at the man.

"I didn't know that," he said, "but I can see where it has its advantages. You don't ever have to be designated driver that way."

Aunt Abigail giggled. "I never thought of that. I like you. You're a smart young man—"

"Oh, there you are, Auntie. I've been searching all over for you!" Dennis appeared around the corner, looking relieved.

"You worry too much, dear boy. I was just making the acquaintance of Jennifer's young man."

"Sorry, Jen," Dennis said, nodding briefly at the man standing beside Jennifer as he led his aunt away. If Jennifer had needed any confirmation that the stranger was one of Tanya's handpicked marriage contenders, she'd just had it. Dennis hadn't been able to escape fast enough.

"I guess I'll go look around. Care to join me?" the man asked. *Damn.* That ponytail interested her more than it had any right doing.

"No, but thanks. I was just leaving," she said. Okay, so she was a coward, but getting involved with a gorgeous man who wanted to settle down was pointless when Teal Automotive was consuming so much of her life. And men with marriage in mind were the only type Tanya ever sent her way. *Damn.*

BRYAN STOOD in the gallery watching Jennifer Teal walk away. He'd never liked society functions, but this one had him more on edge than most. He was a little too warm, his heart beating just a little too fast. And his tie was suffocating him. He desperately wanted to rip it off and get some fresh air, and not just because of the melodious voice still ringing in his ears. He'd just met Nicki's mother. That was all that mattered to him.

Impatient with the time it was taking the private detective he'd hired to find him an in, he'd decided to attend tonight's opening as soon as he'd read about Jennifer Teal's expected presence at the gallery in the morning paper. He'd thought he'd missed her until he'd accidentally bumped into the diminutive artist, Tanya Bradford. That good lady, while involving him in a recitation about one of her paintings, had pointed Ms. Teal out to him, simply because Ms. Teal had been standing in front of the piece in question.

She'd surprised him. He'd expected her poise, her wit, even her intelligence. He just hadn't expected to find her so attractive. He hadn't expected to like her.

Bryan caught a glimpse of the old woman who'd bumped into him earlier across the room. Auntie, Jennifer Teal had called her. And suddenly, seeing Ms. Teal not only as Nicki's birth mother but as a woman with a family, made him feel guilty as hell about what he was doing. Barging into a beautiful woman's life with an agenda of his own, fully knowing he might hurt her. It wasn't his style, but then neither was a home, possessions, the tie he was wearing. But for Nicki...

Jennifer Teal might not look like anybody's mother, but he knew better. Loosening his tie, he turned to go. Nicki was depending on him.

CHAPTER THREE

JENNIFER STILL HADN'T found her man. She and Dennis had interviewed people from more than fifteen advertising agencies in the two weeks since Tanya's opening, both local and out of state, and though several had seemed promising, not one had fully understood what she was trying to do.

Most of the ideas she'd seen would sell One Price to the public. But she didn't only want to sell One Price. She wanted to sell integrity. She needed someone with enough sensitivity to see the difference.

She pushed away from her desk and the file she was supposed to be perusing in preparation for another interview with another representative from another fast-paced, nineties-type ad agency. She didn't need to see the file. She could probably recite its contents by rote, having read fifteen other identical folders over the past two weeks.

She walked around her office, looking at the paintings Tanya had done for her. She wished she had more of her friend's perception, envying Tanya the inner peace that allowed her to see the world around her so clearly.

Her secretary's voice piped into the room. "Your appointment's here, Ms. Teal."

Jennifer punched the intercom button. "Thanks, Rachel. Please send him in."

Dennis wasn't going to be joining her that morning. He'd had to go someplace with Tanya. She'd heard his secretary mention a doctor's appointment. And based on the fact that he and Tanya both had to be there, and the knowledge that neither of them had been sick, Jennifer had a suspicion what it might be about. She wondered who'd be more thrilled, Dennis or Tanya. And she wondered why she wasn't more excited for her two best friends. Maybe she was just feeling a little left out because they hadn't let her in on their secret.

Her office door opened. ''Mr. Chambers to see you, Ms. Teal,'' Rachel said, her tone as professional as always.

Jennifer offered her hand automatically, her mind still in the doctor's office with her friends, until she saw who'd just walked into her office. The man from Tanya's opening. The one she'd been thinking about ever since seeing him that night two weeks ago.

''Oh. Hello,'' she said, hoping she didn't sound as uncomfortable as she felt. She was barely aware of her secretary slipping silently from her office, but she knew when Rachel shut the door behind her. The huge room was suddenly confining, and a little too warm.

''So we finally meet. Officially, that is.'' His deep voice was just as she'd remembered.

He was still holding her hand as he smiled the sexiest smile she'd ever seen. She pulled away from him and moved behind her desk. ''I guess we do.''

She didn't know why he was here, but she wished he hadn't come. He was a little harder to resist than the rest of Tanya's husband prospects. He hadn't told her his name that night at the opening, or she would've known when Rachel announced him that he wasn't the appointment she'd been waiting for.

"You don't sound too pleased. Have I done something to offend you?"

She may have remembered his voice, but her memory had done an injustice to the rest of him. His jeans, so faded they were almost white, were tight enough to leave very little to the imagination. And his shirt was equally sexy. It was faded, too, and cotton, and the sleeves were rolled up to his elbows, leaving his tanned muscular forearms right out in plain view. And his hair...

"I was expecting an ad man," she said, wondering why she was so fascinated by his ponytail.

"And you got one." He settled into the chair in front of her desk.

Damn. She had to admire Tanya's ingenuity. Tanya had known Jennifer was looking for an ad man, but Jennifer had no idea how Tanya had managed to find one who was also ready to get married. Jennifer sat down, feeling foolish standing over him, and overdressed, too, in her stylish business suit. "Okay, you can tell Tanya you tried, but you're wasting your time," she said.

He stood, but instead of leaving as she'd expected, he moved to the couch, taking his sketchbook with him. "I happen to believe I'm using my time very wisely. Coming over?" He indicated the spot beside him on the couch.

His jeans were even more illuminating when he was sitting down. It was hard not to stare. Grabbing a yellow legal pad and pen, she crossed to the couch and sat down beside him. If he'd actually prepared something to show her, the least she could do was listen. But she wasn't going to hire him.

"I'd like to center our campaign around you," he began, "because you *are* Teal Automotive. The entire basis of One Price Selling is integrity, gaining the trust of your customers. They need to trust *you*."

Jennifer got goose bumps.

"One Price Selling is not a gimmick," he went on, "so the usual gimmick advertising will sell it short. Which is why we need to approach this up front, from the top—which again means you. You have a sterling reputation, Ms. Teal. You've built your success on honest business practices, on fairness and customer service, and now it's up to us to make sure that everyone in Atlanta knows that."

The man was good. He was dressed like a construction worker, carried a sketchbook for a briefcase and wore a ponytail, but he knew his stuff. And more important he'd seen what she was trying to do. She suddenly had a vision of him reading Aunt Abigail's health-insurance card.

"What did you say your name was?" she asked.

"Bryan Chambers, of Innovative Advertising," he said, looking perplexed. "Didn't you get the file I sent over?"

The File. She should have read the damn file. "Tanya didn't send you?"

"Your secretary called mine to set up the appointment."

Jennifer could feel herself turning red, a reaction left over from the days when she'd been so aware of being a burden that self-consciousness had become a way of life. "And you weren't at the art gallery that night because Tanya wanted you to meet me?"

"Tanya Bradford, the artist? I'd never met her before that night."

"Oh." Suddenly, as much of a fool as she'd made of herself, Jennifer felt wonderful. She looked at the unusual and oh-so-sexy man beside her and smiled. He wasn't there because he wanted to get married. He was just an ad man. A *gorgeous* ad man.

He smiled back at her. "I'm missing something, aren't I?" he asked. His sensual brown eyes lingered on hers just a little longer than was necessary.

"I'm afraid so, Mr. Chambers. But I'm impressed with your ideas. How soon can you make it back to meet my vice president?"

"Call me Bryan. And is tomorrow soon enough?"

CALL ME, Uncle Bryan. Please call me. Nicki lay on her bed staring at the clock, watching the second hand tick past the two, and then the three, constantly ticking, until five more minutes passed with a still-silent phone. He'd said he'd call.

Her stomach was filled with butterflies. She wasn't going to cry. It made her more scared to cry. But what if he didn't come home? What if...

Her future stretched out before her, a gray scary blob. She blinked, making the picture go away. She wasn't going to be scared. Nothing was going to happen to Uncle Bryan. He'd probably just forgotten he'd said he'd call if he was ever going to be later than five o'clock. 'Cause he'd never had to check in with anybody before.

It was just that he'd always been home by four-thirty—every single day since she'd come to Atlanta. She knew. She watched the clock every day. She always felt tons better the minute he walked in the door.

She loved him so much. She didn't know what she'd do if she lost him, too.

Maybe he was tired of having her around. Other than him dying, that was what scared her most. Sometimes she lay awake in the middle of the night and got crazy just thinking about him not wanting her anymore. She'd heard her mom and grandma joke about Uncle Bryan's wanderlust often enough. But Grandma used to worry about it sometimes, too. Nicki had heard her telling Grandpa once that she was afraid Uncle Bryan's roots were going to shrivel up and die if he didn't plant them somewhere soon. Nicki didn't know about all that, but she knew she just couldn't picture Uncle Bryan ever settling down to a normal boring life.

Oh, God, please help me. Please let Uncle Bryan come home. I promise I won't get in his way. Just let him come home.

Five-thirty. The clock kept ticking. Nicki's eyes were so dry they hurt, but she kept watching the steady rhythm of the second hand going round and round. Her legs were getting stiff, but she wasn't going to move. Not until Uncle Bryan got home. She just had to wait long enough. He'd be home.

He might've gotten in an accident. He could get hurt bad if somebody ran into his Jeep. Especially if he took off the roof and let it all be open. Maybe he was at the hospital. Maybe they were working on him right now! Her stomach started to ache like she might throw up.

Even if he was at the hospital, it didn't mean he was going to die. Maybe he just had some broken bones or needed stitches. He might not be able to take care of them while he was healing, but Nicki didn't care. She could take care of both of them. She'd stay home from school and fetch and cook and clean all day if she had to, and she didn't even care if he was a really grouchy patient like Grandpa when he'd had that heart surgery. Uncle Bryan could yell at her all day if he wanted to, just as long as he came home to her.

Nicki started to shiver. She got cold a lot lately. She thought about pulling her bedspread around her, but she didn't want to move. Her fingers were cold, too, but they were still sweaty against her cheek where she lay on them. Her future stretched out before her, a gray scary blob—

The phone rang.

Nicki's heart started to pound so hard she could feel it in her chest as she stared at the Snoopy phone Uncle Bryan had bought her. What if it was the hospital? Or the police? But they came to the front door, didn't they? Especially since she was just a kid. She started to relax. It must be Uncle Bryan.

Jumping up, Nicki ran to the phone, counting the rings. She knew Uncle Bryan's machine picked up on the fifth ring, so she'd get it on the fourth. She didn't want him to think she'd been waiting by the phone like some ninny. She didn't want him to feel like he had to report to her or anything.

The third ring pealed into the silent house. Nicki took a deep breath. "Hello?" she said, making sure she didn't sound too eager.

"Nick? I'm so sorry, honey. I've been with that new client I told you about for most of the afternoon, taping a series of radio spots, and after I dropped her off there was a huge wreck on Peachtree. And the damn battery on my mobile went dead so I couldn't call, but

I'm back at the office now, and just as soon as I drop these things off I'll be heading home. You okay?''

"I'm fine," she said. He didn't sound like Uncle Bryan the way he was rambling on. He sounded upset. Probably because he'd had to worry about checking in. If it wasn't for her, it wouldn't have mattered that his phone battery was dead.

"I'm sorry if I worried you, honey. I'll buy an extra battery for my phone so next time I'll have a backup."

She was causing more trouble and she didn't even mean to. "It's okay, Uncle Bryan. You don't have to do that. I wasn't worried."

"Oh." A pause. "So whatcha been doing?"

She looked over at the clock, at the name written in little black letters where the second hand connected to the minute hand. "Reading."

"How about if I come get you and we head to the Lightning Bolt? We can get some hot dogs or something from the concession while we play."

Nicki didn't mind about the hot dogs, but she hated the arcade Uncle Bryan seemed to love so much. She wasn't much good at the games he wanted her to learn so badly, and she probably made him bored she was so easy to beat, not that he'd show her he was bored. But even worse than the games, all those people made her nervous. There were more people in the Lightning Bolt at one time than had lived in the whole town of Shallowbrook. And lots of them were boys almost as big as Uncle Bryan, and they wore dirty blue jeans. "Okay," she said. She'd already been enough of a pain for one day.

When they said their goodbyes she hung up the phone slowly, glad that Uncle Bryan was all right. And a night at the Lightning Bolt wouldn't be that bad. Not if she was with Uncle Bryan. She was just going to have to get used to all the people in Atlanta, to going out a lot. She wanted to live with Uncle Bryan forever, and she knew that before she came he'd never stayed home. She couldn't make him change any more than he already had or he was going to get tired of her way before she was all grown-up.

She brushed her hair and changed her clothes, putting on jeans and the Atlanta Hawks T-shirt Uncle Bryan had bought her. She was going to need a bra soon. Most of the girls in her class already had one, and sometimes Nicki wondered if there was something the matter with her that her breasts were only just now starting to grow. She wondered if her mother—her *real* mother—had been a late grower, too. One thing for sure, there was no way she could ask Uncle Bryan what he thought. He'd probably never come home again.

And as she sat on her bed counting the minutes until she heard Uncle Bryan's Jeep pull into the driveway, she wondered for the hundredth time what would happen when she turned eighteen and Uncle Bryan didn't have to keep her anymore. She wondered if he'd be so tired of her, so mad she'd ruined his life for all those years, that he'd leave and she'd never see him again.

Her future stretched out before her, a gray scary blob...

BRYAN CHECKED his mobile as he pulled onto the lot of Teal Hyundai. He was spending the afternoon with Jennifer Teal again, today taping a couple of television commercials, and he wanted to be certain that

Nicki could reach him if she needed to. Not that she'd ever called him. But it had scared the hell out of him the week before when he'd realized his mobile had been dead all afternoon. He'd had visions of Nicki needing him and not being able to reach him, of her being all alone and unable to cope. He'd been tempted to abandon his Jeep in the traffic jam on Peachtree and walk to the nearest phone just to assure himself that she was all right. Only the thought that he'd probably get there faster by waiting out the traffic had kept him in his seat.

Teal Hyundai was a far cry from Teal Cadillac, the dealership he'd visited the day before when trying to determine where to shoot the commercials. Gone were the glitzy mirrored windows and high-tech design he'd first thought would make a good backdrop for the TV spots, and in their place were brick walls and plain glass windows. The only decoration was the Teal Hyundai painted on the windows alongside the blue-and-white Teal logo.

This is where he wanted Jennifer's viewers to see her. Teal Hyundai would appeal to the lower-income car buyers, and her appearance there would make her seem accessible to them. Or so he hoped. He wasn't at all sure how well the classy lady would look in such humble surroundings. Maybe he should have gone with the Cadillac dealership, after all.

And maybe he should never have taken the job in the first place. But when the detective he'd hired had called him with the news that Jennifer Teal was looking for a new advertising firm for a special project she was working on, he'd decided the chance was too good to pass up. He wasn't so sure anymore. He was spending too much time thinking about his newest client.

Jake Landers and Bob McKinney, his film crew, were already set up on the lot just as he'd instructed them. They waved as he parked his Jeep. All they needed now was Jennifer. He got out of the Jeep and crossed the lot toward the tile-floored showroom. She was probably waiting inside.

A sleek blue vintage Mustang pulled onto the lot in front of him, and Bryan stopped, admiring the car. He'd always had a thing for Ford's famous sports car, the older the better. He'd bet this one was at least a '66. Maybe even a '65. Now that he had a garage, he should look into getting one himself. Could be that was just what he needed—a new toy.

Bryan was so busy admiring the car that it took him a minute to realize who'd just climbed out of it.

But only a minute. She looked more beautiful every time he saw her, every bit as sleek and elegant as her car. She was wearing a black short-skirted suit, a perfect contrast to the wavy auburn curls pinned up in that twist thing on the back of her head. He wouldn't mind her for a toy, either, only this one he'd keep in his new bedroom.

Except that she was Nicki's mother.

"Nice car," he said, meeting her in the middle of the lot.

She smiled at him, a friendly glad-to-see-you smile. "Thanks. Sorry I'm late, I got stuck on the phone. I've never been good at cutting people off."

"No problem. I just got here myself." He smiled, too, putting his hand in the small of her back as he guided her toward the camera.

His fears about her looking "right" at this dealership were quickly put to rest. She fit into Teal Hyundai as naturally as she had Teal Lincoln Mercury the week before. After two hours of following her and Bob and Jake around the dealership, Bryan was as perplexed as ever about her. She had a hell of a talent for names. No matter who they passed, from janitor to sales manager, she was outgoing, friendly and called every one of them by name. But what was even more impressive was their obvious ease with her. They treated her with respect, which was probably a given considering that she signed their paychecks, but they seemed to genuinely like her, too.

She turned to speak to an elderly female customer waiting in the service area, and for a second there, he saw Nicki in the tilt of her chin. After listening to the woman's complaints, Jennifer led her into the dealership's waiting lounge and to the comfort of a couch. Then she brought the woman a cup of coffee and promised her she'd get someone on her car as soon as possible.

She did, too. She walked back out to the service area and conferred with the service manager about how to get the woman's car fixed immediately without inconveniencing any other customers. And then, outside in the lot, she apologized to Jake and Bob for the interruption, the Atlanta sunshine catching the gold glints in her chestnut hair. Nicki's hair.

He was puzzled. How was it a woman so outgoing, so giving to others, could keep herself hidden from her own child? He could certainly understand why, at sixteen, she gave up the child, but it seemed odd that a woman like her wouldn't have, at some point, wanted to meet the child she'd given birth to. See if she was well cared for, happy, especially in these days of open adoption.

She obviously hadn't, though, because the birth had not been registered with any of the search-and-find services.

Didn't Jennifer care that her daughter might be out there somewhere, wanting to know her, needing her?

Or was Teal Automotive the only child she cared about? Bryan was aware that public knowledge of her having had a child out of wedlock and giving it up for adoption could damage Jennifer's reputation somewhat and possibly hurt the One Price campaign. So was her business the reason she hadn't registered?

She caught his eye as Jake stopped to load another tape. He gave her a thumbs-up and she smiled, not looking away until Jake called her back to the cue cards Bob was holding. So she felt it, too, this attraction between them. Damn.

He wondered if she was seeing anyone. He knew she lived alone, that she wasn't seen publicly with the same man with any regularity. But that didn't mean she didn't have a private liaison going on. He wondered about Nicki's biological father. Was she still in contact with him?

Nicki's birth certificate had said "father unknown." But Jennifer had only been fifteen when she'd conceived Nicki. Surely there hadn't been a lot of candidates for the daddy. Or, God forbid, had she been raped? Surprised at the rage that filled him at that thought, Bryan determined he had to have some time alone with her, get her to talk to him. As soon as possible. For both their sakes. True, Jennifer was trusting him to do this campaign for her. But Nicky was relying on him, too. And if push came to shove, Nicky's interests were number one.

"As soon as possible" turned out to be two hours later as he and Jennifer sat in her office, viewing the videotape Jake had shot that afternoon.

"I'd like Dennis to take a look at this before we make any final decisions," she said, "but I like the service area for a background better than the lot. What do you think?"

Bryan sat beside her on the couch, smelling her perfume as they leaned forward studying the console television screen. He'd never seen such a naturally beautiful woman in his life. As hard as he looked, and he'd looked damn hard, he couldn't find anything artificial about her.

"I think very few people are going to notice the background," he said.

She looked startled by the compliment, but pleased, too.

"Thank you."

"You're welcome."

He knew he should look away, that their eyes were saying things to each other that should never be said, yet he couldn't seem to break the silent communication.

"How come you've never married?" he asked, the videotape rolling on without them.

She shrugged and turned her gaze away. "Never found the right guy, I guess."

"Maybe you've just been looking in the wrong places."

"Maybe." She glanced back at him. "What about you? I don't see a wedding ring on *your* finger, either."

"I'm a bad candidate for marriage. My soul's too restless."

She laughed. "What's that supposed to mean?"

"Just that I've never been able to stick at *anything* long enough to make me think I could stay with one woman for eternity."

"You're too hard on yourself. I finally read that file you sent over, you know. It said you've had Innovative Advertising for almost ten years. That sounds like sticking at it to me." She grinned at him.

"I also have a partner. I can take my restless soul off when I need to."

"Why do you need to?" Her grin faded, her eyes now serious.

"You ever have the feeling that something great is happening on the other side of the hill and you're missing the whole thing?"

He thought he saw a flash of pain in her eyes. "Sometimes."

"Me, too," he said. "A lot of times. So I guess, until I know why it is I keep feeling that way, I'll keep heading over that hill."

"Be careful you don't get lost."

"Yeah."

He wanted to kiss her. He was pretty sure she wanted him to kiss her, too.

"I'll bet you loved the Ferris wheel when you were a kid," she said, smiling again.

"You think I like going around in circles?"

"No!" She touched his arm, her fingers cool and featherlight. "Don't you remember how high it used to go? Almost to the sky. Certainly high enough to see over that hill."

He couldn't look away from her lips, couldn't stop wondering what they would taste like, how they would feel beneath his. He'd been wondering for weeks.

She was looking at his lips, too, and running her tongue across her own.

Bryan wasn't aware of leaning toward her, but he wasn't surprised when she met him halfway. Her lips were hesitant as he covered them with his own, not really kissing him back so much as allowing his caress. He pulled her into his arms and deepened the kiss, opening his mouth to her, coaxing her to invite him inside.

He lit like a flame to gasoline when she did. No woman had ever excited him as quickly, as completely, as this one did.

Holy hell.

He pulled away from Jennifer, stunned. "I'm sorry," he said, rubbing his hand across his face. "I was out of line there. I don't know what's the matter with me. I've never attacked a client before." His attempt at a joke failed miserably.

"It's okay. It was only a kiss," she said lightly, but she wasn't breathing any easier than he was.

He'd just kissed Nicki's mother. *Where in hell's my brain?*

"So what's the real reason you're not married?" he asked, needing to get his answers and get out.

He reached for the TV control and turned off the videotape, while she scooted farther away from him on the couch.

"I got burned once."

"What happened?"

She got up and went over to her desk, leaning back against it. "Nothing very unusual, I'm afraid. You know the old story... I loved him, he didn't love me back kind of thing.''

Bryan found that hard to believe. The guy must have been crazy. But was he also Nicki's father?

"And you never met anyone else?''

"Believe it or not, I just haven't had the time.''

Bryan stood up. He was getting nowhere. "You haven't had time to date?''

She smiled. "I've dated some great guys. I'm just not ready to invest the time a good relationship takes.''

Did that mean she wouldn't have time for a daughter, either? "What about a family?''

"Tanya and Dennis are all the family I need.''

Bryan would have stopped right then and there. He would have gone home and told Nicki that he couldn't find her mother, that she was dead, anything to keep his niece from coming face-to-face with a mother who didn't have time for her. He would have—if he hadn't seen the wistfulness in Jennifer's eyes. He didn't know if the look had anything to do with Nicki. He had no idea if Jennifer had any motherly tendencies at all. He just knew he couldn't leave it like that.

"I've got tickets for the symphony Thursday night,'' he said, hoping Calvin hadn't already given the tickets away. "A couple of days isn't much notice, but can you come?''

"Yes. I'd like that.'' Her smile had him wanting her all over again.

CHAPTER FOUR

JENNIFER FELT like a girl preparing for her first date. She'd never met a man who attracted her so much, who seemed so perfect for her. He was intelligent, successful, gorgeous as sin—and no more ready to get married than she was.

She wore her navy silk jumpsuit with matching pumps, liking the way the outfit pinched in at her waist and covered enough of her chest to be circumspect, but still left an enticing amount of skin bare. She even pinned a navy silk bow into the twist on the back of her head, which made her feel particularly feminine. Jewelry was something she always allowed herself, and tonight she felt almost sensuous as the cool gold pendant settled between her breasts and gold glinted from her ears and wrists. As she took a last glance in the floor-length mirror in her bathroom, she felt like laughing. She was actually having fun.

She did laugh when she answered the door to Bryan half an hour later.

"What? You don't like my tie?"

It was blue and patterned with little yellow airplanes. "Your tie is fine. It's the suspenders I'm not so sure about."

He hooked his thumbs into the matching blue-and-yellow suspenders. "Too much, huh?" he asked.

Jennifer looked him over one more time. The suspenders held his shirt tightly against his chest, giving testimony to the fact that the man was all muscle. "No, I like them," she said. And she did. A lot. Almost as much as she liked his ponytail.

"Nice place you've got here," he said, looking over her shoulder into the penthouse.

"Thanks," Jennifer said, self-conscious all of a sudden. She had a feeling he hated her home. To a man like him, it probably looked incredibly boring.

She locked the door and followed him out to his Jeep.

BRYAN HATED the symphony. Even more than he hated briefcases. He hated the stuffiness of it, the yuppiness. He didn't want to keep up with the Joneses; he'd left them behind years ago. He certainly didn't need to see or be seen. And he preferred his music with lyrics—and a little more volume.

But he couldn't remember when he'd enjoyed an evening out more. He refused to call it a date; he'd set down the law for himself on that account. But whatever it was, it was the best one he'd had in years. Jennifer was different. She didn't play games or flirt, didn't make him wonder if she had a hidden agenda. She wasn't shy, or coy, or easily embarrassed. And she didn't seem to care about the Joneses, either.

But neither did she say a lot about herself. Teal Automotive, sure. Her activities, the last charity dinner she'd attended, the Hawks' chances to make it to the NBA playoffs, all were open for discussion. But Jennifer Teal, the woman inside the successful entrepreneur, remained a mystery.

The second half of the symphony was well under way, and Bryan was still wide-awake. Amazing. He stole a glance at Jennifer. Her lips were lifted in just a hint of a smile as she watched the stage, engrossed in the music.

His mind wandered from the concert hall to his bedroom, with Jennifer in it, her long wavy hair loose from its pins and spread across his sheet. There were no pillows on the bed. They'd been shoved to the floor hours before, and the covers were gone, too. Jennifer didn't need to cover up. She lay sprawled before him, looking up at him with sleepy eyes and—

Somebody's beeper went off. Bryan was catapulted back to the present, irritated with whoever was being paged. One hell of a great fantasy had been interrupted.

The beeper sounded again. Jennifer nudged his shoulder. "Shouldn't you check that?" she whispered.

His beeper. Damn. It was the first time in all the months he'd been carrying it that the thing had gone off.

He jumped up out of his seat with complete disregard for the people behind him. "I'll be back," he said to Jennifer, already climbing over feet to get to the aisle. He didn't need to check to see who was calling. He knew. There was only one person in the world who had his number. Only one person to whom he'd given twenty-four-a-day access to his time.

His chest felt like it was being squeezed in a vise as he asked the first usher he found for directions to the closest phone. *Dear God, let her be all right.*

Dropping a quarter into the slot, Bryan punched in his number, his finger frustratingly slow on the numerous buttons, and finally heard the line to his home phone ringing.

"Nick? You okay, sweetheart? I can be there in twenty minutes," he said as soon as his niece picked up the phone.

"I'm fine, Uncle Bryan. I'm really sorry to bug you. I wouldn't have, but Calvin called and he's someplace where he can't be reached, so he's calling back in half an hour. He told me I had to page you, or I wouldn't have, honest."

Bryan sagged against the wall in relief. "Bother me already, okay, Nick? It's what I bought the pager for, remember?"

"Yeah."

"So what's Calvin want? He's not coming home, is he?" Bryan's workaholic partner had just left for a vacation with his family, the first he'd taken since he and Bryan had opened their business ten years before. Bryan had a feeling it had been either that or be served with divorce papers.

"He didn't say he was. He wanted to know if you heard from a Mr. Wonderly about some kind of tapes."

"Tell him everything's fine and to quit worrying and enjoy his vacation. Better yet, tell him I'm not taking any more calls from him until next week."

"You want *me* to tell him that?"

"Yep. And if he starts to give you a hard time, you have my permission to hang up on him."

"I can't do that!"

Bryan smiled as he listened to the horror in Nicki's voice. At least he'd managed to get a rise out of her.

"Sure you can. It's easy. You just put the phone back in its cradle without saying goodbye."

"Okay...if you want me to." She sounded like he'd asked her to burn the house down.

"I do. So whatcha up to?" Bryan was reluctant to hang up. Not just because he'd rather talk to Nicki than listen to the symphony, but because she'd finally called him. He wished she'd do it more.

"Watching TV."

"You got all your homework done?"

"Uh-huh."

"And you got Mrs. Baker's number right by the phone?" he asked. Their next-door neighbor was a widow, and a godsend, checking on Nicki for him whenever he couldn't be home.

"Uh-huh."

"Did you feed the fish?"

"Uncle Bryan, we don't have any fish." She sounded like she was smiling.

"Right. I knew that. So, anything sound good for a snack? I can stop by the store on my way home."

"No. That's okay."

And just like that he'd slammed into that brick wall again. It wasn't okay. Not to Bryan. It wasn't okay at all. Because Nicki needed a hell of a lot more than she was telling him. And suddenly he remembered Jennifer, the woman waiting just beyond the doors for him to return. Not his date. Not someone he could fantasize about taking to bed with him. *Nicki's mother.*

"I'll stop for some of those cupcakes you like. If you don't want any tonight, you can take them to school with you tomorrow."

"You don't have to, Uncle Bryan. Honest."

Bryan slouched against the wall, suddenly more tired than he'd ever been in his life. Month after month went by, and they were making no progress. "I know I don't have to, Nick. I *want* to." He paused. "I'll be home soon."

"I can stay home late by myself."

"You do great alone, Nick, but I still don't like to leave you there by yourself. The symphony's almost over, I'll drop my client off, grab the cupcakes and be home. We can watch *Taxi* together. How's that sound?"

"If you want to. But you can stay out later if you want. It doesn't matter."

It doesn't matter. Those were the words that worried Bryan most of all. Nothing seemed to matter to Nicki anymore. He'd been warned to expect apathy from her, as well as himself, as they went through the grieving process, adjusting to losing their entire family in the blink of an eye. But it had been almost a year, and while he sometimes still woke up with that sick feeling in his gut, he was able to look forward to things again. But Nicki wasn't. He was getting more and more concerned that her apathy was passing the boundaries of normal. Nothing mattered.

Nothing, that is, except finding her biological mother. She'd just asked Bryan about it again the day before. And Bryan had lied to her. He'd told her he hadn't found her birth mother yet—because he was still no closer to knowing whether or not Jennifer had a place for Nicki in her life. If he had to guess, he'd guess not. And there was no way Nicki was strong enough to hear that. So, with no other choice, he'd lied to her. Just as he was, by omission, lying to Jennifer. Nevertheless he wasn't going to tell either one of them about the other until he could be surer of the outcome.

He hung up the phone and went back into the auditorium, determined to do whatever it took to get Jennifer to open up to him and get the whole thing over and done with. No more fantasies. Reality was just too important.

JENNIFER LOOKED forward to his good-night kiss all the way home. She'd been thinking about it all evening, every time she'd felt his arm brush against hers or he'd leaned over to whisper something to her. She'd been anticipating his kiss like a silly schoolgirl, and yet she couldn't seem to stop. Had it just been a fluke the other day in her office, the way he'd made her feel?

Her blood was barreling through her veins as Bryan pulled up in the visitor parking at her building. Tonight they weren't at the office. Tonight they weren't working. Tonight the kiss would be more than an accident.

"I love this time of year," he said as they walked together toward the ornate front doors of her apartment building. The Georgia air was warm, balmy. A gorgeous spring evening.

"Because of the basketball play-offs, right?" It was all Dennis talked about when they weren't talking about work or Tanya.

"Nope. The flying." He held open the door for her before the doorman could get it.

She looked at his tie. "Flying."

"Mmm. It stays light longer now, but it's not summer vacation yet, so the skies aren't too crowded."

"You're a pilot?"

"Yeah. Since I was a teenager. I was barely eighteen when I bought my first plane."

She pushed the button for the elevator. "Do you still have your own plane?"

He nodded. "A Cessna four-seater. There's nothing like being up there in a world all your own. You're never going to get freer than that. Do you like to fly?"

"I don't know. I've never flown in anything smaller than a 737, and I'm usually working the whole time we're in the air."

"I'll take you up some time, if you like. We can go to dinner at a great place I know in Huntsville."

"Alabama?"

"Yeah, and they've got the best red snapper I've ever had."

The man was incredible. And maybe just what she needed. "If you're serious, I may just take you up on that."

The Day, Jennifer thought, was coming up fast. Another couple of weeks and it would be twelve years. Twelve long years, and facing that day never got any easier. No matter how she tried to convince herself otherwise, the what-ifs, the recriminations, the guilt were always there. And the wondering. But maybe this year she wouldn't have to be alone with her guilt. Maybe, if she spent the day with Bryan, she wouldn't hurt so bad.

"I'll give you a call next time I'm going up," he said.

The elevator came and Jennifer stepped inside with him, glad to find they had it all to themselves. She put in the key for the penthouse and pushed the button that would take them up to the top floor. And when she turned, he was looking at her.

"So what did you think of the cello concerto?" she asked, nervous again.

He grinned at her. "The truth?"

She nodded.

"I think the Wonderly-soup account is going to benefit from it greatly."

"The Wonderly-soup account?"

"Mmm. I think it was during that concerto thing that it finally hit me what was missing from the campaign."

She grinned. "You didn't enjoy the symphony, did you?"

"There were some good parts," he said, holding her gaze with his own. Jennifer felt as if she was going to melt right there beneath his sexy brown eyes.

The elevator doors opened, and she stepped out, sliding her key into the lock that would let them into her penthouse.

She didn't really know what to do next. She'd never brought a man here with anything intimate in mind.

The penthouse door opened and she turned. *Invite him in, idiot.* "I really enjoyed myself tonight."

He brushed his fingers along her cheek. "I did, too."

"In spite of Mozart?"

"He wasn't that bad. I think half my problem is the setting. I'd probably like him a whole lot more if they'd put on an outdoor concert, up on Stone Mountain, say, with everybody wearing shorts and lying around on blankets in the grass."

It sounded wonderful to her. Especially if he took her along. "I'll let you know if I ever hear of one," she said.

"You do that."

He was looking at her the way he had in her office right before he'd kissed her. And this time she was ready for him. She wanted him to kiss her. She wanted to feel his arms around her again more than she'd wanted anything in a long time.

"Well, good night," he said, and stepped back into the elevator.

Jennifer hadn't even noticed that he'd been holding it open. Before she had a chance to respond he was gone.

"HOW'S TANYA?" Jennifer asked Dennis the next day over a midmorning cup of coffee in his office. She hadn't slept much the night before and it was her fourth cup of coffee so far.

"Great! Just great. Her show was a huge success. Requests have been pouring in for more paintings. She even had a call from someone in New York. He wants to set up a one-woman exhibition for her."

"A New York show? All by herself? How long will it take her to get ready?"

"It'll have to be after—" Dennis stopped.

"After?" *After another five or six months?*

"After she, uh, gets enough new paintings done to carry another show," he said, stirring more sugar into his coffee.

Damn. How long were they going to wait before they told her they were expecting a baby? She knew lots of people who'd had babies.

Just none that were close to her.

She pictured herself listening to the intimate details of the growth of Tanya's baby and having to celebrate every development with them. She thought about walking into an infants'-wear department, of looking at the overwhelming array of garments, holding them up and hearing Tanya marvel at how tiny they were.

"How long will that take?" She should just tell Dennis that she knew about Tanya's pregnancy. That she'd probably known before Tanya did. That even if Dennis's secretary hadn't slipped the news, Jennifer had recognized the symptoms, anyway.

"She told the guy it would have to be next summer."

"And he's willing to wait that long?"

"Yeah. He's already booked the date. The second week in July."

"So you're going to New York," Jennifer said, forcing a smile. She was happy for her friends. They deserved it—and more.

Dennis fidgeted with the picture of his wife he kept on his desk. "Tanya's counting on you coming with us, Jennifer. She says she can't do it without you there."

Jennifer thought of the baby Tanya was carrying. It would be seven or eight months old by then, and the focus of every moment of their lives. She started to sweat. "I don't know if we should both be gone at once," she said, hating herself for her sudden weakness. She didn't understand what was the matter with her.

"We'll see what happens when—" His phone rang and Dennis broke off.

Jennifer couldn't help noticing he hadn't tried very hard to persuade her. Was Dennis really that unsure about her ability to handle being around their baby? Even for a few days? He knew her better than anyone else on earth. And yes, she generally avoided being around babies because they made her remember, but it wasn't like she couldn't handle those memories if she had to.

"Yes, I did see them . . . I agree . . . Great, we'll look forward to seeing the finished product." She listened to Dennis's conversation, telling herself she was over-reacting. Dennis was probably just waiting for Tanya to tell her their news. And she'd be excited about their new baby long before it arrived; she just needed a lit-tle more time to get used to the idea.

"Sure, she's right here," Dennis said, holding out the phone. "It's Bryan Chambers."

Jennifer stood up. "I'll take it in my office."

"He's on line two," Dennis said, his brows lifting in surprise.

But Jennifer wasn't thinking about Dennis's reac-tion as she left his office. She needed to know what she'd done wrong the night before. And she certainly wasn't going to ask within earshot of her vice presi-dent.

"Hi," Jennifer said, picking up the phone as soon as her office door was closed behind her. She sank into the blue upholstered high-backed chair behind her desk.

"Jennifer? Good." Without waiting for her to speak, he went on, "I'm working on the next series of television ads for One Price, and I've got an idea I'd like to run by you." He sounded so formal. So imper-sonal.

"Shoot," she said, picking up a pen to sign a cou-ple of letters Rachel had left for her.

"So far we've appealed to your wealthier custom-ers, to businessmen and to the working class. This time I want to go for the housewife, the family man and Grandma."

"All at once?" She put the signed letters in her out tray.

"If we can."

What had happened to the man who'd come to her door wearing bright blue-and-yellow suspenders the night before? "How?"

"By including children in the scripts. We show you in a series of short spots, giving a Teal Automotive coloring book to a couple of kids while their parents shop for a car, explaining One Price to a little boy who's in with his parents buying a car, and fastening a baby into the built-in child seat in a Windstar."

Jennifer set her pen down slowly, deliberately. "I'd rather you think of something else." She pushed up the sleeve of her pale pink suit, looking at her Rolex.

"Of course, if you insist, I will, but I think you ought to at least give the idea some thought. Talk it over with Dennis, if you'd like. A series of spots like this would not only be cost effective, but time effective, as well, reaching several markets at once."

She didn't hesitate. "I don't need to talk to Dennis. I'd rather not do it."

There was a pause on the line, and Jennifer knew she was handling the situation badly. Still, she felt like she was being bombarded with babies all of a sudden. It should have helped her to realize that her reactions were largely because of the impending anniversary, that she was always a little sensitive this time of year, that she'd be fine once The Day had passed again, but she still didn't feel any more inclined to hold someone else's baby.

"Mind my asking why not?" Bryan's voice, softer now, made her feel like a heel.

"I'm not very good with kids."

"What's to be good about? They say their lines, you say yours, you smile at them, and it's done."

Except for the baby. If it cried in her arms, they could have to redo the take. Heaven only knew how long she'd have to be holding it. "I'd just feel better if you could come up with something else," she said, looking over her schedule for the rest of the morning.

"Well, whatever you say..."

She'd disappointed him. "Bryan?" She pushed her calendar aside.

"Yeah?"

"Did I do something wrong last night? Something to send you away?" She was beyond caring if she made a fool of herself. She needed to know.

"No. Why do you ask?"

"One minute we were having a good time, and the next you were gone."

"The symphony was over."

"But that didn't mean the date had to be. It wasn't even ten o'clock."

"Is that what it was? A date?"

"I thought so," she said.

"So is that how you treat all your dates? With vague answers any time they get too close?"

"Is that what I was doing?"

"You're doing it again. You answer my question with a question."

"I don't have many dates that mean anything. I really don't know how I treat them."

"Are you saying ours meant something?"

"Maybe. You're different, Bryan. And you don't apologize for it or flaunt it. And you don't seem to care that I'm the owner of Teal Automotive. It's refreshing. It also helps that you're no more interested in marriage right now than I am."

"It may not matter overly much to me that you *are* Teal Automotive, or that you're one of the richest single women in the city, but I do like to know the people inside the women I date. Getting to know you is like trying to break into a cement cell."

Jennifer's hand started to shake. "It's...it's hard when you're in my position. You never know what people want from you, or if they even want you at all, rather than what you can do for them. You tend to get cautious after a while."

"Poor little rich girl, huh?"

"Maybe. Except that I have a couple of close friends I'd trust with my life, so I don't consider myself all that poor."

"So what does it take for someone to become your friend?"

"Are you saying you want to?"

"Maybe."

She smiled. If his "maybe" meant anywhere near as much as hers had, things were going to be all right.

"Then I guess you ask me out again and see what happens."

"I'm getting kinda hungry for some red snapper."

"If that's an invitation, the answer's yes."

"Monday for lunch?"

"Okay."

"Good. And, Jennifer?"

"Yeah?"

"You're right to be cautious—about what people might want from you, I mean. See you Monday."

Jennifer held the phone long after the dial tone was humming in her ear. He understood. And she was in trouble. For the first time in her adult life she'd met a man she could fall in love with.

But just how attracted would he be if he learned the truth about her? How much would he admire a woman who'd apparently once had the morals of an alley cat? Who'd been stupid enough to get pregnant?

CHAPTER FIVE

SOMETHING WAS WRONG with her—in the head. Nicki didn't know what. She'd never been around a crazy person before to know what one was like. But she knew something was wrong. Nothing was fun anymore.

She tossed aside the book she was reading and stared into space. The book was stupid. The kids in it had stupid problems. They spent all their time worrying about who their best friends were inviting to parties, and whether or not their moms were going to let them go to the movies with boys. Like any of that stuff really mattered. Nicki couldn't believe she'd ever found books like that any good.

She heard Uncle Bryan turn off the shower. As soon as he got ready, he was driving her to the mall to shop for summer clothes. He was making a really big deal out of it, taking the whole day, since it was Saturday, and even taking her out to a fancy lunch like her mother used to do when they came to the city to Christmas-shop. Nicki used to look forward to those trips for weeks, counting the days and making lists so she'd be sure not to forget anything. She used to love shopping.

But not anymore. Shopping was stupid. Who cared about all the fancy stuff in the store windows? Clothes were clothes. They didn't really matter. They didn't stop things from happening. And what did she care if she looked good? There was nobody around to dress up for. Uncle Bryan mostly just wore jeans and T-shirts, and it didn't matter to him if that was all she wore, too. Besides, dressing up was dumb. A waste of time. It wasn't going to bring back her parents.

"Ready to go, Nick?"

Uncle Bryan came into the living room, still pulling on his shirt. His hair was wet, but already the long part was in its ponytail. Grandma would've had a fit if she could see it, but Nicki thought it was neat.

"Yeah. I've got my list, just like you told me," Nicki said, getting to her feet. She was going to try really hard to make herself have fun today. Uncle Bryan wanted her to, he was trying really hard to make the day good, and she so badly wanted to make him happy with her.

He didn't get it about what colors didn't look good with her hair or which stores carried the nerdy clothes, but he was friendly with all the clerks, and Nicki didn't mind shopping with him at all. He made her try on every outfit they picked, and then come out so he could see her in it. Which made her feel sort of special, even if he *was* only doing it because of her mother.

She pulled on a baby T with a big daisy on the front and a pair of matching daisy shorts, and looked at herself in the dressing-room mirror. The outfit seemed okay, and she'd seen lots of girls at school wearing daisies lately. And it didn't have any red or orange that would look bad with her hair. But still, she wasn't sure if she looked geeky or not.

She peeked out the door of the dressing room to make certain nobody but Uncle Bryan was out there, and then slipped out.

"Is it comfortable?" He'd asked that same question with every outfit.

"I guess."

"Well, I gotta tell you, Nick. You look wonderful in it. That top shows how slim you are, and the shorts make your legs look miles long."

Nicki blushed, but she felt like smiling.

"But I don't know," Uncle Bryan continued, and her stomach tightened up again. "It might be a little old for you. Maybe you should wait a year or two before wearing those short shirts."

"Okay," Nicki said, trying really hard to hide her disappointment.

"You're only eleven, Nick. We don't want boys noticing how cute you are for a while yet."

Nicki nodded and went in to change. He didn't have to worry. Boys didn't notice her. But she didn't feel so bad about not having the outfit if it was because Uncle Bryan thought she was cute.

Uncle Bryan paid for her clothes, including a longer daisy T-shirt to go with the daisy shorts. She added the bag to her other packages and followed him out into the mall, wondering again what was wrong with her. She was glad to have all her new things. She just wasn't excited about them. In the old days, when she'd come to the city to shop, she'd thought over and over again about each new thing she got, pretending different places she was going to wear it. Sometimes she even got an excited feeling in her stomach that lasted for the whole day. But now they were just clothes, things she had to have.

She saw a big advertisement in the mall for a Six Flags amusement park, and remembered the only time she'd been there, the time Uncle Bryan had taken her on the roller coaster and she'd thrown up. It had still been the very best time she'd ever had. She'd always wanted to go there for a whole week and spend nights in a hotel and everything. She knew Uncle Bryan would take her if she asked him to. But she didn't want to go anymore. She didn't see what was so fun about going upside down and throwing up. She'd been such a stupid little kid back then.

They passed a drugstore, and Uncle Bryan stopped. "How about a chocolate bar to tide us over till lunch?" He named her favorite kind.

"Okay," Nicki said because he seemed so glad to get it for her. But it didn't really sound too good.

And neither did lunch when they finally finished their shopping later that afternoon. Uncle Bryan took her to the Mexican restaurant she used to beg to go to every time they came to Atlanta on a visit. And she ordered her usual burrito with extra beans, but it wasn't hard at all to wait for it to come, and she ate it because she knew she had to, not because she really wanted it. She just didn't feel hungry anymore. Besides, no matter how much she ate, it didn't make the empty feeling inside her go away.

Uncle Bryan was eating a steak, which the restaurant also had on the menu. He didn't like Mexican food. "You haven't mentioned your birth mother in a while, Nick. You giving up on her?"

Nicki's heart started to beat fast. "No. But you said you'd let me know when you found out something, and I didn't want to nag you. Mom always used to say

I nagged a lot and she'd get mad about it some-times.''

"So it still means as much to you that we find her?"

Nicki nodded. It meant everything to her. She'd spent hours imagining what her other mother would be like, how their first meeting would go. Whenever thinking about her mom and dad, and never seeing them again, made her feel like she was just going to curl up and die, she'd think about finding her other mother, and the scared feeling would go away a little bit.

Uncle Bryan was paying attention to his lunch again.

"So have you found out anything?" Nicki hoped it wasn't nagging to ask, since he'd brought up the sub-ject.

"Not yet, but they're narrowing it down." He put a big bite of steak in his mouth.

Nicki put her fork down, too excited to eat any more. "Narrowing it down" had to mean they'd found out something. And if they'd found out some-thing, they could probably find out more. So maybe there *was* a chance she'd know where her other mother was before Uncle Bryan wanted to get rid of her.

Uncle Bryan was keeping her because he knew her mother and grandma would have wanted him to, but there were no real ties—no *blood* ties—to hold him to her when she started to bug him too much. And she would. She didn't know when, and she hoped it would take longer because she was trying very hard not to get in his way, but she knew that eventually he'd be climbing the walls. Not because he wanted to be that way, just because that was Uncle Bryan.

"You remember the time when I was really little and I asked you if you had crabs in your pants?" she asked him. It made her feel better when she thought of those days.

He grinned at her. For an uncle, he was really handsome.

"Yeah, I remember. I wondered what Lori was telling you about me."

"You got really mad at her. I've never seen you and Mom yell at each other like that."

"And all because you had big ears and a little memory," he said teasingly.

"Can I help it if I didn't know the difference between ants and crabs?" she asked.

She'd been so happy in those days. She hadn't even known how great it was—or that it could all go away so fast, either.

And that was why she had to find her other mother. She needed to in case Uncle Bryan got tired of her before she was old enough to be on her own. Even if her other mother still didn't want her, maybe she had an aunt or a grandma someplace who did.

It had never bothered Nicki that she was adopted when she lived in Shallowbrook. Actually it had made her feel special because her mom and dad had picked her, her especially, to love. But Uncle Bryan hadn't picked her. She'd been forced on him.

There was another reason she had to find her other mother. Nicki had to know why that lady had given her away. Nicki hoped that she hadn't meant to, that she, Nicki, had been taken away without her knowing it. She was afraid, sometimes, that Uncle Bryan thought about how it wasn't fair that he *had* to keep her when even the woman who'd actually had her didn't want her.

She knew that he had to think it wasn't fair, 'cause Uncle Bryan hadn't ever wanted any children, not even his own. She'd heard him arguing with Grandma about it the last time he'd come to Shallowbrook for vacation. Grandma was always wanting him to get married and give her some more grandchildren. And he'd said he wasn't the marrying kind and he wouldn't make a good father. Nicki thought he'd make the best dad ever next to her own, and she loved him as much as any kid ever loved a dad. She just wished he felt differently about wanting kids.

JENNIFER CHATTED EASILY with him when he flew her to lunch on Monday. In fact, she spent the entire meal telling him about the celebrity tennis match she'd attended over the weekend. But her describing, in great detail, how two professional tennis players had faced off against each other with two professional basketball players partnering them wasn't exactly what he'd had in mind when he'd encouraged her to open up to him.

On the way back to her office, he'd asked her again about the television spots he wanted her to do with children. She'd still refused to do them, but he had a feeling she was weakening. The idea almost guaranteed success. And the more time he spent with Jennifer the more important it became to him to make her One Price campaign a success.

But apart from the campaign, there was another reason he couldn't let the idea die. She'd refused to do the commercials because she wasn't good with kids. That worried him.

Nicki was sound asleep when he got home that afternoon, but because she hadn't slept well the night before, he didn't wake her up for dinner. He spent the evening thinking about her birth mother, instead. The woman was perplexing. She seemed so up-front and honest, yet there were times when he sensed things simmering under her polished surface that he couldn't begin to understand. She always appeared so together, but she had a past that wasn't together at all. And what made him even more uncomfortable was how much she just plain intrigued him. Somehow he had to get her to relax enough to open up to him.

The idea came to him Wednesday morning. A picnic. A quiet intimate lunch for two. And he knew just the spot—a lush green patch of land up on Stone Mountain. Telling Jacci to cancel his afternoon appointments, Bryan checked with Mrs. Baker to make certain his cheerful neighbor would be available in case Nicki had a problem at school, then dialed Jennifer's private number.

"Have you got anything comfortable to wear stashed at work?" he asked as soon as she picked up the line.

"Bryan?" She sounded pleased to hear from him.

"Uh-huh. I was thinking about kidnapping you for a couple of hours, but you'll need to change out of that suit you're wearing."

"How do you know I'm wearing a suit?"

"Aren't you?"

"Yes."

"See?"

"Okay. Well, it just happens I do have a change of clothes here. I always keep some jeans handy in case I want to have dinner with Sam," she said, sounding sassy, egging him on.

"Who's Sam?" He pretended to sound aggrieved.

"Only the best mechanic I've ever met."

"And you have dinner with him often?"

"Fairly often. Anything else you want to know?"

"Yeah, why can't you wear your suits for Sam?"

"Because they might get greasy."

Bryan grinned. "Greasy?" He pictured a couple of black handprints on the derriere of the green linen suit she'd been wearing at lunch on Monday. "Jeez, Jennifer, have some class."

"Don't get gross on me, Chambers. Sam's almost seventy years old, and whenever we work on my car together, I bring him dinner."

That got him. "*You* work on your car?"

"Guess I'm not so predictable, after all, huh?" she asked. He could tell she was laughing, though she had the grace to do so silently.

He wanted to throttle her and kiss her at once. Except that she was Nicki's mother.

"Just change into those jeans. I'm on my way," he said, and hung up.

"IT'S BEEN YEARS since I've been here," Jennifer said an hour later as he pulled into the west gate at Stone Mountain. He'd taken the sides and top off the Jeep, and strands of her auburn hair had pulled free of their twist and feathered her cheeks and neck.

She was smiling—and beautiful.

"Not too much time in the life of a busy executive to stop and smell the roses, huh?" he asked.

"There probably should be. I just don't slow down enough to find out."

He pulled around to the service drive that led to a big parking lot by the youth camping area. "Why not?"

She'd made her way in a man's world and he admired her for it. But didn't she long for some of the things she'd passed up? Things like marriage and motherhood?

She shrugged, and he sensed another of her vague answers on the tip of her tongue. And then she looked at him, really looked at him, her hazel eyes a little unsure.

"I'm happiest when I'm busy," she said.

Bryan could understand that. He was, too.

He pulled a blanket and the deli basket from behind his seat and led her into the park. He could hear children in the distance, yelling, laughing, having the times of their lives.

She helped him spread out the blanket and divvy up the turkey and roast-beef sandwiches, chips and apples. He opened a couple of wine coolers.

"I would've figured you for a beer man," she said, taking a long swallow from the bottle he handed her.

"Usually when I drink I go straight for the hard stuff, not that it happens often, but I was trying for a more romantic effect here." He'd fought with himself when he'd purchased the bottles at the deli next door to his office. No matter how much she attracted him, he had no business pursuing a personal relationship with her. But he'd gone ahead and bought the wine, anyway.

"Romance is good." The sun-draped mountain was a perfect background for her smile.

He stretched out across from her, taking a couple of sandwiches with him. "I wasn't sure you took time for that, either."

"I don't very often."

He was curiously glad to hear that.

They ate and drank, the sound of trees and grasses rustling in the light breeze, just enough to mute the noises of the park, enveloping them in their own little world. Jennifer looked more relaxed than he'd ever seen her, and more beautiful.

"This was a great idea," she said halfway through her second sandwich.

Looking across at her, feeling more content than he'd felt in a long time, Bryan had to remind himself of his reason for bringing her there.

"I hoped you'd enjoy getting away. You work too much."

"I know."

"So why do you? Surely there are other ways to stay busy." *God, woman, tell me what I have to know before I fall for you and hurt us both.*

She put her sandwich down, turning to look up at the mountain. The chair lift taking visitors up one side of the mountain was visible from where they sat.

"I'm in a man's world, and I've always had the feeling that if I relax too much, if I let go for even a minute, I may lose it all."

He looked at her profile, the delicate features. What a contradiction she was. So feminine, yet so driven to succeed. "You're talking about a multimillion-dollar empire!"

She turned her head, looking straight at him. "And do you know how many men are just waiting for me to make that one mistake that'll let them eat me alive?"

"Then what made you get into the business to begin with, if you feel that way?"

"I took it over from my parents."

"Couldn't you have sold it, used the money to invest in something else?"

"No, I couldn't." She shook her head, looking back at the mountain. "I needed to make a success of it, not sell it. I needed to do it for them."

Bryan sat up. "Why?"

"I was born late in their marriage. My mother was already in her forties and had thought herself beyond child-bearing age. They were good people and they loved me, but I was an intrusion in their lives, one they never really, wholeheartedly accepted."

Bryan thought of his own family, feeling the familiar pang as he remembered how close they'd all been. "It must have been rough growing up," he said, thankful suddenly for Shallowbrook and the years of his youth.

"It wasn't that bad. They weren't mean to me or anything. It just seemed like I was always trying to be perfect in order to avoid their irritated frowns. Half the time I don't even think they knew they were frowning. They just didn't know what to do with a child around."

She was still facing the mountain, but at least she was talking.

"And so you grew up and made them millionaires to repay them for making your childhood miserable?" he asked.

She looked at him then and smiled, a self-deprecating, knowing smile. "Is that what it sounds like?"

"From where I'm sitting."

She shrugged. "I don't know, maybe it was a little like that. But they tried, Bryan. They were always honest with me, and fair. They gave me opportunities, including a college education they couldn't afford. After I graduated with a degree in business, I found out what a bad state Teal Motors was in. They asked me if I could help them. Finally there was something I could do to please them, to pay them back for the twenty-year disruption I'd been in their lives, something to show them I loved them. Something I could do to make them happy again. And as it turned out, pleasing them pleased me, too. I love the car business."

He admired her determination. "So how long did it take you to learn the ropes?"

"I already knew them inside and out. I grew up at the dealership and worked there for most of my teenage years. I rebuilt my first car engine, with Sam's help, during my junior year in high school."

Before or after she'd given Nicki away? "What happened to the car?" he asked.

"Nothing. I'm still driving it."

"The Mustang?"

"Mmm."

"You wouldn't be interested in selling it, would you?"

"Never. God willing, I'll be driving that car when I'm eighty."

"Somehow I believe you will be," Bryan said, gathering up the remnants of their picnic. She really cared about certain things in her life—her parents, her business, her car. But what about her child? How had Nicki missed out on that caring?

Bryan loaded their things back into the Jeep and then suggested a walk. He wasn't any less confused now than he'd been before the day had begun. How could a woman who'd grown up as she had, who'd spent her entire life trying to earn the love of her parents, not at some point have given a thought to the child she'd given birth to? Why hadn't she at least registered someplace in case the child needed her?

The path to the petting zoo was heavily traveled and swarming with kids. A couple of little boys, around five or six years old, zoomed past, racing each other to a tree up ahead, and Bryan couldn't help but smile at their antics.

"Shouldn't their parents be watching them more closely?" Jennifer asked, frowning.

"They're probably right behind us."

"I hope so. Those boys look awfully young to be on their own."

Her shoulder brushed him and he had to restrain himself from putting his arm around her and pulling her closer. She didn't need his protection. There was nothing there for her to be afraid of.

"Have you ever thought about having children?" he asked, losing sight of the boys as they rounded a bend.

"I have no interest in being a mother."

His heart sank. "Isn't that a little strong?"

"I feel strongly about it."

She'd put more distance between them, moving closer to the side of the path. "What about Teal Motors? Don't you ever think about having an heir to pass it on to?"

"Not really."

"But girls always want to grow up and have babies," he blurted. *Great, Chambers, now there's an intelligent statement.* But he was frustrated and scared for Nicki. He just didn't want to believe that Jennifer had no place in her heart for the daughter who needed her. He'd seen her with her employees, with an old lady she didn't even know. She was compassion personified. Something wasn't adding up.

"Why is it that just because I'm a woman, I'm automatically expected to produce babies? If I were a man, would you be pressuring me to procreate? And what about you? I don't see you out there lining up to be a daddy."

Because I'm already a father, and mother, too, to your child. They fell into an uneasy silence as they continued to walk, and Bryan wondered if she was wishing she'd never set eyes on him.

They'd reached a fork in the path, and Jennifer swerved onto the different route. "Let's see what's up there," she said, glancing back to make sure he was behind her.

What was up there turned out to be a birthday party for Molly, who was just turning eleven, according to the banner strung across the path. He and Jennifer walked to the end of the path, silently passing beneath the banner, before they turned around and headed back the way they'd come.

Bryan watched the birthday girls as they passed the party a second time. The girls were gathered in a huddle, squealing and giggling, right beside a table piled high with presents. Bryan got a sick feeling in his gut as he saw a woman, probably Molly's mother, call the girls over and give each of them a slip of paper and a shopping bag. A scavenger hunt.

Nicki had had a scavenger hunt for her tenth birthday. And a tornado for her eleventh. And, dear God, her twelfth one was coming up soon. His heart froze as he realized just how soon. In a little over a week, Nicki was going to be twelve years old. In a little over a week, it was going to be a full year since Lori and his parents had died.

He had no idea how he and Nicki were going to celebrate the day, but he was pretty certain she wouldn't be enjoying it the way Molly obviously was.

"Excuse me, lady. We're having a scavenger hunt. Do you have a bobby pin I could have?" A girl stood before them on the path, looking cute and carefree as she grinned up at them. Her lips were stained purple.

"No. I'm sorry," Jennifer said. She kept on walking. Bryan stared at the pinned-up hair on the back of her head.

The pigtailed girl walked backward, staying in front of Jennifer. "Would you look at my list then and see if there's anything here you might have?" she asked.

"I'm sorry, honey, I have to get back," Jennifer said, smiling as she stepped around the child.

"Thanks, anyway," the child called as she scampered off.

The whole thing had only taken a couple of seconds, but it worried Bryan more than anything that had gone before. Jennifer had been as pleasant as always, but she'd still just brushed off that child with an ease that told its own story. A story that might well contain an unhappy ending for Nicki.

CHAPTER SIX

"MAMA? MAMA! *Ma-ma-a-a!*"

Bryan shot out of bed, pulled on his cutoffs and raced into Nicki's room as he heard the familiar cry. It had been almost a month since the last time. He'd been hoping they were past this point.

He pulled the sweating body of his niece from beneath her covers and into his arms. "It's okay, Nick. I'm here, baby. It's okay," he said softly over and over as he stroked the damp strands of her hair away from her face.

He felt her shudder and knew she'd come back to him. "Uncle Bryan?" Her voice was weak and frightened.

"I'm here, baby. Right here," he said, choking down the emotion that had been so close to the surface for the past year. As hard it was for him to accept the loss of his family, he knew it was ten times harder for Nicki.

She started to cry, sobbing against his chest so hopelessly that it hurt him just to listen to her. God, he hated the Fates that had done this to such a sweet sensitive child.

He held her and rocked her, soothing her with words of love, and long before the storm had passed, a few of his own tears had mingled with hers.

"I'm sorry, Uncle Bryan. I didn't mean to," she said some time later, pulling away from him.

He reached out, brushing the tears from her cheeks, aching inside as he saw her swollen eyes. "Don't apologize, sweetheart. It isn't your fault. None of this is your fault."

She shivered and scooted back from him, sitting on her pillow with her knees curled up to her chest. "Sometimes I think it is," she whispered.

Bryan froze. "No! Nicki, you're not to blame for anything. Don't even think it."

She looked up at him, her soft hazel eyes filling with tears again. "But if it hadn't been for me, for that stupid party I had to have, everybody wouldn't have been together outside like that."

Bryan slid down to kneel at the side of her bed, leaning over to bring his face even with hers. "The tornado would still have come, honey, and even inside, in different houses, they would have died if it was their time. It had nothing to do with you."

She studied his face, her eyes wide. "Do you really believe that, Uncle Bryan? Really?" she whispered.

"Yes, I do, honey. With all my heart."

Nicki held out her arms and asked, "Can I have a hug?"

"Of course, sprite. Always." He sat back down beside her and pulled her into his arms, silently cursing his inability to shield her from her demons.

"I just wish it didn't hurt so much," she said after a minute or two.

Bryan felt her words clear to his soul. "I know, little one. I wish that, too."

"Do you still miss them?"

"More than ever, honey. All the time."

"Do you think we'll ever stop missing them?"

Bryan weighed his words carefully. "Not completely. I don't think we'd want to. We never want to forget them or how much we loved them. But I do think that someday we'll smile more often than we cry when we think of them."

"Sometimes I try not to think of them because it hurts too much, and then I feel bad, like I'm trying to forget them. But I don't want to forget them, Uncle Bryan. Not ever, and sometimes I'm scared I will."

"I know, sweetie. But you don't have to worry about that. There's a part of each one of them in you, and no one can ever take that away from you."

"I love you, Uncle Bryan." She snuggled into his chest.

"And I love you, Nick, more than anything."

He held her until she fell back to sleep, thanking the Lord for saving her from the ravages of the tornado that had taken the rest of his family. He'd willingly lay down his life for this child. Or his heart. She came first. No matter what.

JENNIFER SAW BRYAN twice more that week. He was still after her to do some commercials with kids and had stopped by on Thursday to show her the specs for the spots he'd reserved, including a projected return on her investment. It was impressive.

On Friday he came by to bring her the scripts. He wasn't taking no for an answer. And Jennifer found herself weakening. Probably because she knew he was right. They were a great idea.

Nevertheless, as she sat across from him in her office, she said, "There have to be other good ideas."

"Good, sure, but not great." He tapped the folder against his jeans. "At least read the scripts, and then we can talk again."

Jennifer took them. There was no reason not to. "Okay, but I can't promise to like them." But she knew she would. And maybe, after next week was over, she'd even feel better about doing the commercials. She wasn't good with children, but she didn't dislike them. It was just the time of year. She was overreacting.

"All I'm asking is that you give them a chance." Bryan rubbed his hand over his eyes and down his face, the second time he'd done it in the five minutes he'd been there.

"You look tired," she said, concerned.

"I am. My partner is in the middle of the first vacation he's had in ten years, and it's been hell at the office. I'd never realized just how much he does there."

"Maybe we shouldn't have gone to Stone Mountain the other day, huh?" She still wasn't sure why they'd gone. If he'd been after a romantic interlude as she'd thought when he took her up there, wouldn't he at least have tried to kiss her?

He stood up. "It was worth it," he said, his gaze penetrating. "I wanted to see you. Besides, I worked late last night at home."

"Do you work at home a lot?" She came around her desk to walk with him to the door, wishing he didn't have to leave so soon.

"More now than I used to." He tucked his sketchbook under his arm and pulled his sunglasses out of his shirt pocket.

"You have an office there?" She didn't even know where he lived.

He stopped at the door. "I'm working on it. I just bought the place last summer and I'm furnishing it a little bit at a time."

"It's the first home you've owned?" Jennifer didn't know why she wasn't just letting him go. She had more work to do than time to do it. And apparently he did, too.

"Yeah. Ownership always sounded like chains to me."

"So what made you change your mind?"

"It was time."

A master at issuing vague answers, Jennifer knew she'd just received one. She wondered why.

"By the way, I like the dress." His eyes moved slowly over her, lingering on her breasts, the dip at her waist, before continuing downward.

"Thank you. I guess I was kind of in a rut with the suit thing."

He looked at her lips and then opened the door. "Read the scripts, Jennifer," he said, and nodded at Rachel on his way out.

SHE WAS WORKING at home herself that evening, dressed in a short black shift that she only wore around the house, when her buzzer sounded, signaling a visitor for her downstairs. She pushed the button on her intercom. She hoped it was Bryan.

It wasn't. It was Tanya.

"I want to know why you've been avoiding me," her friend said the minute she was in the penthouse. She slid out of her sandals and plopped down on one of Jennifer's white overstuffed couches.

"I haven't been avoiding you," Jennifer said, sitting on the opposite couch.

"You know about the baby, don't you?" Tanya asked.

Jennifer couldn't escape Tanya's piercing stare. She nodded.

"Who told you?"

"Dennis's secretary, indirectly. I heard her talking about your doctor's appointment."

It was Tanya's turn to look away. "I didn't mean for you to find out that way, Jen. I wanted to tell you myself."

"Then why didn't you?"

"I just wasn't sure you'd want to hear about it—especially with next week looming so close and all."

Jennifer didn't want to think about next week. "It's been twelve years, Tanya. I think I can handle it," Jennifer said dryly.

"I don't, not when you use that tone of voice. Which is just what I was afraid of." Tanya was as blunt as ever.

Jennifer's chest tightened, making it harder for her to breathe. "What? I said I could handle it. It's not a big deal."

Tanya's eyes softened, but Jennifer saw the hurt in them. "Yes, it *is* a big deal. To me and Dennis, anyway. And you're not happy about it."

"Of course I'm—" Jennifer broke off, unable to continue lying to her friend. "It's just the time of year, Tan, like you said. You know me. I get a little weepy, the day goes by, and then I'm fine again. I'll be happy for you long before the baby comes." At least that was what she'd been telling herself.

"That's what Dennis and I figured at first. It's why we decided to wait until after next week to tell you about it. But I'm not so sure anymore."

"What do you think I'm going to do—fall apart at the seams?"

"No! Of course not. You're stronger than that. What you're going to do is keep avoiding me until we drift apart, and eventually we'll only see each other at the annual Christmas party."

"Isn't that a bit melodramatic?" Jennifer smiled at her friend.

"I don't think so, Jen, and neither does Dennis."

"You guys are my best friends. We see each other all the time," Jennifer said, doing everything in her power to believe that everything was going to be just fine.

"You see Dennis at work every day, but how long has it been since you came out to the house or even met me for lunch?"

Jennifer couldn't remember the last time.

"Next to Dennis, you're the best friend I've ever had, Jen. I'm not going to lose you because I want to be a mother."

"You're not going to lose me."

"Then why have you been avoiding me?"

Jennifer looked away. "I've just been busy at work overseeing the introduction of One Price. I'm spending a lot of extra time at the dealerships."

"So's Dennis, and I still see him."

"He lives with you."

"He also meets me for lunch."

"All right! I'll meet you for lunch. Pick a day."

"And have you cancel on me? Uh-uh."

"What is it with you, Tanya? You want me to have lunch with you, so I've said I'll have lunch with you."

"I want you to admit you're bothered by this baby."

Jennifer felt as if she was suffocating. "Why would I be bothered?"

"I was with you on her first birthday, Jen, remember?"

No! Jennifer's mind went blank. She felt numb. It was understood that that chapter in her life was over.

"I remember that day like it was yesterday. We were both at Florida State, checking out the campus before applying."

Pain seared through Jennifer as she remembered, too. All of it. Every painful, lonely, empty second. No. She'd come through that. It was over.

"And I got drunk and cried in my soup. I never have been able to hold my liquor worth a damn." She forced the words past the constriction in her throat.

"You cried because your heart was breaking."

Jennifer jumped up. Why had she ever thought Tanya was her friend? Friends didn't do this to people. "Okay, I was dying inside. Is that what you want to hear?"

"No."

"What, then? What do you want from me, Tanya?" She was nearly yelling. *Deep breaths. Calm down. It's over.*

"I want you to let go of the guilt, for starters."

"Leave it, Tanya."

"I can't, Jen. I'm going to lose you if I do. And you're going to lose, too."

Jennifer sat back down, her head in her hands. "I can't do this again."

"You haven't done it yet. That's my point. All these years, I've thought you handled everything so well, but instead, what you've been doing is beating yourself up every year on her birthday until you're crazy with pain, and then you run from it the rest of year."

Jennifer couldn't breathe. "You've deduced all this because I'm not happy you're pregnant?" Jennifer couldn't believe how awful those last five words sounded.

"No!" Tanya rubbed the slight mound of her belly as if apologizing to her baby for Jennifer's horrible words. "But when you started avoiding me, it got me thinking about a lot of things. Made me see them in a different way."

"What things?"

"Look at how you are around children, Jen. Or, rather, how you're *not* around them. You avoid them like the plague. At last year's Christmas party you even arranged it so they'd be in a different room altogether."

"I hired a Santa, Tanya! He had gifts for every one of those children. Can you imagine what a ruckus there'd have been if they'd been in the same ballroom as several hundred adults?" She went over to the wet bar and poured Tanya a glass of the sparkling water she always kept on hand for her.

"It might have been fun. There's nothing like seeing that glow in children's eyes when they're opening presents from Santa. Besides, that doesn't explain your refusal to speak to all those eighth graders at that young businessmen's convention last fall, or your insistence that we shop during school hours. And what about that time they wanted you to appear at the children's home to raise money for the new roof? You bought the damn roof yourself so you wouldn't have to go."

"I'm just not good with children, Tanya," she said, handing Tanya the glass.

"Baloney."

"I'm not. They make me nervous. I don't know, maybe I get it from my parents, but I always feel uncomfortable when I'm around kids."

"Maybe it's because you can't look at them without remembering, without all the old guilt coming back, and that makes you feel unworthy all over again. I don't think it's the children who make you uncomfortable, Jen. I think it's the relapse into low self-esteem that does that."

"Since when did you get your degree in psychology?" Jennifer asked, going back to pour herself a glass of wine. Her hands were shaking and some of the wine spilled over the rim of her glass.

"I love you, Jen. I think that counts more than a degree."

Jennifer couldn't continue to fight Tanya. She knew her friend well. Tanya had a stubborn streak the size of Georgia when she believed she was right. And Jennifer had a feeling Tanya *was* right this time. She took her wine over to the couch, needing to sit. Her legs were shaky, too.

"What do you want from me, Tanya?" she asked softly, meeting her friend's concerned gaze.

"I want you to forgive yourself for giving away your baby. I want you to let yourself grieve for your loss."

"Oh, I grieve, Tanya. More than I realized."

Tanya shook her head. "You don't grieve, honey. You just hurt. Grieving means letting go."

Jennifer couldn't hold back the tears any longer. They welled in her eyes and rolled slowly down her face. "I wish it were that easy, Tan. But maybe it isn't possible to have a baby and then just let go." Jennifer felt alien saying the words. She hadn't talked about her daughter since the baby's first birthday when she'd poured out her soul to Tanya. But maybe Tanya was right. Maybe she hadn't recovered from that time in her life as she'd thought she had. She *should* be feeling happy for her friends' upcoming parenthood. So maybe, as Tanya said, it was time to take a close look at herself, come to terms with her past.

And suddenly, as the walls she'd built so many years before came tumbling down, Jennifer was swamped with emotions, with thoughts, she hadn't dared let herself acknowledge. And every one of them hurt.

"I never said it was easy, Jen." Tanya's voice brought Jennifer back up from the abyss. She'd forgotten, for a moment, that her friend was even there in the room. "But I'm afraid you're never going to get on with your life if you don't let her go."

Jennifer saw the love in Tanya's eyes, and it gave her the strength to continue into territory she'd thought never to visit again. "It doesn't seem right that I turn my back on my firstborn and then go blissfully on with my life."

Tanya grabbed a tissue from an end table and sat down beside Jennifer. "You didn't turn your back on her, honey. You gave her a shot at a much better life than you could have provided for her."

Jennifer sniffed, her tears still streaming down her face.

"Oh, Jen," Tanya said, holding Jennifer the way she had that day so many years ago.

Jennifer cried until she didn't have any tears left, leaning on Tanya, needing her friend's strength. Tanya continued to hold her, murmuring soothing words. At last Jennifer sat back on the couch, her mind clouded by the anguish she'd kept bottled up inside.

"You know, there're places you can go now, places you can register yourself as her mother in case she's looking for you." Tanya's soft words broke the silence. "There are even ways you can find out where and how she is."

"I've thought of that," Jennifer said, her voice still thick with tears. "During those first years, I drove myself crazy thinking about finding her. Do you have any idea how many times I've stopped in a crowd because I saw a child who looked her age and had my color hair?"

"Then why haven't you registered? What could it hurt?"

"I promised I wouldn't." But until that moment, Jennifer hadn't even realized she still put any stock in that childish promise. She had at first, of course, during those early difficult years. But she was an adult now. She hadn't thought of those hospital-bed promises in years.

Tanya frowned. "Promised who?"

"I don't know. God maybe. Or myself. I promised I wouldn't look for her, and I wouldn't ever let anything or anyone ever take her place in my heart, if only she could have a happy life." She'd promised something else, too. She'd promised never to make love again. But surely she wasn't still holding herself to that vow, was she? The reason she hadn't been with another man was simply that she hadn't had the time to develop a close enough relationship.

"When, Jen? When did you promise that?"

"The night before they took my baby away. A nurse brought her in to me." If she closed her eyes, Jennifer could still feel the softness of her daughter's skin, still smell that new-baby smell. "I held her." Her words were barely a whisper, but they conveyed twelve years' worth of anguish.

"Oh, Jen," Tanya said, her eyes filling with tears. "I'm so sorry. But surely you haven't been holding yourself to a promise made under those conditions. You were only a child!"

"I know. And it's not like I've even thought about that old vow for years, but I thought about it a lot those first few years, and I guess upholding it just became habit."

She drew a shaky breath. "Besides, in my heart, I know I don't have the right to hunt her down. If she does have a happy life, if her family is everything I chose not to be, it would be cruel for me to breeze in now and stake my claim to her. She may not even know she's adopted. And what if she hates me for what I did? Or worse yet, what if I'm like my mother? What if I'm just not good with kids? With her?"

Tanya wiped away her tears. "You need to quit worrying about that right now, Jen. You're too good with people not to be good with kids. After all, they're just miniature adults with a huge dose of innocence thrown in. All you need to relate to kids is some compassion, and you're one of the most compassionate people I know."

Jennifer smiled through her tears. "What about that time Ralph Goodwin brought his kid to the Teal corporate offices and then got tied up with the accountant for over an hour? Rachel went home sick and

I got stuck with the child. He must've told me ten times he hates me. He even stuck his tongue out at me."

Tanya laughed. "He was a brat, Jen. He stuck his tongue out at everybody."

"Okay," Jennifer conceded, serious again. "But how about that time here in the building when the electricity went out and I was in the elevator with that little girl who lived downstairs? She huddled in the corner the whole time and acted like I was the big bad wolf, ready to eat her at any second. That had to be the longest two hours of my life."

"She was scared. She wanted her mother. It wasn't anything you did."

"I wish I could believe that."

"You'll see. You'll have your chance. Just as soon as junior's born."

Jennifer didn't think so. She'd always been afraid of being like her parents, unable to relate to children, but she'd been pretty sure of it that night in the elevator. She'd been unable to reach that little girl, unable to offer any comfort. And there hadn't been a single instance since then that had proved her wrong.

But Tanya was right about one thing: it was time to stop running. She'd had no idea she'd let herself get so out of whack over the years, and wondered if that vow she'd made as a child had had other far-reaching effects. Maybe it, and not lack of time, had stood in the way of her ever developing a lasting relationship with a man. She didn't know, but it was a possibility she was going to have to face, and she would, just as soon as her One Price policy was up and flying. And until then, no matter how painful she might find the next several months, she was going to be there every step of the way for her friends, just as they'd always been there for her.

Tanya broke gently into the silence that had fallen. "Even if you don't search for your daughter," she said, "you can still register yourself as her birth mother."

The prospect was exhilarating and frightening at once. What if her daughter needed her? But what if she failed her daughter? "Maybe."

"Just maybe?"

Jennifer thought of Bryan. Of the commercials he wanted her to do. "I don't know. You may not think I'm a failure around kids, but I'm not so sure. I never know what to say to them."

But if the lines are written for me, if they're rehearsed, if I know in advance what the children are going to say...

"At least think about it, Jen. Don't be so ready to condemn yourself."

"Maybe..."

The two sat silently for a couple of minutes, absorbing the peace of the penthouse. And then Tanya got up to retrieve her glass and sit back down on the other couch.

"Now that that's out of the way, tell me about this gorgeous hunk you've been seeing," she said, typical Tanya-style.

"I'm not seeing him. We're just friends. And you can tell your husband that his big mouth is going to get him into serious trouble if he doesn't watch it," Jennifer replied, feeling more like herself again.

Tanya grinned. "Oh, my! I didn't realize this Bryan guy was such a big deal. There may be hope for you yet."

Jennifer threw a pillow at her friend, hitting her square in the face.

"Now look what you've done," Tanya said, laughing as she jumped up with the glass she'd been holding. "You've spilled water all over your pretty white couch."

Jennifer stood up, too. "Either come help me answer some charity letters or go home, Tanya. I have work to do."

"But what about the couch?" Tanya asked.

"It'll dry."

Tanya answered more than thirty letters, including checks from Jennifer in each, before she finally went home. She didn't mention Bryan or the baby again.

JENNIFER WAS BUSY all weekend, working both at home and at the office, visiting a couple of her dealerships as she usually did on weekends and holidays so her people knew that while she expected them to work the off-hours, she wasn't asking anything of them she didn't do herself. She attended a Hawks game on Saturday night with her finance managers and their spouses, and an art exhibit with Tanya on Sunday. And afterward, she had dinner with Dennis and Tanya at their home in Snellville, just west of Atlanta.

She saw the nursery her friends were setting up, picked up a tiny white T-shirt and cried all the way home. But at least she was no longer running.

She didn't hear from Bryan all weekend.

But he called her first thing Monday morning, before she'd even had a chance to pour herself a cup of coffee. "Did you read them?" His voice was wonderfully familiar and exciting at the same time.

"Don't you ever say hello?"

"Hello, did you read the scripts?"

"Yes."

"And?"

"They're good."

"And?"

He sure didn't make anything easy. "I want your word that I have the final say on anything that's aired, and that you'll destroy any tapes I don't approve of."

"So, you're going to do them." The approval she heard in his voice almost made the rough weekend she'd spent fighting with herself over her decision worthwhile.

"On a couple of conditions."

"Which are?"

"You'll be there for the filming of each and every one of them."

"Of course."

"And if I say stop, we stop."

"You're the boss. How soon can you clear a couple of days to get it done?"

She looked at her calendar. Friday—The Day—was blank. She was hoping to spend it with Bryan—but not working. It was going to be hard enough just to get through those hours.

"Is next Monday soon enough?"

"Monday's good. Calvin'll be back by then to hold down the fort here, and it'll be easier for me to spend a few days away from this place. It'll also give me time to find the kids. I'll let you know the details later in the week."

"So I won't see you before then?" she asked. She couldn't come right out and ask him for a date on Friday. Just like she hadn't been able to look up his home phone number and call him over the weekend, no matter how badly she'd wanted to. She might be a nineties woman, she might live in a man's world, but she'd been labeled "easy" once. It wasn't going to happen again.

"Would you like to?"

"Yes."

"Then I'll see what I can do to juggle things here."

Jennifer pulled out the tickets she had. They weren't for Friday, but she'd told him she'd let him know if she heard of a concert more in his style. She wasn't asking for a date, merely doing a favor for a friend.

"Boston's playing at Fulton County Stadium on Wednesday night. Somebody gave me a couple of tickets." Someone had. The girl she'd bought them from at the ticket outlet where she'd stood in line on Saturday.

"Boston. Quite a band. Now that brings back some memories."

"I don't know about blankets in the grass, but it'll be outdoors and blue jeans."

"Just my style. Okay, lady, you've got yourself a date. What time's the concert?"

"Eight."

"Then how about if I come for you at five and we can stop someplace for dinner on the way?"

"I'd like that," Jennifer said, feeling better than she had in weeks, years maybe.

Just two more days until she saw him again.

CHAPTER SEVEN

BRYAN WANTED TO KICK himself for agreeing to go to the concert. He could have gotten out of it easily. He could have simply told her he was busy all week with Calvin out of town. She'd have understood. And he would have told her that if she hadn't agreed to do the commercials, if she hadn't given him another spurt of hope.

But he still should have turned her down. Because the concert was a date. Pure and simple. He had a date with the most beautiful woman he'd known in a long time, a woman he'd been fantasizing about since he'd spoken to her in that art gallery all those weeks ago, the first woman he'd seen more than three times without getting bored. Nicki's mother. A woman who was off-limits.

A woman who might very well hate him when she found out he'd been seeing her as a means to his own ends. One thing he'd learned over the past weeks with her was that she didn't trust lightly. But she trusted *him*. She was opening up to him in ways she apparently hadn't done with a man in a long time. And he was breaching that trust at the same time he was encouraging her to open up more.

But what choice did he have? Nicki had had another nightmare over the weekend. He'd figured the recurrence was probably due to her upcoming birthday, but that didn't make it any less painful—for either of them. He wasn't sure how much more his niece could take. He wasn't sure how fair he was being to her by having the information she wanted more than anything else and not giving it to her.

And yet, could he risk the chance that Jennifer might reject her? Could he risk Nicki's falling apart on him completely? Bryan didn't have any answers, but he knew one thing: he was living on borrowed time.

THANK GOD it wasn't blankets on the grass. Bryan didn't think he'd have been able to keep his hands off her if they were lying down. As it was, he was having as hard a time keeping his mind on the show as he had at the symphony. And Boston was one of his all-time favorite rock bands.

But Jennifer was wearing one of those short shirts Nicki had wanted, minus the daisy. The tanned strip of bare waistline only inches away from him was sheer torment. Her hair was up as usual, but a few tendrils had escaped and brushed his arm every time she turned her head.

The chords from the beginning of "More Than a Feeling" blared out across the stadium, and Bryan felt the familiar rush of adrenaline he always got when he heard the song. He sat forward to watch the lead guitarist, his hand dropping to the arm of his seat.

But it didn't land on the arm of the chair. It landed on Jennifer's hand. And before Bryan's lust-fogged brain could demand that he remove his hand immediately, Jennifer's fingers curled around his.

He looked over at her silently, unable to hear or be heard above the deafening roar of the band. He wasn't sure what he had to say, anyway. She smiled at him, her eyes promising him things he couldn't have. He smiled back, wondering what it was about her that made her so different from all of the other women he'd dated.

It had been far too long since he'd had a woman. Too long since he'd felt the soft gliding of a woman's fingers on his body, pleasuring him, getting tangled in the hair on his chest, digging into his back. Too long since he'd kissed the delicate flesh of a woman's body, since he'd heard her cry out in passion and delight.

And it was going to be even longer. His first and only concern right now was Nicki. And if it turned out that Jennifer didn't want Nicki, then he would never have Jennifer.

But he held Jennifer's hand throughout the remainder of the concert, and he took it again as they walked to his Jeep afterward. "I, uh, don't have all the times set for next week yet. I'll have Jacci give you a call with them on Friday," he said, as if talking business with her somehow made the fact that he was touching her less dangerous.

"I won't be in on Friday."

Bryan helped her over a knee-high wall as they took a shortcut between parking lots.

"You're taking the day off?"

He'd wondered how she was going to spend Nicki's birthday, if she even remembered what day it was.

"We're having the carpets cleaned in the executive offices. It's an annual thing."

The carpet cleaned. Nothing more profound than that. He released her to unlock the passenger door of the Jeep. "As it happens, I have the day off, as well. I have some personal business to attend to."

"Oh. Will it take all day?"

"Uh-huh. I'm driving up to Shallowbrook."

"Isn't that where you said you grew up?"

"Yeah. It's a great little town." Or at least it was. Before a tornado swept in and destroyed everything in its path.

He told himself not to be disappointed that she hadn't remembered Nicki's birthday. He didn't expect her to have spent the past twelve years thinking about the daughter she'd given away. And she had no way of knowing how difficult this particular day was going to be for Nicki. And for him.

She didn't know because he chose not to tell her. And he was no closer to doing so. He hated the indecision. He preferred to act and deal with the consequences. But this wasn't about him. It was about Nicki. And so far, all he knew was that Nicki's mother didn't want children, and apparently never thought about the one she'd had. But how would Nicki react if he told her he couldn't find her mother? Would she break down completely?

"Would you like to come in for some coffee?" Jennifer asked half an hour later as she unlocked the door of the penthouse.

The vulnerable look in her eyes was almost his undoing. She hadn't offered lightly. But he knew what would happen if he stepped inside that door.

"I'd love to, but I'll need to take a rain check. I have work to do with Calvin being gone."

She looked disappointed. "You're going to work tonight?"

"For a while." It might help him sleep.

"And you thought *I* didn't take enough time to smell the roses."

Bryan reached out, brushing aside the hair framing her face. He wished he'd met her in another lifetime. "I'll take time to smell them. Just as soon as Calvin returns," he promised.

It was a promise he wasn't going to keep. And he wasn't going to kiss her good-night, either. He saw the confusion in her eyes as he stepped back into the elevator. He was hurting her, but there didn't seem to be any way not to.

BRYAN WAS UP early on Friday, creeping around his kitchen furtively, trying not to make a sound as he prepared Nicki's favorite breakfast—pancakes with blueberry syrup, and grits. He piled it all on a tray he'd decorated with linen and a china plate he'd bought specifically for the occasion and topped it off with a single yellow rose. He was going to make her feel special today if it was the last thing he did.

"Up and at 'em, kid," he said cheerily as he pushed into her room.

"But it's the first day of summer vacation," came the sleepy voice from the bed.

"It's more than that, and you know it. Now open your eyes and see what I've brought you."

She turned over reluctantly and sat up, her eyes still only half-open.

Holding the orange juice steady, he set the tray down across her legs. She looked at it and then at him.

"Oh, Uncle Bryan," she said, her eyes filling with tears.

"Happy birthday, Nick."

She looked back down at the tray. "My very own breakfast in bed. Just like a grown-up."

"Just like a princess," Bryan corrected, handing her a tissue from her nightstand. "Now eat up before it gets cold. The chef'll get mighty cranky if his food goes to waste."

She ate every bite.

THEY'D BEEN BACK to Shallowbrook several times since the tornado. Nicki had insisted on it during those first months when visiting the cemetery was the only thing that seemed to give her any comfort. But it had been a couple of months since their last visit, and Bryan headed north toward his hometown reluctantly. A lot of plans had gone into the day. But he still wasn't sure he was doing the right thing taking Nicki back, especially on the anniversary of the tragedy that had changed their lives.

He left the sides and top on the Jeep for the trip, and Nicki stared silently out her window as he drove. "We couldn't have asked for a nicer day," he said after they'd been on the interstate for several minutes. The sun was shining. No clouds in the sky. No storms on the way. Thank God.

Nicki nodded warily.

"We could run across the border to Tennessee before we go if you'd like, pick up some fireworks for the Fourth of July."

"Okay," Nicki said with the same lack of enthusiasm.

"Would you rather we stay in Atlanta, Nick? We can go back to town and find something fun to do there, or we could take the plane up."

"Nah, that's okay."

They passed a billboard advertising the Gold Rush museum in Dahlonega with promises of gold-panning opportunities, reminding Bryan of the first time he'd taken Nicki off on his own. Lori and Tom had been driving down to Atlanta to stay with Bryan after Christmas one year when Nicki was about four, but instead of driving straight through, as Bryan was doing, they were going to take a detour and stop at an outlet mall on the way. Rather than travel with her parents to the mall, Nicki had begged to ride to Atlanta with him in the Jeep. He'd told her it was fine with him, certain that Lori, who never let her daughter out of her sight for more than five minutes, would refuse. He'd had the shock of his life when she'd agreed. Apparently shopping with a four-year-old wasn't exactly a picnic.

So he'd buckled Nicki in and started out for home, but Lori and Tom, in spite of their detour, had arrived there long before he did. That was because Nicki, asking questions about everything she saw, had insisted when they'd passed a colorful sign advertising the Gold Rush museum that they stop and put gold in pans, too. She'd conned him into three more stops along the way—for fudge, a hamburger and, the last, a traveling carnival she saw when he'd pulled off for her to use the rest room—before he finally got her home.

Lori had been furious, waiting in the parking lot of his condo when he pulled in sometime after dark. Crying with relief and hollering at him at the same time, she'd taken one look at Nicki sleeping soundly in the seat beside him and hit him in the chest with both fists over and over. He'd never seen his sister so angry.

What he'd give now to have her angry at him again. To have her there at all. Or even to have back that talkative little elf who'd gotten him into so much trouble. He looked over at Nicki now, trapped in her silent world of grief, and wanted to pound his fists into something, too.

"Calvin's due home this weekend, so what d'ya say we give him a week or two to get settled in and then we take a trip to the beach?"

"Okay. If you want to."

"Don't you want to go, Nick? We could do some snorkeling."

She shrugged. "It doesn't matter."

He saw a sign for her favorite burger joint. "You want to stop for lunch?"

"Okay."

Damn. I could tell her now, if I wanted to.

He bought her a hamburger, french fries and a chocolate shake, and refused to leave the restaurant until she'd finished all of it. But he gave up on conversation when they got back in the Jeep. He was too concerned about what lay ahead of them, or rather, Nicki's reaction to it, to force a cheerfulness he was far from feeling.

They'd been back in the Jeep for about half an hour when Nicki broke the silence. "Uncle Bryan? I have something to ask you . . . and I don't want you to get mad at me."

They were the most words she'd strung together in days. "Ask away. I never get mad at you."

"It's about my other mother. I just wondered if you'd heard anything yet."

He glanced over, expecting to see her staring out the window. She wasn't. She was looking straight at him, trying to hide the hope in her young eyes.

"I…" He couldn't do it. He couldn't just crush that hope. "We're making progress, Nick. They have her name."

"They do? What is it?" Her eyes were almost bright, her voice sounding more like a little girl's than it had since he could remember.

What is it. He wasn't ready. "I don't know yet, honey, not until I get the report. And don't get too excited. They haven't found *her* yet—they just have her name. She could be anywhere in the country, or even out of it, and there are probably several women with the same name."

"Yeah, but if they could get this far, they just *have* to find her. I can't believe they really know her name. I wonder what it is…" She looked out at the road as if the answer was written there. "Maybe Ariel or…or Cameron. That would be neat, don't you think? Cameron sounds like a cool name."

I feel like scum, he thought. "It's probably something ordinary, honey, like Debbie or Sue." *Or Jennifer.*

"Maybe. I can't wait to find out. I wonder how soon they'll find her?"

"It's hard to say, sprite. Just don't get your hopes up too high."

"I know. I won't. And about that trip to the beach?"

"Yeah?"

"I guess it'd be good."

Just the mention that her birth mother had a name, and suddenly she *wanted* to go to the beach. She actually *wanted* to do something. It was going to be damn near impossible to tell her her mother couldn't be found. But what would happen if he told Nicki who she was and Jennifer walked away from her? Again.

They stopped for some flowers at the local florist, now set up in a brand-new shop on Main Street rather than the historical building Bryan remembered from his youth, and went out to pay their tributes to Lori and Tom and Bryan's parents.

Bryan cried inside for the young girl who knelt so carefully on her parents' grave, telling them she loved them as she left her flowers there for them, explaining to Lori through her tears that she'd brought her carnations because they smelled the best and lasted the longest. He stood back, allowing her time with them, thinking that if it were up to him, they'd never visit the graves at all. What he needed from his family he had in his heart. But he knew Nicki wasn't old enough to understand that yet.

She didn't say much else, just pulled some grass from around their stone, and then stood and turned away. Bryan put his arm around her and walked her back to the Jeep.

"I wish birthdays had never been invented," she said, trying not to cry again.

Bryan pulled her into his arms and held her, a few tears of his own escaping from his tightly clenched eyes, while she sobbed out her anguish. He held her until her breathing evened and he knew she'd spent all the hurt inside of her. For now.

"Let's go," he said.

Nicki gave him one last squeeze. "I love you, Uncle Bryan."

"I love you, too, Nick. Always."

"Do you think Mom'll be mad at me for finding my other mother?" she asked as she climbed back into the Jeep.

"No. Your mother was prepared for the time you might have questions. She knew she was your real mother, and that was all that mattered to her." Bryan had stretched the truth a little bit. It wouldn't do Nicki any good to know that though Lori had been prepared for the questions and would have encouraged the search, she'd also worried about losing Nicki to her biological mother someday. He thought that was probably a normal reaction, though.

Instead of heading to the interstate, Bryan turned the Jeep back toward town.

"Where're we going?" Nicki looked nervous.

"There's someone here who wants to see you, Nick," he said, hoping she was up for it. She hadn't wanted to see any of her old friends since she'd left Shallowbrook, but they had a surprise waiting for her. One he hoped she'd like.

"Who?"

"Just wait and see."

He turned a couple of corners and pulled onto a street that hadn't been touched by the tornado.

"Sally's house?" Nicki asked as he pulled into her best friend's drive. She didn't seem happy to be there.

Bryan turned off the ignition. "C'mon. Let's go in."

Ten girls were waiting on the covered porch, all dressed in shorts and tops like Nicki's, several of them sporting the daisies Nicki wore, and all talking at once. They stopped when they saw Nicki, probably not sure what to make of the changes in their once lively and

talkative friend, and then Sally ran forward and threw
her arms around Nicki's waist.

"Nicki! I can't believe you're finally here!"

Nicki stood awkwardly in Sally's embrace, looking
over her shoulder at the group of friends waiting behind Sally.

Come on, Nick. You'll be okay. Bryan didn't know
why he'd ever thought this might help.

The other girls rushed forward then, surrounding
Nicki, and Bryan lost sight of his niece as they tried to
make her feel welcome. They were all talking at once,
telling Nicki about the party they'd planned for her,
wishing her happy birthday. He didn't hear Nicki utter a word.

His gaze sought Betty Sanderson, Sally's divorced
mother, over the girls' heads. Her eyes were full of
sympathy.

"Come on, girls," Betty said cheerfully. "Let's go
inside and show Nicki what we've got for her."

He waited until they'd all pushed their way through
the door before walking up the steps himself. "It'll be
all right," Betty said as she held the door open for
him.

He'd grown up with Betty. He'd even dated her a
time or two. She'd filled out a little since then, and her
dark hair had a couple of strands of early gray, but she
still looked great. She'd always been smart, and per-
ceptive beyond her years, too, even back in high
school, and he'd learned to trust her judgment. This
time he was counting on her being right.

Nicki was sitting on the couch, the girls beside her
and on the floor in front of her, their talking making
up for Nicki's near-silence. They didn't seem to no-

tice she was answering their questions with only one or two words, sometimes just a shrug.

"How are you doing?" Betty asked Bryan quietly, standing just inside the room with him.

"We're getting along."

"She's still not opening up much, is she?"

"I'm beginning to wonder if she ever will. Maybe the tornado did something to her we'll never be able to fix."

"I doubt that, Bryan. She's young yet. Give her time. Maybe our little surprise today will help."

"Or make her miss what she lost even more."

"I don't think so."

Bryan watched his niece parry questions, hating the lost look in her eyes. She used to be the noisiest one in the bunch. But she wasn't a part of their chatter anymore. Not only had she moved away physically, she'd moved away emotionally, leaving her childlike trust and innocence behind.

"Have you made any progress on your search for her birth mother?"

"I found her."

"Nicki's met her? What happened? Didn't it go well?"

"Nicki doesn't know I've found her. She thinks we're still looking."

Betty frowned. "Don't you think you ought to tell her? The last time you called you made it sound like it was all that mattered to her."

"Which is exactly why I'm waiting. Look at her, Betty. I'm not sure she can handle it if her mother doesn't want to acknowledge her."

Betty looked over to where Nicki sat, quiet and solemn, with her friends.

"She doesn't want her?"

"I don't know yet, because I haven't told her about Nicki, either, but it doesn't look good. She's uncomfortable around kids. Says she doesn't ever want to be a mother."

"Oh, no," Betty said sadly.

"Well, she's not as bad as she sounds. That's why I haven't given up on the whole thing yet. The woman's really something. She's the most honest, fair, compassionate person I've ever met. She's tough when she needs to be, she's a first-rate mechanic, though not by trade, she's got a great sense of humor and very loyal friends." Bryan stopped.

"It sounds like you've gotten to know her rather well."

"I took a job creating a new campaign for the company she owns."

Betty's eyebrows raised. "You work for her and she doesn't know about Nicki?"

"Not yet. But I don't think I'm going to be able to keep them a secret from each other much longer."

"How do you think the woman'll take the news?"

"She'll probably never speak to me again."

Betty yanked on the end of his ponytail. "Turn on some of that charm of yours, Chambers. She'll come around."

Bryan grinned at his friend, glad he'd kept in touch with Betty over the past year. "So," he said, ready to be done with what he and Betty had planned, one way or the other, "let's get this show on the road."

Betty walked back out to the hall and opened the door to the dining room. "Nicki! Look who's here," she said, releasing a furry dynamo of brown and gold and white from captivity.

A Shetland collie—a miniature Lassie—came barreling into the room, leaping and barking.

"Lucy? Lucy's here? She's alive?" Nicki jumped off the couch, stumbling over the girls in her path as she ran to meet the Sheltie. She dropped to the floor, clutching the dog to her with all her might, laughing and crying as Lucy covered her face with kisses.

"Look, Uncle Bryan! Oh, look! Lucy's alive!"

Bryan's throat was thick as he hunkered down beside his niece. He scratched the excited dog behind her ears, a little surprised by just how glad *he* was to see Lucy again. He and Nicki had conspired to get the dog for Tom and Lori for Christmas three years before.

"A farmer found her about five miles out of town," Betty said. "She was dehydrated, but not hurt. He put notices up, but everybody was too busy taking care of things after the tornado to pay much attention. Then last week, Sally and I were driving by the farmer's house, and Sally saw her. We stopped and called her name, and sure enough it was Lucy."

Nicki's gaze was glued to the dog, her fingers stroking her pet as she listened. Suddenly she froze, squeezing the little dog so tightly Lucy squirmed to escape. "We can keep her, can't we, Uncle Bryan? We're gonna take her home with us, right?" she asked, her young face filled with fear.

"Of course, Nick. Happy birthday, honey."

"Oh, Uncle Bryan, thank you. Thank you. Thank you. Thank you." She got up and threw her arms around Bryan's neck, tears streaming down her cheeks. But for once, Bryan knew, they were happy tears.

His eyes met Betty's over Nicki's shoulder. She was crying, too, but she was also smiling. She gave Bryan a thumbs-up.

"Okay, who wants cake?" she asked a couple of minutes later. The girls were crowded around Nicki again.

"We do!" Ten girls screamed their approval. One sat oblivious, hugging her dog in the middle of the floor.

NICKI SLEPT most of the way home with Lucy nestled in her lap. The dog was obviously as happy to be reunited with Nicki as Nicki was to have her. Bryan breathed a huge sigh of relief. He'd been afraid seeing Lucy would make Nicki lonelier for her parents. He'd even gone so far as to think she might refuse to have anything to do with the dog. He'd never given any thought to his own reaction. He'd certainly never expected to find that he'd have any affection for the animal.

Fancy that. Bryan Chambers, bachelor extraordinaire, comforted by a family dog.

CHAPTER EIGHT

JENNIFER HAD SPENT The Day as she always had—trying to forget. She hadn't heard from Bryan all weekend and she'd missed him. A lot. Now it was Monday, and she stood in the service drive at Teal Pontiac waiting for him, nervous and worried about the upcoming filming and trying not to show it. And he was late.

"You've done it again, Jennifer. One Price Selling has only been in place for a couple of weeks, and already there's a noticeable increase in sales volume," Ralph Goodwin said from beside her. She hadn't even realized the general manager had joined her.

"It's still too early to really judge, but thanks for the vote of confidence." She'd noticed the increase herself; she'd been monitoring sales reports daily since the first commercial had hit the air two weeks before. But she was too cautious to get her hopes up yet. Advertising in general usually brought in increased business at first.

Ralph rested his elbow on his other arm, his hand under his chin. "The place is buzzing with positive feedback. The general consensus seems to be that customers are fully embracing the idea of being able to buy a car without the pressure of haggling for it."

Where's Bryan? The film crew's already in the showroom. "How about your sales staff? They giving you any trouble?"

"A little. Not a lot. We've had an occasion or two when a customer wouldn't buy a car unless he could dicker, not believing, of course, that we wouldn't dicker when push came to shove. When we wouldn't, the customer walked. There's a little grumbling each time it happens."

"But the numbers the guys'll gain in the long run when people understand we mean what we say will be well worth the loss of a sale or two."

"I know. It's just a hard concept for salespeople to swallow—letting a deal walk out the door. But none of them are quitting yet. I'd even go so far as to say that the majority are happier. We've taken away a lot of the negative pressure of the job by giving them a good product and reliable service to sell, rather than price."

Jennifer nodded. It still sounded right to her. It could work. It *had* to work.

She saw a familiar vehicle pull onto the lot. Bryan. Finally.

She walked over to meet him as he hopped down from the Jeep.

His gaze sought hers immediately. "How're you doing?" It wasn't an idle question.

Okay, now that you're here. "Better than I expected." He looked great. He was wearing lightweight cotton pants today, instead of jeans, and a polo shirt. The short sides of his hair were windblown, but the back was in its usual ponytail.

He studied her. "I thought you might dress a little more casually today, since we're going for kid ap-

peal,'' he said, walking with her toward the showroom.

"I just felt more comfortable this way. Besides, suits
are my image. I've worn them for every commercial
I've ever done. I was afraid the whole thing would
look fake if I wore something different now."

Bryan conceded the point. "I like your hair," he
said.

It was up in its usual twist, but she'd added a couple of gold-and-black clips that matched the buttons
on her suit. "Thanks."

He looked over at her again, his sexy brown eyes
warm, approving. "I'd like to see it down even more."

Jennifer felt his regard all the way down to her toes,
although she'd been telling herself all weekend to for-
get·him. She'd decided he obviously wasn't interested
in her—not as a woman. In all the times they'd been
together, he'd only kissed her once. That time in her
office. And it wasn't like he hadn't had the opportunity.

But when he looked at her like that...

"Hey, boss, we're ready to start whenever you give
us the go-ahead," Jake Landers said as she and Bryan
walked into the showroom. Bryan stopped to have a
few words with him.

Jennifer continued on into the showroom, her gaze
immediately seeking out the little boy standing with his
mother by the electric red Pontiac Firebird Trans Am
Coupe. About four feet tall, blond and dressed in
shorts and a Hawks T-shirt, he looked harmless
enough. So why did her stomach suddenly feel as if she
was going off to war?

"Ready, Jen?" Bryan said, crossing to her. Nobody but Tanya and Dennis had ever called her Jen. She liked the sound of it coming from Bryan.

"Ready," she said, smiling at him. As ready as she'd ever be, at least.

"Okay, you remember Bob McKinney and Jake Landers, don't you?" he asked, leading her over to the two men.

She smiled and reached out to shake their hands. "Of course. How are you, gentlemen?" She'd liked them the last time they'd worked together. She'd liked the films they'd turned out, too.

"Just fine, ma'am," Jake said for both of them. "If we can have you right over here, we'll get this show on the road."

With one last look at Bryan, Jennifer put herself in the hands of his crew.

The morning wasn't too bad. Jennifer found that if she kept her own counsel, watching the proceedings from the side except when she said her lines, making this commercial was no different than any of the other ones she'd done. The little boy, in spite of his youth, was a professional. She wasn't expected to entertain him, or even watch out for him. He had his mother there to do that. And she didn't have to make him like her—Bryan's lines took care of that.

She'd been convincing her staff of over six hundred employees about the merits of One Price Selling for weeks. And she believed in it herself. So the part she was playing, explaining One Price to the boy's mother, felt almost natural to her. Answering his questions, in slightly less formal terms, was simply a matter of reciting the lines Bryan had written. By the end of the morning, when Jake and Bob were finally satisfied

they had enough on tape, she was feeling pretty relaxed. The next few days might not be so bad, after all.

"It was nice meeting you, Ms. Teal," the boy said
as he and his mother were leaving. It was the first time
he'd spoken to her apart from the scripted lines.

"It was nice meeting you, too, Taylor. You're pretty
good at what you do, you know." Jennifer was glad to
have a chance to tell him. She'd been impressed, and
she always made it a point to offer praise for a job
well-done.

The little boy smiled and blushed. "Thanks. You're
not so bad, either. And I love your cars."

If he were old enough to drive, she would probably
have given him one. Jennifer continued with her
goodbyes, all the while hearing Taylor's words ringing in her ears. *You're not so bad, either.* She could
have hugged him right there on the showroom floor.

Tuesday, at Teal Hyundai, was even easier than
Monday. There were two kids, a boy and a girl posing
as brother and sister, and all Jennifer had to do was
walk up while their parents were busy working out the
financing, smile at them, offer them a Teal Automotive coloring book and walk away. A voice-over introduced One Price Selling, pointing out that the
bank's financing paperwork was the only time-
consuming part of buying a car at any of the Teal Automotive dealerships.

They ran through the take half a dozen times, and
each time, Jennifer smiled at the children, and each
time, they smiled back. She knew they'd been told to,
that their smiles were written into the script, but they
made her feel good, anyway.

They were about halfway through the shoot when
the little girl came over and stood in front of Jenni-

fer. "I love your earrings," she said. "My diary has hearts on it and so does my jewelry box."

Jennifer's fingers went automatically to the heart-shaped gold studs in her ears. She'd forgotten she'd put them on. "Thank you," she said, smiling at the child.

"Ready to roll," Jake called, putting an end to the impromptu conversation before Jennifer could worry about finding something to say about diaries or toy jewelry boxes. It was back to the safety of rehearsed lines and staged smiles.

But the little girl smiled at Jennifer when she came over to tell her goodbye, and that wasn't rehearsed at all.

"What were you so worried about?" Bryan asked her as they walked out to their cars afterward. He was smiling at her, too, and her heart beat faster.

She shrugged. "I'm not sure at the moment, but let's get through tomorrow before we celebrate."

"Tomorrow's going to be the easiest of all. You put a baby in a built-in car seat and you're done."

Jennifer knew that. It was the thought of picking up the baby to begin with that was keeping her up at night. Tanya's pregnancy had shown her how much she'd been fooling herself all these years. And she hadn't held a baby since...

She didn't want to think about that now. "Are you and Calvin still going over things?" she asked. He'd had to rush away the day before to meet with his partner.

"Yeah, but we got a lot done. He came to the house last night, too. One more afternoon and we should just about have it wrapped up. I'm looking forward to a little time off, I can tell you. It's been two weeks since I've been up in the air."

They reached her car. She unlocked the door, but didn't immediately climb inside. "Speaking of time off, how'd last Friday go?" she asked. She couldn't help but wonder about the personal business that had taken him back to his hometown. It had dawned on her that while he demanded she open up to him, there were parts of his life about which she knew nothing. She didn't even know where he lived.

His expression grew solemn. "Better than I expected."

"You were expecting a bad time?" she asked. She hadn't thought of that when she'd tormented herself with visions of what he might have been doing. Like seeing an old flame—or a current one.

He looked at her, as if searching for something, and then seemed to come to a decision. "Do you remember the tornado that ran through northern Georgia this time last year?"

"Of course." That part of the state had been declared a national disaster area. She'd donated heavily to the cleanup cause herself. And then it hit her.

"Shallowbrook was right in its path. It was one of the towns worst hit, wasn't it?"

He swallowed, looking out over the top of her car, and nodded. She felt a sickening sense of dread even before he spoke.

"I lost most of my family in the blink of an eye." He sounded as if he still couldn't quite believe it.

Jennifer reached out to him, uncaring for once of who she was, of where they were. She cupped his jaw with her palm. "I'm so sorry, Bryan." There was nothing else she could say.

"I was driving up when the storm hit. There was a family party at my parents' house. Everyone was there—my sister and her husband, cousins, aunts and uncles. I was two hours late and so..." He didn't have to explain any further. She could only imagine the hell he was revisiting.

"I'm so sorry," she said again, her eyes filling with tears.

He looked down at her, taking her shoulders in his hands as if touching her somehow grounded him in the present, away from visions of the past. "Thanks," he said, looking at his hands on her shoulders, then letting go of her all of a sudden, as if he'd only just realized his hands were there.

"So it wasn't as bad going back as you'd thought it would be?" she asked.

"I've been back many times, and it's always hard. But a friend of mine had found something she thought I'd want. I wasn't so sure until I got there, but she was right."

Curious, Jennifer asked, "What was it?"

"My sister's dog. The damn thing had been wandering around for several days after the tornado, and this farmer found her and took her in." He went on to tell her how Betty and her daughter happened on the Sheltie, took the animal home and called him right away.

"Did the dog remember you?"

"Oh, yeah, she remembered all right. She's been underfoot ever since."

Jennifer smiled. "So you brought her back with you?" she asked, liking the picture of this big, strong, free-spirited man driving home with a dog in his lap.

"Yeah. She's at home. She's part of the reason Calvin and I didn't finish last night. We took her out back for a game of ball that lasted longer than it should have."

"I'm glad you have her," Jennifer said. It made her feel better for him to know that he had at least a small piece of the family he'd lost.

"Me, too." He was smiling again.

Jennifer was perfectly content to bask in that smile.

BRYAN STOPPED HOME after he left Teal Hyundai. Nicki had still been asleep when he'd left that morning, and he didn't like not having shared breakfast with her before he went off to work.

She was still sleeping when he got home shortly before lunchtime, but she'd moved from her bed to the living-room couch, probably because she'd had to get up to let Lucy out back. Bryan frowned as he looked down at his sleeping niece. She'd been asleep yesterday afternoon when he'd called from the office, too.

Lucy was jumping up on his leg, and he reached down with one hand to grab the dog into his arms. "What are we going to do with her, Lucy my girl?" he asked, scratching the dog behind the ears. He was rewarded by a lick on his chin. He laughed.

Nicki sat up suddenly, disoriented. She pushed the hair out of her face. "Uncle Bryan?" she said when she saw him. "Why are you home? Is it dinnertime already?"

"No. It's not quite lunchtime," he said. He was worried about her, sure that sleeping through summer vacation was not healthy.

She rubbed her eyes. "Then how come you're here?" she asked, yawning. And then she stopped midyawn to stare at him.

"Did you find her? Is that it?" She studied his face. "Is it bad?" she whispered, looking frightened again.

He hated that look.

"I didn't find her yet, Nick. I just stopped in to take you to lunch," he improvised. He'd give her a reason to stay awake if he had to, give her hundreds of them. She wasn't going to break down on him. He dropped the dog to the floor.

"You didn't have to," she said, scooping Lucy up and burying her face in the thick fur.

"I know, Nick." Lord, he was tired of not reaching her. She'd looked so excited when she'd thought he had news. But her answers might not lie in finding her birth mother. He had to help her find the will to live within herself.

She looked at him as if waiting for something.

"Go on. Get some clothes on. We're going to the Burger Barn. And bring a swimsuit." To hell with Calvin and Innovative Advertising. He was taking Nicki to Splashtown. Even she couldn't sleep through an afternoon at the water park.

He called his partner and arranged to meet him later that evening. Calvin's family had stayed at the beach for an extra week, so Calvin didn't mind working another evening. Bryan didn't mind, either. The busier he stayed, the less time he had to think.

BRYAN DROVE to Teal Ford bright and early Wednesday morning. He'd finished filling Calvin in on the projects at hand and had cleared his schedule for the day. As soon as they wrapped up the filming, he was going to have a talk with Jennifer. He couldn't go on this way any longer. He wanted the woman so badly he went to bed aching at night, and his dreams were filled with fantasies so wild even he couldn't believe his subconscious had conjured them up.

She wanted him, too. He'd read it in her eyes. He'd known it the night of the Boston concert. If he'd gone into her apartment then, they would have made love.

But more than the wanting, she cared about him. He knew that when he'd told her about the tornado. The damnable thing was, he was beginning to suspect he cared about her, too. More than he'd ever cared for a woman before. More than just physically.

But she was Nicki's mother. And if she didn't want Nicki, then they had no future. Even if she did, they probably had no future, Bryan admitted as he pulled into the lot of Jennifer's largest dealership. Because as soon as she found out who he was, why he'd really met her, she'd never trust him again. And he wouldn't blame her. He'd knowingly abused her trust.

Of course, her wanting Nicki was a big "if." She wasn't comfortable around children, and the possible damage to Jennifer's reputation alone might be reason enough to keep her away. Especially now that she'd embarked on her One Price campaign.

Bob and Jake were just setting up when Bryan arrived, and Jennifer was talking with a couple of salespeople on the showroom floor. Bryan hoped the crew would be ready to start soon. He wanted to get this over with. He pulled his cellular phone out of his back pocket, unfolded it and dialed Nicki.

"Hello?" Her voice was groggy with sleep.

"It's me, Nick. Listen, I need you to do me a couple of favors this morning."

He listed the chores he'd invented on his way to work that morning. They should be enough to keep her up and moving around for most of the day. He and Nicki were going to beat this thing if it killed him.

The morning's filming promised to progress as smoothly as it had the previous two days. Thank God. His patience level was impossibly thin. The baby's mother was a pleasant woman, and she was delighted to meet Jennifer. Jennifer looked a little tired, but she smiled at the other woman and welcomed her to Teal Ford.

Jake ran through the take with both women, indicating just when the mother should hand her baby to Jennifer without getting into the picture herself. Jennifer hadn't looked at the baby once, as far as Bryan could tell, and she seemed a little tenser than she had the previous two days. Nevertheless she nodded at Jake and took her position by the Windstar they'd picked for the take.

Everything went as planned until Jennifer reached for the baby. Bryan wasn't sure what went wrong, but suddenly the baby was screaming and Jennifer was making a beeline for the baby's mother, getting rid of the angry little bundle as fast as she could.

"Cut!" Jake's voice rang out over the baby's wails.

Bryan walked over, noticing all the curious hangers-on. He motioned to Frank Dorian. Jennifer had introduced him earlier as the general manager of Teal Ford.

"Clear these people out, would you, Frank?" Bryan asked.

"Consider it done," Frank said, motioning to a man on the other side of the room.

"What happened?" Bryan asked when he finally made it over to the small group clustered around the squalling baby.

Jennifer stood back from the group, her hands clutched in front of her. Her face looked pinched. She didn't say a word.

"He's just scared. He'll be fine in a second," the mother assured everyone, rocking the baby against her shoulder. "He's usually pretty good about going to people, but every once in a while he gets a mommy attack."

True to her word, the baby calmed almost immediately. They waited another couple of minutes for the tears to dry on his lashes, and then Jake called everyone to their positions. Jennifer came forward, but she didn't look at all sure about what she was doing. Catching her eye, Bryan smiled at her encouragingly. He stayed closer this time, wanting to be certain they got it right. It didn't look like Jennifer was going to hold up for many more takes.

"Roll 'em," Jake called, and Bob held up the cue cards. Jennifer ran through her lines perfectly, the poised confident businesswoman, and then Jake swerved in for a close-up of the built-in baby seat through the open side door of the Windstar, giving Jennifer a chance to take the baby from his mother.

Bryan saw her reach for the child. She held him gently in her arms, about an inch from her body. But before she could get him the two feet to the van, the baby started to scream again.

Jennifer returned the baby to his mother immediately. "That's it, guys," she said to everyone present. "This one isn't going to happen. Sorry for wasting everybody's time."

Without another word to anyone, she turned and left the showroom.

Bryan made it outside just as she was pulling off the lot.

Yanking his keys from his pocket, he jumped into the Jeep and took off after her. He'd never seen her so upset, and he couldn't let her leave like that. Not as a professional, and not as a man who cared about her, either.

She was heading toward her office building, he guessed, and he pulled onto Peachtree right behind her. He couldn't figure out what had gone so wrong back there. In spite of all his weeks of getting to know Jennifer, it seemed as if he didn't know her at all. He would never have believed she'd run out like that. She was a fighter, not a quitter.

About two miles from the Teal corporate offices, she finally noticed him behind her. Catching his eye in her rearview mirror, she shook her head. He nodded. She drove for about another quarter of a mile before she suddenly cut across two lanes of traffic and swerved into a deserted parking lot. Horns honked behind him as Bryan followed, pulling his Jeep up beside her Mustang.

He jumped down and opened her car door.

"I can't do it," she said, looking straight ahead through her windshield. Her hand still rested on the ignition, as if she was prepared to take off at any second.

"I'm not going to ask you to go back there," he said. He'd already dismissed his crew. "I just want to talk."

She glanced up, the look in her eyes shocking him. It reminded him of Nicki, of the emptiness he saw sometimes when he looked at his niece. He wouldn't be surprised if she was going to refuse to discuss what had happened that morning.

"So talk," she finally said.

He leaned on the door frame of her car. "What happened back there?"

"I told you I'm no good with children. Did you think I was just making that up? I've been through this before. Oh, not commercials, but anytime I'm alone with a child, he or she either ends up huddling in a corner, crying or wrecking the place."

"You've been working with kids all week, Jen, and you did fine. They liked you."

"They were professional actors."

"They were kids! They were well behaved, yes. And they'd been taught how to memorize lines, but if little Taylor hadn't liked you, you can bet we wouldn't have had such an easy time of it on Monday. I've worked with him before. I know."

"You wrote every word I said, Bryan."

Damn, Bryan thought. What was it with the females in his life?

"That little girl yesterday worshiped the ground you walked on."

"She liked my earrings."

Patience, he reminded himself. Jennifer was one of the most confident people he knew. Yet it was as if he'd never met the woman sitting in her car. This woman reminded him a lot of Nicki—a mass of insecurities. But at least he knew what had caused Nicki's problems.

"Jennifer, that baby today was only three months old. He was hardly old enough to hold up his head by himself, let alone take an instant dislike to someone. He just didn't want to be separated from his mother."

"He didn't cry the couple of times Jake took him, when he was demonstrating the take."

He'd forgotten that. "Jake probably reminded him of his father."

"He didn't like me, Bryan. I'm not good with children. I don't understand them, and I don't know how to act around them. They make me nervous, and children can sense things like that."

"Okay, let's say for a minute you're right, but that still doesn't explain this." He reached out and took her hand off the steering wheel.

"What?" She wouldn't look at him.

"You've been gripping that wheel so tightly your knuckles are white." He held up her hand. "And you're shaking, too."

Bryan hunkered down beside her, keeping her hand in his. "Come on, Jen. What gives?"

"I don't like to be put in situations where I'm not sure of myself." Her words were almost a whisper. It sounded like tears weren't far away.

Suddenly he was no longer the professional, and he wasn't Nicki's uncle, either. He was simply a man trying to comfort a woman he cared about.

"No one does, but that doesn't explain why you're so upset. I thought we'd become friends over the past few weeks. Can't you tell me what's wrong?"

"I just...I just haven't held a baby since..." Her voice was filled with tears and she broke off, trying to compose herself.

Bryan pulled her from the car and over to his Jeep. Opening the passenger door and leaning back against the side of the seat, he settled her between his legs and held her against him.

"Since when, honey? You haven't held a baby since when?"

"Since I..." She looked up at him, her eyes full of shadows. "Since I...gave my own away."

CHAPTER NINE

EVEN KNOWING what he did, Bryan was shocked at Jennifer's revelation. He wasn't sure what he should say. She hadn't held a baby in twelve years? As punishment? Or because she really didn't like babies?

Finding no answers or even words to comfort her, Bryan simply held her, rubbing her back, smoothing her hair away from her face, just as he'd done for Nicki so many times in the past year. So much pain.

He knew now that she hadn't forgotten Nicki. There was no doubt that she hurt for her lost baby. That didn't mean she'd accept Nicki, but it was time to find out. He was beginning to hope as he held her, as he wanted to continue holding her, comforting her, that maybe this bizarre situation could somehow work out happily for all three of them. Maybe.

If she ever forgave him for the deceit he'd been practicing since the evening they'd met.

She pulled away from him, wiping tears from her eyes. "Sorry, I didn't mean to go all blubbery on you. I don't make a habit of it, I promise."

She was embarrassed. Bryan lifted her chin until her eyes met his. "Don't. Don't apologize or get all distant on me. You've had a rough morning—you needed a friend. After the past year I can certainly understand that. I'm just glad you chose me."

She reached up and cupped his cheek. "Dear Bryan. I don't know where you've been all my life, but I'm certainly glad I finally found you."

Looking down into her beautiful face, Bryan knew he was lost. She was everything he'd ever wanted in a woman and more. He leaned over the couple of inches it took to close the distance between them and touched his lips to hers. He kissed her the way he'd wanted to kiss her for weeks, totally, intimately, the way a man kisses a woman he desires beyond all else.

She melted against him, her lips pliant and eager. She'd obviously been wanting the kiss as badly as he had.

Bryan couldn't keep his hands still. He ran them over her, down her back, up over her waist, brushing the sides of her breasts, before tilting her head to allow him better access to her mouth. He deepened the kiss.

She moaned, pressing her hips against his; he might have forgotten himself completely if a horn hadn't honked on the street behind him.

He lifted his head slowly, holding Jennifer's gently between his hands, looking into her eyes for confirmation of what he already knew. That she wanted to make love to him as much as he wanted to make love to her.

But there were things they had to settle first. And once they were done settling them, there might never be an afterward.

She leaned her head against his chest. "It's scary to think I might have lived my whole life and never felt like this," she said.

"Surely you've felt it before." *Some*one had fathered Nicki.

She stepped back. "You'd think so, wouldn't you?"

"I'd like you tell me about it, Jen."

"And I will—someday. But not today. Please don't ask me to go through it all again right now. I think I've had about as much as I can take."

"But—"

"I know I'm being unfair, Bryan. I can't lay this on you and expect you not to wonder, but I need a little time. I've never told another living soul about that part of my life, with the exception of two very special friends who helped me through it. I've only realized in the past week how much of it is still unresolved for me, and I'm just not ready to talk about it yet."

"Can you just answer one question?"

"I'll try."

"Do you think you did the right thing giving your baby away?"

"I was young, Bryan. I did what I thought was best, and, yes, I still think I did the right thing—especially after today. I'm just not good with kids. When God handed out mother's instinct, I guess he skipped me. My mother was the same way—my father, too, for that matter—and believe me, if I'm like them, my baby's better off with someone who wanted her badly enough to go through the adoption process to get her."

If she'd been anyone else Bryan would simply have accepted that here was a woman who wasn't meant to be a mother. But she wasn't anyone else. She was Nicki's mother. And he couldn't help wondering if Jennifer wasn't good with kids because she did indeed take after her own parents, or just because she'd convinced herself she did.

Whether Jennifer *wanted* Nicki or not was no longer even the problem. If she was convinced she didn't have a knack for mothering, she probably wouldn't even try. Hell, knowing Jennifer, judging by what she'd just said about her child being better off without her, she'd probably convince herself that she'd be doing Nicki a favor by staying away from her.

He had to find out if she was right. He had to know if Nicki was better off without her, if knowing her would do Nicki more harm than good, before he even considered introducing them as mother and daughter. And the only way he could find out if they were good together was for them to meet.

"I have a confession to make."

She frowned, looking confused. "What?"

He had no idea how to break it to her gently. "I don't live alone."

She froze. "You have a roommate, you mean?"

He'd never thought of Nicki as a roommate, but he said, "Sort of." After Jennifer had spent the morning telling him how uncomfortable she was around children, how did he just blurt out that he had one?

"Male or female?"

"Female."

She backed up another step, her face draining of color.

And then it hit him how the conversation must sound to her. "She's *twelve*, Jennifer. And she's mine."

"You have a daughter?" She didn't look much less horrified.

"Technically she's my niece, but I'm raising her now. She was my sister's daughter. She's all the family I have left."

Jennifer gave an audible gasp and her eyes shimmered with emotion. "Oh, Bryan...the sister killed in the tornado. Of course. Oh, God, I'm so sorry. For both of you."

"She's mine now, Jennifer. Legally, but emotionally, too. I love that kid so much it hurts. And it hurts a lot, because she's having a really tough time of it. She lost even more than I did that day, because she lost her childhood. I'll always have great memories of mine."

Jennifer gazed at him in silence for a moment. Then she said, "You're one special man, Bryan Chambers."

"I do what I have to do," he said, shrugging off her praise.

"Still, I'd say she's very lucky to have you."

Bryan hoped so. At the moment he wasn't sure he was doing anything right. "The reason I told you about her is because I wanted you to meet her. I have a feeling she's going to like you as much as I do. You could come and have dinner with us tonight."

She stepped back. "Uh, thanks, but I don't think so," she said, looking toward her car.

Bryan turned her back to face him. "Jennifer. Nicki and I are a package deal. I care about you more than I can ever remember caring about a woman, but Nicki and I are a team. You see me, you see her, too."

"Why didn't you ever mention this to me before?"

Good question. One Bryan wasn't ready to answer. And if she couldn't handle *his* having a child, how would she react if she knew that child was hers, as well? He needed to convince her she was good around kids first, good around Nicki, and then he'd think about telling her the rest. Otherwise he was going to lose before he'd even begun. And Nicki would lose, too. And all because Jennifer thought she'd been born without the ability to mother a child.

He couldn't believe she was right. He remembered her hand cupping his face when he'd needed comfort, the hero worship in the little girl's face as she'd followed Jennifer around the dealership the day before.

Jennifer was still watching him, waiting for an answer to her question. He might not be able to answer her honestly as Nicki's uncle, but he could as a man who wanted a relationship with this woman. "By the time I knew that I wanted to bring you home, that you were more than just a casual attraction for me, you'd already told me you weren't comfortable with children."

"Wasn't that even more reason to tell me?"

"Probably. I just didn't want to lose you before I had a chance to convince you it might be worth your while to hang around."

Jennifer wanted to hang around. More than she'd ever wanted anything in her life—other than her baby a long time ago. But *twelve*... The same age now as the baby she'd given away. She just wasn't strong enough to handle that. Not yet. Not when she was just discovering for herself how much of the past she had still to face.

"I'm sorry, Bryan. It just isn't a good idea," she said.

His stricken expression was the last thing she saw in her rearview mirror as she drove away.

IT HAUNTED HER in the two days that followed, as well. She worked incredibly long hours, even for her, waiting for the moment Bryan would call to say he had the tapes ready for her to view, even while she dreaded speaking with him if it was only going to be about something so superficial. She'd never made love with the man, never shared any real physical intimacies with him, and yet she had the feeling he knew her as well as she knew herself.

Part of her couldn't believe the cruelty of fate that would allow her a taste of all life could be, all that her life had been without, only to make it all unobtainable. But the other part of her, the weak part, knew that it was only what she deserved. What right did she have to love, to be loved, to live happily ever after, when she'd withheld her love from her own child?

He finally called Friday afternoon.

"The tapes are still in the lab. They should be ready sometime early next week," he said as soon as she picked up the phone.

Jennifer smiled. It was just so damn good to hear from him. "Hello yourself." She wrapped the phone cord around her finger.

"How you doing?" His voice was softer, more personal as he asked the question.

"I've been better. I miss you."

"Enough to have dinner with me tonight?"

Her heart began to slam against her ribs. "Just you?"

A heavy silence hung over the line, as if he was only just then deciding the answer himself. She held her breath, hoping with all she was worth that his answer was yes.

"Me and Nicki," he finally said.

She thought about all the what-ifs and what-might-have-beens she'd been torturing herself with for the past couple of days. And she hadn't even met his niece. She was afraid to find out how much worse it would get if she did what he wanted.

"I can't, Bryan."

"You don't know what you're missing, Jen. Nicki's a great kid."

She closed her eyes. That was exactly what she was afraid of. Meeting Nicki was going to make her need to have what she could never have all that much worse. And more, she was terrified that if she met Nicki, it was only going to prove, once and for all, that she was a failure with kids. Bryan wouldn't be able to make any excuses for her if his own kid didn't like her. And she wouldn't be able to make any, either.

"It's not Nicki that's the problem, Bryan. It's me. I'm sorry. I can't have dinner with you tonight."

He said, "You can't run forever, Jen. Think about it." And he hung up.

As awful as Jennifer felt, she also knew a huge sense of relief when she dropped the receiver back into the cradle. He'd invited her to dinner again. He'd had time to think about the bombshell she'd dropped in his lap on Wednesday, time to calculate the years, time to figure out what she'd been doing when most fifteen-year-olds were still having their parents drive them to the movies. And he'd still invited her to dinner.

It was then that Jennifer admitted she'd been worrying herself sick that he wouldn't. She'd been afraid, after blurting out her secret, she'd lost Bryan's respect.

Jennifer packed up her briefcase, cleared off her desk for the weekend and told Rachel she was leaving for the day. She might not be ready to face Bryan's niece, but there was something she *could* do.

She called Tanya from her car phone.

"I have the afternoon free," she told her friend as soon as she answered. "I thought maybe we could do a little bit of shopping for that package you're carrying."

"Where are you?"

"In my car approaching Lenox."

"Phipp's Plaza is on Lenox. I'll meet you there in fifteen minutes."

Tanya hung up and Jennifer had no chance to change her mind. Not that she was going to. She wasn't about to lose the only real friends she'd ever had. Which meant she was going to have to come to terms with the new person in their lives. She could do it, too. She was a survivor. She wasn't going to live out the rest of her life running away from a past she couldn't change. But she couldn't afford to fall apart at the seams, either. Not with the One Price campaign resting in the balance. She'd just have to take things one step at a time.

Tanya pulled into the mall parking lot with two minutes to spare. She jumped out of her car with a determined grin on her face and said to Jennifer, "I'm not letting you off easy now that you dragged me over here."

Tanya needn't have worried. Jennifer wasn't about to back down. "Lead the way," she said, trying to ignore the knot in her stomach.

They walked into the department store, and Tanya headed right to infants' wear with an ease that told Jennifer she'd already been there many times.

"I've got a full layette of T-shirts, newborn through twelve months, but I haven't started on sleepers and socks yet," she told Jennifer as they walked past a display of cribs.

"You're *buying* clothes already?" Jennifer asked. She'd expected they'd just look for now.

"I have to have something to do. Dennis won't let me paint until after the baby's born. He's afraid the turpentine fumes might harm it."

Jennifer's hands were shaking as she tried to look around the department without seeing it. "Did you ask your doctor about it?" she asked.

"Nope. It wouldn't matter whether she said I could or not. If Dennis is worried the fumes'll hurt the baby, I won't mess with them. But if he tries to tell me I have to sit home all day and watch soap operas and knit booties, I'll have to give him a severe piece of my mind."

Jennifer smiled as she pictured Tanya doing just that.

Tanya stopped at a rack filled with tiny garments on hangers. "We need to start with newborns and work our way up," she said, pulling a sleeper off the rack. "I want fourteen of these in each size."

Jennifer was sweating as if she'd just jogged, not driven, to the mall. "Fourteen?"

"I've heard that babies go through a ton of clothes, sometimes three or four outfits in a day, and I'm not gonna lose what little sleeping time I'll have to do laundry," Tanya said.

It made sense to Jennifer. She looked at the plastic tags along the top of the rack, searching for one that said newborn. She found it, moved toward it and grabbed a hanger off the rack. "How about this one?" she asked.

"It's cute, but we can't do pink, or blue, either, since we don't know if it's a boy or a girl."

Jennifer looked at the sleeper. She hadn't been aware she'd picked a pink one. But once she looked at it, she couldn't look away. It was so incredibly small she could hardly believe a body could be small enough to fit in it. The feet were barely two inches long. And it was such a pretty pink, soft with a white lace ruffle across the bottom. It reminded Jennifer of one she'd picked once. She used to go to stores and choose outfits she'd like to buy for her baby, back in the beginning when she'd thought she'd be strong enough to stand up to her parents and keep the child growing inside of her.

"You okay?" Tanya's voice pulled her back.

Jennifer blinked the tears from her eyes. "Yeah."

"You wanna go? I didn't mean it when I said I was going to hold you to this, you know."

Jennifer nodded, putting the garment back on the rack. "Yeah, I know. But it's okay. We can stay. And why don't you know if we're shopping for a boy or a girl? You're almost four months along." Ultrasounds were usually done as a matter of course, and when she'd been pregnant, she'd been told the sex of her baby by her fourth month.

"We don't want to know," Tanya said. "Neither one of us gives a rip what it is so long as it's healthy, and we decided to do it the old-fashioned way. Wait until it's born." She put a couple of little garments over her arm.

Jennifer picked up a purple sleeper. It was terry cloth, and she liked the hearts embroidered on the chest. Love was what a baby needed most.

"Here," she said, handing it to Tanya. Tanya took one look at Jennifer's face and added it to the bunch.

They found four sleepers in all, a couple of pairs of newborn shoes and a comforter that doubled as an activity table before Tanya announced that they'd exhausted that department. Jennifer insisted on paying for all of the purchases. It was something she wished she'd been able to do twelve years before.

"Where to next?" she asked Tanya as the two made their way back out into the mall.

"You sure you're up for more?" Tanya settled her bag against her hip. It was almost as big as she was.

Jennifer wasn't sure. But she wasn't giving up. "Lead the way," she said, "and give me that." She took Tanya's package, stopped to buy a handled shopping bag to put it in and then carried it herself.

They went through the next store, a baby boutique this time, with a fine-tooth comb, adding several more sleepers and a sterling rattle set to their pile of purchases. At last Tanya suggested they stop for burgers and malts in the food court. And the entire time they stood in line, she critiqued the children walking through the mall, or rather, critiqued their parents, telling Jennifer what she was going to do the same or, in many cases, differently with her baby.

"How do you know all this stuff?" Jennifer asked her as they sat down at a table for two in the old-fashioned burger joint.

Tanya shrugged, swallowing a bite of her big juicy hamburger with everything on it. "Common sense."

"Aren't you the least bit worried you might not be a good mother?"

"Hell no!" Tanya said loudly enough to draw several pairs of eyes their way. "All it takes to be a good parent is plenty of love," she said, lowering her voice. "And that I've got in excess. I can't believe how much

I love this kid already, and I haven't even felt it move yet.''

Jennifer smiled sadly, remembering. ''I know.'' But she didn't agree with Tanya's assessment of parenthood at all. Her parents had loved her, yet in a lot of ways they'd been awful parents.

''Have you thought any more about registering someplace?'' Tanya asked softly, looking at Jennifer over her malt.

Jennifer remembered a tiny hand brushing her cheek. ''Constantly,'' she told Tanya, pushing her unfinished burger aside. ''I want to, but I keep wondering if it's the right thing to do. Say I find her, say she wants to meet me and her parents are even agreeable to it, and, hell, while we're at it, let's pretend she likes me, will I be able to handle seeing her knowing she's not mine? Will I try to take over, not even meaning to, or will my mere presence interfere in her relationship with her mother? At the very least, it would be complicated. And sometimes I think it would be best for all of us if I just left well enough alone and got on with my life.''

''Can you?'' Tanya asked, blunt as always.

Jennifer thought of Bryan, of his niece—Nicki, he'd called her. ''I thought so,'' she said. But even if she wasn't getting on with her life, was searching for her daughter the answer?

''What if she needs you, Jen? What if something's happened and she really needs you? You have so much you could give her now. And even if she doesn't need you, even if she's perfectly happy, wouldn't you like to know that? Honestly?''

Jennifer felt a panic attack coming on just thinking about it. ''Of course. But she doesn't need me, Tan.

If I'm at all like my mother was, the last thing my daughter would need is me."

"You're nothing like your mother, Jennifer Teal. That woman had ice for a heart. Your only problem is that you're too perfect for your own good, my dear," she said.

"What are you talking about?" Jennifer scoffed. Perfect was one thing she'd never been. Not even as a baby, according to her mother and the tales of colic and diaper rash she'd heard about while she was growing up.

"You are, Jen. You always have been. You're so damned good you have to invent things to worry about. Dennis says it's because you always tried so hard to please your parents, and the worst part was they never even noticed."

"That's not true. They noticed me a lot, and always when I seemed to be screwing something up. Dennis is right about one thing, though. I did try. And it paid off in the end. I finally did something right when I took over the business and they were able to retire in luxury."

"And did they thank you for it?" Tanya asked somewhat bitterly.

Jennifer loved her friend for her loyalty, even if it was misplaced. "They would have if they hadn't died before they had the chance."

"The car accident was six months after they left!"

"But they were in the Orient most of that time."

"I remember," Tanya said.

Jennifer wondered if Tanya also remembered that she'd been unable to cry at their funeral. It was something she'd never understood.

"So what's up with your hunk?" Tanya asked later as they strolled through the mall. They had too many packages to carry already and had decided to leave any further shopping for another day.

Jennifer thought of the relief she'd felt when she hung up from Bryan that morning. "Well, he doesn't think I'm easy."

Tanya hooted. "I don't see how he could. You're the biggest prude I've ever met."

"I am not," Jennifer said, laughing as she hit Tanya with one of the sacks she was carrying. "I remember skinny-dipping in a very cold lake with about ten other people for club initiation."

"We were all *girls,* Jennifer. That doesn't count."

"I'm not a prude, Tan," Jennifer said, suddenly serious. "I just learn from my mistakes. Unfortunately I learned too late that you're often judged by them. No matter what I did those last two years in high school, I was treated like a . . . a cheap slut."

"That was all a long time ago, Jen. You were a kid. You made a mistake. No man worth his salt is going to hold that against you today. Besides, Bryan doesn't know about it, anyway, does he?"

Tanya stopped suddenly and stared at her friend. "*Does* he?"

Jennifer couldn't miss the astonished, but hopeful look on Tanya's face. "I told him about the baby."

"Well, hallelujah!"

CHAPTER TEN

SHE WAS HOLDING her baby, smelling the baby-sweet smell, gazing into her daughter's bright blue eyes, and everything was as it should be, as it always would be.... And suddenly the nurse was there, taking her baby away, and there was nothing Jennifer could do about it. Her arms wouldn't work, her hands were numb, and no matter how she cried out, the nurse didn't seem to hear her. Her parents were there, too, and the doctor, but no one saw her. They were all looking at her baby. And then, ignoring her protests, they all walked out of the room together, taking her baby with them....

Jennifer woke up feeling sick to her stomach, her tears mingling with the cold sweat on her face and neck. She lay shaking in her bed, trying to tell herself that it was only a dream, that she had to be up in just a few hours, that she should go back to sleep. But she didn't want to go back to sleep. She didn't want to dream anymore.

Getting up, she wiped her tears away, but to no avail. They kept right on falling. As if she had no will of her own, she was drawn to her wallet, to the tattered picture waiting there to torment her. She pulled it out, looked again at the image she knew better than her own face and remembered. Remembered things she hadn't thought about in years...

She'd lost her virginity on her fifteenth birthday. She'd been hoping for a quiet celebration, just she and her parents and a good meal someplace where they sang "Happy Birthday" to you and brought you a little cake with a candle in the middle. She'd had a quiet party, all right—a TV dinner at home, alone. Her parents had forgotten what day it was.

But Billy Wilson hadn't forgotten. A couple of years older than Jennifer, he'd taken her out a time or two, and while his experience had made her uncomfortable, she'd basked in his attention. No one had ever made her feel special before. Billy brought flowers for her birthday, red roses, and told her he loved her. He asked her to drive out to the lake with him, to let him make the day really special. Anxious to get out of the empty house, Jennifer grabbed a sweater and followed him to his car.

His kisses excited her at first. And though she knew it was wrong, she even liked the feel of his hands on her breasts. But when his fingers slid beneath her skirt, she wanted him to stop. He told her that she wasn't being fair to him, that she couldn't lead him on and then just expect him to stop. He said that he loved her, that he wanted to show her how much, that he wanted to marry her as soon as she turned seventeen. That if she loved him, she'd let him do what he wanted.

Jennifer wasn't even sure what love was, yet she knew she wanted to be loved more than anything else on earth. Feeling awkward and scared, she lay down in the back seat of his car and let him climb on top of her. It hurt. A lot. But he held her afterward, so gentle with her she almost cried. And she was glad she'd let him love her that much.

She wasn't nearly so glad a couple of weeks later when she caught him out with a girl from the cheerleading squad at school. Or when, that same day, she heard some girls talking about her in the locker room. They knew what she'd done with Billy.

She wanted to die then. She went to her favorite place, the last mechanic's bay at Teal Motors, and worked on an old Pontiac her parents had given her. They'd taken it in on a trade, and even the wholesalers hadn't wanted it. She could keep it if she could get it running. She cried a bucket of tears as she worked, hating Billy Wilson, but mostly hating herself for being such a fool.

Her only comfort in the days that followed came when she'd gotten her period. Billy hadn't made her pregnant . . .

Jennifer looked again at the picture in her hand, wondering just when she would have atoned for the sins of her youth. If there would ever be a time. She didn't know, but one thing was for sure. Until she did, she couldn't see Bryan and his niece. She just couldn't handle it. . . .

"DAMN!"

Nicki huddled back into the couch as she heard Uncle Bryan in his office swearing again. He'd been working all morning, even though it was Sunday, and things didn't seem to be going too good.

He'd been a grouch all weekend, though he'd stayed nice to her—so far. She was probably what was causing his bad mood. She was bugging him, and there was nothing he could do about it.

"Nick!"

She jumped up and rushed to the door of his office. "Yeah?"

"Would you make us some lunch, honey? I think there's enough bread in there for peanut-butter-and-jelly sandwiches. That'd be easy."

"Sure, Uncle Bryan," she said, and hurried away before she did something to make him mad.

She tripped over Lucy on the way to the refrigerator for the jelly, but she didn't mind. She couldn't believe how happy she felt when she hugged the dog. It was almost like hugging her mom again.

Lucy began to bark as soon as Nicki had the jar of peanut butter open, and Nicki quickly scooped up a fingerful for the dog, telling her to hush. Lucy was a peanut-butter freak. She ate an awful lot of food, in fact, and she ran around the house a lot, too, sometimes knocking things over. She was probably part of the reason Uncle Bryan was so grouchy. He'd never had to take care of a kid before, let alone a pet. Nicki hoped they found her other mother soon. She needed some other family out there somewhere just in case Uncle Bryan couldn't stand to keep her anymore.

And she hoped they liked pets. She'd just die if she lost Lucy now.

She put two sandwiches and some chips on a paper plate, about the only kind Uncle Bryan used, not like the china ones her mom and grandma had always used, grabbed up a napkin and a glass of milk, and took it all into Uncle Bryan's office.

"You didn't have to do this, Nick. I could've come out there with you," he said when she set the plate down beside him.

"That's okay. Lucy'll share mine," she said.

He looked at her over his drafting table. "Just make sure you get the bigger share."

Nicki went out to the couch and curled up again. She'd have liked to snuggle up on her bed, but it seemed to bug Uncle Bryan when she did that. Anyway, she didn't want a sandwich. She wasn't hungry. She hadn't been feeling too good since she'd woken up that morning, and she was really afraid she might be going to start her period. She'd just die if she did. She couldn't go to the school nurse with it being summer, and they lived too far away from the store for her to go there by herself and get stuff. Besides, she didn't have any money and she wasn't even totally sure what to get. But one thing was for sure—she couldn't go to Uncle Bryan for help if it happened.

He'd probably faint if she asked for those pad things. She'd probably faint, too.

Nicki thought again of her other mother, something she did almost all the time lately. She thought about how wonderful it would be if she found her mother *before* she started her period, and if her mother wanted her, she'd have a woman there to help her through the whole yucky thing.

She thought about how happy Uncle Bryan would probably be to have his freedom back again. And she tried not to think about how sad that made her feel.

JENNIFER SPENT all day Sunday with Sam, changing the plugs and belts and oil and filter on the Mustang, and eating ribs Sam barbecued himself on the old grill he kept outside his apartment building. Sam had been living in the same six-unit building Jennifer's whole life, though he was no longer a tenant. He'd bought the building a few years before when Jennifer had promoted him to corporate mechanic, a fancy title that allowed her to pay him a lot of money to do what he loved to do. And he was worth every penny.

When she went back to work on Monday she was ready for business. The first thing she did was refuse all calls. She instructed Rachel to pick up her private line for her through the remainder of the week and to send Bryan Chambers's calls to Dennis from then on. Her vice president could handle the rest of the One Price campaign himself.

She made it through the day better than she'd expected to, and by Tuesday morning she was certain she'd done the right thing. She got a lot more work accomplished when she wasn't waiting for her phone to ring. It was also easier to pretend she wasn't missing Bryan so much when she wasn't constantly hoping to hear his voice on the other end of the line.

Dennis's familiar knock sounded on the door of her office shortly after nine.

"Come on in," she called. She hadn't seen Dennis since before her shopping spree with Tanya on Friday.

"Mornin', Jen. Did you get my message about the newest One Price films? Chambers is bringing them over tomorrow morning for us to take a look at them. He says they're dynamite." Dennis took his usual seat in the armchair next to her television set.

"Rachel told me, yes, but I can't make it. I'm meeting with Peterson tomorrow," she said. John Peterson was the architect they'd hired to put up the new truck building next to Teal Chevrolet.

"Put him, off, Jen. We need to get these commercials on the air."

"I trust your judgment, Dennis. You can okay them without me."

Dennis settled his ankle on the opposite knee. "Chambers expects you to be there."

"Then he's going to be disappointed." She tapped her pen against her desk pad. She'd made her decision.

"What happened?" Dennis asked, frowning. "I thought you two had a thing going."

Jennifer knew it would be useless to deny it, especially since his wife had almost as big a mouth as he did. "We did. But I'm having a little trouble dealing with his niece."

"I didn't even know he had a niece."

"I didn't know it, either, until last week. She lives with him."

She figured that was all she'd have to say. Dennis would figure out the rest. Tanya would've filled him in on Friday's conversation, as well as the one she'd had with Jennifer that day in her penthouse. He'd know what she was dealing with. More so than Tanya really, since Dennis had been with her since the very beginning. He'd already been working for her father when she'd met Tommy Mason. He'd watched her jump through hoops for the older boy. And he'd also been her sole emotional support in the year that followed.

"So is she a delinquent or what?" he asked, leaning forward with his forearms resting on his knees.

Jennifer looked at him, surprised. "I don't know. I haven't met her. She's twelve," she said.

Dennis's eyes filled with understanding. "I can see where it might be a little rough at first, but I still don't see that as a reason to avoid the man if you're really interested in him."

"I do."

"You're twenty-eight years old, Jen. Don't you think you've been punishing yourself long enough? Isn't it about time to forgive yourself?"

"It's a little hard to forgive someone for being ir-responsible enough to create a life with no means to care for it," she said. Peace, she'd thought she'd found. Acceptance, she knew she'd found. Forgive-ness, she didn't think she'd ever find.

"If you'd done it consciously, maybe, but you didn't, Jen. And you've paid for your mistake. Ten-fold."

"I was paid for it, you mean."

"What in the hell are you talking about?" Dennis asked, getting up and sitting on the corner of her desk.

Jennifer didn't like having him tower over her. She already felt menial enough as it was. "I took their bribe, Dennis, remember? Give up the baby and get the car I'd always wanted."

"That's bull, Jennifer. Even *your* parents wouldn't offer a car in exchange for a child. They gave you that car to appease their guilt, not buy you off."

Jennifer hadn't seen it that way. "I still took it. I still gained by giving the baby up," she said.

"But you'd have given the baby up either way, Jen, because it was best for the baby. You took the car to please your parents, just like you'd been doing your whole life. You knew it would make them feel better if you allowed them to do something nice for you."

"I loved that car, Dennis."

"Sure you did. You still do. It's a great car. And it served you well back then, too, giving you the distraction you needed."

Jennifer smiled sadly. "I'd love to think you're right, my friend. I'd love to think I wasn't as awful as I've always thought, but pretty words can't change the past. If I'd been stronger, I could've fought them. There are places I could've gone where they'd have helped me find a job and take care of my baby."

Dennis leaned down, holding her gaze with his. "And what kind of life would that have been for that child, Jen? Could it have competed with the two-parent, financially secure family you sent her to? You're one of the strongest people I know, lady. It took one hell of a lot of guts to give away the one thing you loved most in the world."

Jennifer's eyes filled with tears as she listened to her friend. He'd pulled her through some hard times in the past, taught her how to hold her head up high again when she'd gone back to high school branded a tramp.

"So you think two people with money raising her compensates for the fact that she'd been denied her own mother's love?" she asked. She'd driven herself crazy all weekend, the questions going round and round in her head.

"I think if they love her as if she was their own flesh and blood, she's just the same as every other kid on the block."

"Except that she knows she has a mother out there someplace who didn't want her."

"If her adoptive parents love her enough, it doesn't matter. You wanna know what I think?" he asked, his eyes filled with challenge.

"What?"

"I think you're getting a little stuck-up in your old age, lady, placing so much importance on yourself in that girl's life. I'd wager a guess that if she ever thinks about you, it's fleetingly."

A slow grin spread across Jennifer's face. Dennis had always known just what to say to make her feel better. "Why couldn't I have fallen in love with you?" she asked him.

"You knew I was saving myself for Tanya," he said, grinning back at her. But they both knew there'd been a time when he'd have married Jennifer in an instant if she'd have had him.

"Yeah, and you'd better be saving your money, my friend. That woman plans to buy out the stock in every baby store in the city over the next five months."

"Yeah. I saw all the loot she bought on Friday." He sobered. "So you're really okay with our having a baby?"

Jennifer set her pen down. "It might be a little hard at times seeing Tanya go through all the stages I went through, but I'm ready for it. I have to let the past go."

"If you really mean that, why not let Chambers introduce you to his niece and see what happens?" Dennis asked. "Maybe spending some time with a twelve-year-old would help you get on with life, rather than avoiding it."

"You think that's what I've been doing?"

"Isn't it?"

Jennifer shrugged, not sure of anything anymore. "Don't press me on this, okay? Meet him for me tomorrow?"

Dennis got up. "If that's what you want," he said, heading for the door. He didn't bother to hide the fact that he thought she was making the wrong decision.

"It's what I want," Jennifer said. But she heard the lie in her words even if Dennis didn't. She honestly didn't know what she wanted, except maybe to be fifteen again, to have the chance to do it all over—and get it right this time.

HER MEETING with Peterson took as long as Jennifer had expected, but just to ensure that she missed the meeting with Innovative Advertising, she stopped at the drugstore on her way back to the office. Walking up and down the aisles, buying an extra deodorant when she already had a spare at home, stopping for more of the toothpaste and bubble bath she'd picked up over the weekend, she wondered how strong Dennis would think her if he could see her now.

By lunchtime, having stopped at the cleaners and her favorite jewelers, as well, she figured it was safe to return to the office. She'd have Rachel order her a sandwich of some kind while she caught up on the work she'd missed that morning. She wanted to get moving on Peterson's plans as soon as possible. Which meant she had several phone calls to make to get the city permits they needed.

She spent a frustrating twenty minutes talking with the mayor's office, ten of them with the mayor himself, which only resulted in having to make more calls than she'd started with. If the pollution didn't suffocate the world, she figured the red tape would. It made no sense that she had to beg the city to allow her to spend her own money to develop a garbage dump into a valuable piece of property that the citizens of Atlanta could be proud of.

The door to her office burst open and Jennifer glanced up, her heart rate accelerating at the sight of Bryan Chambers.

"I'm sorry, Ms. Teal. I told him you weren't to be disturbed," Rachel said behind him, wringing her hands.

"I didn't figure that meant me." He held his ground as if he owned it.

Jennifer stood. "It's okay, Rachel," she said, dismissing her secretary. As much as she'd done to avoid him, she didn't have the strength to demand he leave now that he was there.

"You weren't at the meeting." Bryan strode into the middle of her office, challenging her.

"Hello to you, too," she said, stalling. She'd come to no decisions about him. About them.

Had she?

"I wanted you to see the tapes."

"I'd planned to look at them tonight. I had an appointment this morning. With my architect."

His brow rose. "You're building a house?"

"A truck building next to Teal Chevrolet."

Their eyes caught and held as they stood across the office from each other, as if neither knew where to go from there. He was dressed as usual in blue jeans and a short-sleeved pullover, his ponytail hanging down over his collar. He looked wonderful.

"Have dinner with us tonight," he said, his words soft, seductive.

She let out a breath, one she hadn't realized she'd been holding until he'd asked the question. And it was then she knew she'd made her decision. Dennis had said a lot of things the day before that had struck home. Things she'd needed to hear.

"On two conditions," she said.

He took a few steps toward her, his face slowly breaking out in a grin. "What might those be?" he asked.

"We go someplace neutral, a restaurant, and we drive there separately."

"Giving yourself an escape route?" he asked, but he didn't seem to care. He was still grinning.

"Maybe." She wished she could take this as lightly as he was. She felt like she was strangling.

"Then I have a condition, too." He was no longer smiling.

"What?"

"If you run out on us, you make certain Nicki knows it doesn't have anything to do with her. Fake a sickness or something, I don't care, but I don't want that little girl upset. She's been through enough."

"Of course," Jennifer said, hurt that he'd found it necessary to warn her, as if he wasn't sure he could trust her around his niece. But then, she couldn't blame him. She didn't trust herself, either.

She agreed to meet Bryan and Nicki at seven o'clock at a steak place closer to her penthouse than the office, and she wondered suddenly if she was doing the right thing, if she shouldn't have followed her instincts and left well enough alone....

CHAPTER ELEVEN

NICKI DIDN'T WANT to go to dinner. Bryan had thought his niece would've been eager for some female companionship for a change, but though she hadn't argued, he'd seen the resistance in her eyes. Eyes that were exactly like her mother's.

"What's up, Nick? I thought it'd be fun for us to get out," he said.

Apparently he'd said the wrong thing. That fear was back in her eyes. And he had no idea why. Hell. He'd climb a damn mountain for the child, if only she'd tell him which one.

"You can go, Uncle Bryan. You don't have to drag me along on your date."

"Who said anything about it being a date?"

"It's with a woman, isn't it? The same one you took to the symphony, you said, and out to Stone Mountain that day."

Bryan's eyes narrowed. Apparently Nicki paid more attention to what went on around here than he'd thought. "It's with the same woman, yes, but tonight's not a date. She wants to meet you, Nick."

Nicki's eyes widened. "Me?"

"Of course, you. It's the whole reason for the dinner. We're a pair now, Nick. You and me. My friends need to be your friends, too. Besides, why wouldn't she want to meet you? You're a pretty spectacular kid."

"And you're positive I wouldn't be bugging you if I'm there?"

He grabbed her by the shoulders, holding her steady while he looked her straight in the eye. "Positive."

"But what would I wear?" she asked, her expression worried again.

"How about that flowered thing we bought a couple of weeks ago, the one with the thin straps?"

Her brows came together as she considered his suggestion. "The one that's shorts that looks like a dress?"

"Yeah. The color looked great with your hair."

She smiled, nodding. "Okay. When do I have to be ready?"

Bryan looked at his watch. "A couple of hours," he said.

"Then I better get moving." She was already pulling her long hair out of its ponytail as she headed toward her room.

Bryan watched her go, well aware that she could be ready in an eighth of that time, but he'd give her all night if she wanted it, as long as she kept looking as happy as she'd looked walking down that hall. She had a purpose.

Bryan went in to change, uncomfortable with the power he unwittingly held over the two most important people in his life. He was orchestrating something between them that was highly personal for both of them, and neither one of them even knew about it. But when he considered his options, he couldn't see any other way.

And it might just possibly be the right one, too. First Jennifer had surprised him by agreeing to the dinner at all, and now Nicki actually appeared to be looking forward to it. Maybe it was meant that mother and daughter finally meet.

Nicki was as quiet as usual as they drove the couple of miles to the restaurant, and just in case she was worried about meeting Jennifer, he took the time to tell his niece a little bit more about her. He told her things he thought might interest a twelve-year-old, such as that Jennifer drove a convertible and was friends with a famous artist, but that was all.

He saw her sitting at a table as soon as he ushered Nicki into the crowded restaurant. She looked beautiful. He'd never wanted a woman so much just from looking at her. Or was it because he could only look that he wanted her so much?

With one arm around his niece, he led her toward Jennifer's table, surprised to find that his hands were sweating. So much rested on the evening. Far more than either of his guests knew.

He could tell the second that Jennifer noticed them. He saw her stiffen, saw her glance run over Nicki and then away. His heart sank. She was meeting her own daughter for the first time. Shouldn't she feel something, some connection, even if she didn't know why?

"Is that her?" Nicki whispered.

"That's her," Bryan said. He wished he could tell Nicki that the woman she was heading toward was her mother. She deserved to know that. Jennifer deserved to know it, too. It was unfair of him to walk her daughter up to her as if she was a total stranger. And yet, as he saw Jennifer's eyes shy away from the child at his side, he knew he couldn't tell her. He couldn't tell either of them. Not yet.

"Jennifer, this is Nicki," he said as they reached the table. He held Nicki's chair out for her. Waiting.

"Hi." Nicki grinned, a hint of the imp he'd once known.

"It's nice to meet you," Jennifer said, returning Nicki's smile, then looking away.

Nicki didn't seem to notice Jennifer's reticence. She sat down, picked up her menu and started to read it as if she actually had an appetite to appease.

Jennifer picked up her menu, too, and Bryan looked from one to the other of them, a man truly between a rock and a hard place. He was amazed, once he saw them together, how very much they resembled each other, with their long auburn curls and striking hazel eyes, and knew a moment's unease when he considered the possibility that someone else might pick up on the resemblance, as well.

They ordered dinner, but as soon as the waiter left, silence fell over the table again. Bryan refused to let the evening fail and spent the next ten minutes trying to keep the conversation rolling for all three of them. But between Jennifer's monosyllabic replies and Nicki's shy smiles, it seemed an impossibility. He was relieved when their dinners arrived and they could occupy themselves with the business of eating.

"My steak's great. How's your, Nick?" he asked.

"Good."

Bryan looked to Jennifer. She wasn't eating much, which was unusual. "How about yours?" he asked.

"Fine."

Silence descended again. Bryan was beginning to think he'd made the biggest mistake of his life.

"Could I have the salt, please?" Nicki's soft voice broke the silence.

The saltshaker was by Jennifer. She picked it up, passed it to Nicki with a tight smile and turned her attention back to her plate.

"Thanks," Nicki said.

"You're welcome."

Great. These two had spent nine intimate months together and now the most they could manage was polite platitudes? Bryan's appetite was rapidly dwindling to nothing as he sat between them, needing to make things right for both of them and suspecting it might be impossible.

Nicki put her fork down on a near-empty plate. "Your hair's the same color as mine," she suddenly said, looking at the twist of hair on Jennifer's head.

Bryan almost choked. Their hair color *was* unusual. Would either of them be suspicious of the resemblance? Would Nicki? She knew he'd been looking for her birth mother.

"Yes, it is." Jennifer glanced at Nicki's long auburn curls, then away.

"I guess you have to be careful with colors, too," Nicki said, her voice tentative.

Jennifer smiled at her before looking away again. "Always."

Nicki looked over at Bryan. "You know what Lucy did today, Uncle Bryan? She fell asleep in the dirty clothes," she said, a smile on her lips. It didn't quite reach her eyes, but it was a start.

The evening ended as soon as they finished dinner. Bryan and Nicki walked Jennifer to her car.

"It was nice meeting you," Nicki said, somehow making the words sound sincere, rather than merely polite.

Jennifer glanced at his niece only briefly. "It was nice meeting you, too, Nicki. Bye," she said before climbing into her car.

Bryan couldn't let her just drive away. He was afraid he'd never see her again. He leaned down and kissed her fully, if much too briefly, on the lips. He'd have liked to have spent the next several hours kissing her—and more. But Nicki was there. And Nicki came first.

"Bryan?" Jennifer's voice called him back as he turned to go. "Call me." The two words sounded ominous.

He nodded, leading Nicki away.

"Bye," Nicki said one last time, looking over her shoulder as she and Bryan headed to the Jeep.

"She's nice," Nicki said on the short drive home.

Bryan was amazed. How could Nicki say that? Jennifer had barely acknowledged her all night.

"I think so," he said.

"She eats her salad without dressing, same as me. And Mom always said I must be the only person in the world who does that."

So she'd noticed, too. "She does, huh?" *Intelligent, Chambers.*

"Do you think we can go out with her again sometime?"

Bryan glanced at his niece, seeing the interest sparking in her eyes. "I'll ask her," he said, knowing he couldn't promise any more than that, and worried he was setting Nicki up for a disappointment. He wouldn't be at all surprised if Jennifer planned to end things once and for all the first chance she got.

He'd just have to see that she didn't get the chance.

Bryan had some papers to drop off at Teal Automotive the next day, and he stopped home to get Nicki on the way to Jennifer's office.

"Are you sure she won't mind if I come to her work?" Nicki asked, already slipping into her sandals.

"I'm sure," Bryan said, though he wasn't at all. After the way Jennifer had acted the night before, he wasn't sure she ever wanted to see Nicki again. Which was why he couldn't give her a choice. She had no idea how much was resting on her learning to care for Nicki.

Not only was Nicki's happiness hanging in the balance, but Bryan's, as well, and, he suspected, Jennifer's. He'd only begun to realize how much he'd grown to feel for Jennifer over the past weeks, how much his future happiness had begun to depend on her. He'd intended to insinuate himself into the woman's life, find out what made her tick for Nicki's sake. He hadn't expected to want to stay there.

And if she didn't accept Nicki, he'd never get the chance.

SHE WAS SUCH A YOUNG LADY, so grown-up. Jennifer hadn't realized how mature twelve was. And yet, there'd been a true air of innocence about her—

"Hey, Jennifer! You in there?"

Jennifer's gaze flew from the window of her office to the man who'd been sitting across from her most of the morning. "Sorry, Dennis. Where were we?" she asked, looking at the figures in front of her.

"I've been right here. It's you who keeps leaving us. We can put this off, you know. We didn't finish this year's projected budgets until last August. Next year's can certainly wait another week or two."

Jennifer gathered up the papers on her desk. She really had it bad. There had never been a time when work didn't take care of what ailed her. "If you don't mind, I guess we better stop for now. I'm having a little trouble concentrating."

"I've noticed," Dennis said dryly, putting his copies of the Teal Automotive projected profits back into a folder. "You wanna tell me what's got you so tied up?"

"I met his niece last night," she said softly, remembering the long excruciating ordeal.

Dennis froze, his papers half-in and half-out of their folder. "And?" he asked, watching her carefully.

"She was older than I expected."

"She's not twelve?"

"Yeah, she's twelve. Twelve is older than I expected. She knew exactly what to order for herself and didn't have to be reminded of her manners even once."

"You sound disappointed."

Jennifer shrugged. "Silly, isn't it? It's just that whenever I've pictured my baby out there, growing up, it's always been with the idea that she still needed mothering. But Nicki's so self-sufficient."

"I'm sure not all twelve-year-olds are, Jen. And just because she can eat by herself doesn't mean she doesn't need a mother. You certainly could have used one at that age."

She looked up, surprised. "I had one."

"In fact, maybe, not in deed, but I'm not going to debate with you about it again. So how'd it go otherwise?"

Jennifer fiddled with the magnetic paper-clip holder Sam had given her for Christmas one year. It was in the shape of a Mustang. "It went okay," she said.

Dennis didn't say anything. He just sat watching her.

"I liked her."

"You two hit it off?"

"Not exactly, but I don't think she hates me."

"She'd be nuts if she does. What'd Bryan say about it?"

"I don't know. I haven't talked to him yet today." She'd been waiting for his call all morning.

Dennis pushed his files aside. "Was it as hard as you thought it would be?"

"Harder." Jennifer was appalled when tears sprang to her eyes. She'd thought she'd cried them all out during the long dark hours of the night.

"I'm sorry, Jen," Dennis said awkwardly, leaning forward to brush the top of her hand with his fingers.

Jennifer swallowed, then wiped her eyes, willing the tears to stop. "Her hair's the same color as mine," she said, her words barely above a whisper. "I kept watching her in my peripheral vision and wondering if my own daughter looks like that, if she smiles so sweetly, if her bone structure is as fine. If she eats her salad without dressing."

"Bryan's niece ate her salad without dressing?" Dennis asked.

Jennifer nodded.

"And I thought you were the only one who did that," he said, smiling across at her gently.

"I know. And she seems to like catsup as much as I do, too." Jennifer stopped, composing herself. She'd never been so confused in her life, but she was *feeling* again. She just hadn't decided if that was a good thing or a bad thing.

Her intercom buzzed, startling her.

She pushed the call button. "Yes, Rachel?"

"Mr. Chambers is here to see you, Ms. Teal."

Jennifer's eyes flew to Dennis. She wasn't ready to see him yet. Not like this.

Her office door opened. "Oh, but— I'm sorry, Ms. Teal," Rachel said over the intercom as Bryan stepped into her office.

He wasn't alone. Jennifer's gaze fluttered to the child hovering nervously at his side.

"Hello, Nicki, it's good to see you again," she said, her heart floating. Dear God, was it right for her to feel such an immediate bond with this child? She flooded with guilt when she thought of her own child, the one she'd abandoned, the one who had the right to expect her affection—

"Hello, Ms. Teal. Uncle Bryan said you wouldn't mind if I came along with him."

Her voice was as sweet as Jennifer remembered.

"I don't mind at all," Jennifer said, looking at Bryan. He smiled at her in that way he had that made her feel like the only woman alive.

And then, coming farther into the room, he shook Dennis's hand. "Good to see you, Dennis," he said. "I've got some schedules for you two to approve." He pulled a folder out of the sketchbook under his arm.

Nicki wandered over to the couch, and Jennifer wanted to leave the two men to their business and join the girl there. But she couldn't think of a thing to say. She didn't have any idea what twelve-year-old girls were interested in. Did they play with Barbie dolls? Or did they think fashion dolls were dumb by the time they reached twelve? Did they still watch cartoons and think boys had cooties? She couldn't remember how it had felt to be twelve. She started to get nervous.

"Let me see what you've got," she said, joining the men.

Nicki sat quietly on the couch, looking at the pictures on Jennifer's office walls.

BRYAN CALLED Jennifer later that afternoon to invite her to his place for dinner the following evening. He didn't expect her to accept, but he wanted her to know he wasn't going to give up. He was shocked when she agreed to come. His house wasn't ready for guests.

She'd never seen his home before, and picturing the cool perfection of her penthouse, he spent the entire next day at home cleaning, much to Nicki's amusement. But as much as his niece teased him about his unusual behavior, she helped him, too. She seemed almost excited herself at the prospect of company.

Nicki was a whiz in the kitchen, having learned to cook from her mother and grandma, and when she offered to make a meat loaf with all the trimmings, Bryan didn't have the heart to tell her he'd been thinking of something a little fancier.

She was wearing her daisy outfit and had been pacing between the living-room window and the kitchen for almost half an hour by the time Jennifer pulled into the driveway.

"She's here," she announced. Bryan dropped the stack of magazines he'd been trying to find a home for right back where they belonged—in the middle of the coffee table. He was what he was, blue jeans, ponytail and all.

Nicki hung back when he answered the door, but not too far. Jennifer looked beautiful as always, slim and cool in a short white dress that flared just over her hips. He brushed her lips with his and invited her inside.

"Hi," Nicki said from behind him.

"Hello." Jennifer smiled over his shoulder at Nicki before turning back to Bryan.

"I like your house," she said, looking around at the interior with its open-floor plan.

"It's not quite a penthouse." He cursed himself for saying that. Possessions didn't matter to him. And he'd be damned if he'd start apologizing for what he was just because he'd met a woman who mattered.

"It's a lot nicer than a penthouse." Jennifer walked into the living room, turning around. "You don't have to wait for an elevator to get home, for one thing," she said.

"You live in a penthouse?" Nicki asked, following her into the room.

Jennifer nodded, glancing at Nicki only briefly before looking around again. "Where's your dog—Lucy, didn't you say her name was?"

"Uncle Bryan made me keep her outside. She barks a lot when she meets someone new."

"She also jumps up on people, and I didn't want her to get hair all over you before you even got in the door," Bryan said, leading Jennifer over to the couch.

Jennifer sat down, sniffing the air. "Something sure smells good," she said.

"It's meat loaf. Nicki made it."

"I hope you like it," Nicki added, sounding apologetic.

"I've always liked meat loaf," Jennifer told them both, jumping up to peer at the books in Bryan's bookcase.

They'd been his mother's. The wall they'd been on since before Bryan was born hadn't been touched by the tornado that had torn up most of the house.

Nicki went out to put the finishing touches on dinner, and Bryan poured a couple of glasses of wine. As tense as he felt, it was still great to be alone with her for a moment.

"Here, this is for you," he said, taking her a glass. But he didn't hand it to her immediately. He bent down to kiss her first. A kiss that exploded between them the minute their lips touched. A kiss that would have continued if Nicki hadn't called from the kitchen to say that dinner was ready.

By the time they met his niece in the dining room, Bryan had his breathing a little more under control. The rest of his body wasn't so quick to cool down. He took his seat at the head of the table, wondering if he was ever going to find out what it was like to make love with Jennifer, to have her moaning beneath him, begging for satisfaction. Somehow he couldn't picture Jennifer begging for anything.

Nicki passed around plates and bowls, and the conversation was as scarce as it had been the other night. Bryan still hadn't seen Jennifer look directly at Nicki for more than a few seconds, but at least she was eating better tonight. He hoped that meant she was getting a little bit more comfortable being around Nicki.

"You know what, Uncle Bryan? I think you've set a record for the number of times in a row you've seen Ms. Teal," Nicki said about halfway through the meal.

Bryan nearly choked on his baked potato. Jennifer offered him his glass of water, solicitous as always, but he saw the grin she was trying to hide.

"You might even fall in love with her," Nicki continued. Bryan didn't know whether to shout with glee at this glimpse of the Nicki he used to know or to strangle her.

"Finish your dinner, Nick," he said, trying to sound stern and fatherly.

"I *am* finished." Nicki motioned to her empty plate. "Grandma always used to say that it would take the love of a good woman to bring peace to your wandering soul," Nicki said.

She sounded just like his mother when she said it, too. "Having you here brought peace to my soul, sprite. Now go get us some dessert or something."

"I made brownies," Nicki said, taking her empty plate into the kitchen.

He watched the door swing shut behind his niece, hearing again the words he'd just said. Having her with him, having someone he loved at home, needing his care, did seem to have brought peace to his soul, at least for the time being. He'd been feeling a lot of uncomfortable things lately, but claustrophobic wasn't one of them. Of course, knowing himself as he did, he knew that the dreaded restlessness could attack at any time.

"She's sweet," Jennifer said, looking at the door Nicki had left through.

"She's the best," Bryan said. Now all he had to do was convince her mother of that.

AN HOUR LATER Nicki and Jennifer stood in front of the video cabinet in the living room trying to decide which movie to watch. They'd let Lucy inside as soon as the dishes were done, and Jennifer, after confessing she'd never been allowed to have a pet while she was growing up, took an instant liking to the dog. The three of them played tug-of-war with her until Lucy, finally tired out, curled up in a corner of the room and went to sleep. That was when Bryan suggested a movie. He didn't want Jennifer to leave when they were all finally starting to relax.

Nicki grabbed a movie from the cabinet, but Bryan had a feeling she didn't even know which one she held. She was spending more time looking at Jennifer than at the movies in front of her. He waited by the video-cassette recorder, watching them both. Their resemblance was amazing.

"I like your jewelry." Nicki's words were soft, hesitant.

"Thank you." Jennifer glanced at Nicki briefly before returning her attention to the triple stack of movies.

"I had a baby ring," Nicki said. She was looking at the gold chains around Jennifer's neck. "It had my name and my mom's engraved on the inside."

"Oh," Jennifer said, pulling out a movie to read the blurb on the back.

Bryan remembered the ring. Lori had bought it for Nicki for her first birthday, their first birthday together. Come to think of it, he hadn't seen it since the—

"I used to wear it on a gold chain around my neck, but I took it off to go swimming and then the tornado came and I never saw it again."

Oh, God. He should have realized. He should have remembered how important that ring was to Nicki. They could at least have looked for it in the rubble.

"Your uncle told me about that tornado," Jennifer said gently. "I'm sorry."

"Me, too." Nicki shrugged. "Have you ever seen *The Lion King?*" she asked, pulling another video out from the cabinet. Bryan was amazed. It was the first time Nicki had ever mentioned the tornado without crying.

Jennifer looked at the movie Nicki held out. "No."

"It's a great movie. You and Uncle Bryan should watch it."

"What about you, Nick?" Bryan asked. "I thought you were going to watch with us."

"I've already seen it a hundred times," she said. "I'd kinda like to go to bed."

He should consider himself lucky. Nicki had stayed up an hour later than usual already.

And it wasn't like time alone with Jennifer was going to be any hardship for him.

Grabbing Lucy, Nicki kissed Bryan on the cheek. "Night, Uncle Bryan," she said.

"Night, Nick. Be sure you brush."

Nicki grimaced at him. "I will. Night, Ms. Teal."

"Good night, Nicki. Thank you for the meat loaf. It was very good," Jennifer said, standing awkwardly in the middle of the living room.

If she'd been watching she'd have seen the glow that spread across Nicki's face at the polite praise, but she was still looking at the movie cassette Nicki had given her. Bryan couldn't figure it out. Though she was gentle about it, Jennifer continued to shy away from Nicki as if the child had some kind of disease, yet

Nicki was blossoming before his very eyes simply having Jennifer around.

Jennifer seemed to relax the second they heard Nicki's bedroom door close behind her. "We don't have to watch this if you don't want to," she said, handing him the movie.

Bryan reached for the video, pulling Jennifer up against him as he did. "As good as this is, there *is* something I'd rather be doing," he said, nuzzling her neck.

Tilting her head back, she gave him better access. "Mmm. I see what you mean."

They were alone and in private, and he'd been wanting her too long to just stop. He covered her lips with his, hungry for the taste of her. She was warm and sweet, and far too sexy for his peace of mind. Her lips opened beneath his and his body quickened as he accepted her invitation, deepening the kiss.

Never had a woman affected him so powerfully. His body surged against hers, aching with the strength of his yearning to take her with him on the wildest ride of his life. She was perfect. Her slim body filling his arms was like heaven, her breasts pressing into his chest an exquisite torture.

Bryan started to shake with the effort it took him not to lower her to the floor and pump himself into her until he found the blessed relief her kisses promised. She deserved better than that. So did he. And Nicki was right down the hall.

He dragged his lips from her mouth, resting his forehead against hers. "I guess we better watch that movie, after all," he said, his breathing heavy.

"Probably." Jennifer smiled wryly. "Nice girls don't seduce their hosts when they're invited to dinner, do they?"

"Is that what you were doing, seducing your host?"

"I don't know. If I was, was it working?"

Bryan grinned at her, still holding her against him. "What do you think?"

"I think that you're one hell of a man, Bryan Chambers."

"Because I'm so hard it hurts?"

"No!" She burst out laughing. "Because you don't let your physical desires overpower your brain—"

"You haven't seen me at four o'clock in the morning," Bryan interrupted, thinking of all the cold showers he'd taken since he'd met this woman.

"—and you don't put pressure on me to satisfy those desires," she finished.

"One thing I've never done was coerce a woman into bed. Either she wants it as badly as I do, or we don't do it."

"See, that's what I mean." She looked up at him. "Why couldn't I have met you when I was fifteen?" she whispered.

Bryan tensed. "Who *did* you meet?" It was important for him to know the details, to understand.

She pulled away from him and sat on the couch. "No one really," she said, looking down at the dainty white sandals on her feet.

"You had a baby, Jen. There had to be someone."

Her head shot up. "I had a baby, yes, but I didn't say it happened when I was fifteen." She looked at him, puzzlement furrowing her brow.

Bryan froze, thinking back to the day she'd told him about her giving up a child. No. She'd never said *when* she'd had the baby. That was something he'd figured out on his own, because he knew how old Nicki was. Good Lord, what had he just done?

CHAPTER TWELVE

MORE THAN ANYTHING, Bryan hated the lies. He sat down beside Jennifer on the couch, leaning forward with his elbows on his knees. "I guess it was the way you said you wished you could've met me when you were fifteen," he replied. "I just assumed that was when you got pregnant." He tossed the truth around like a hot potato.

"Oh." That was all. Nothing else.

"I won't pressure you to tell me about it, Jen. But whenever you're ready to talk, I'll listen."

She slipped her hand through the crook in his arm, resting her cheek against his shoulder. "I was too young, Bryan. But old enough to know better. And I don't want you to know. I don't want you to think any less of me."

He couldn't promise her it wouldn't matter. It was his niece she'd given away. "The woman I care for is the woman you are today. Who you were with in the past is just that—in the past." He spoke to her bowed head.

"I hope you mean that," she whispered, raising her head, studying him, as if to determine the sincerity of his words.

"I'm more concerned with how you and Nicki get along than in how old you were when you lost your virginity."

She pulled back. "I'm not sure she likes me," she said, sounding just about her daughter's age.

"She likes you, honey. After dinner the other night, she asked if we were going to see you again."

"Maybe because she was hoping you weren't."

"Trust me. She wasn't. She almost got excited when I told her you were coming for dinner tonight."

"She barely said two words to me."

"You barely said two words to her, Jen."

"Because I don't know what to say."

"You say what you'd say to me, within reason of course. You just need to learn to relax around her a little bit. She's a great kid once you get to know her."

Somehow he had to convince Jennifer she was good with children. She was having a hard enough time sticking it out with Nicki merely being his niece. She'd bolt for sure if she knew the true significance of winning Nicki's regard.

It wouldn't be like it was the first time she'd abandoned her daughter.

"She's really strong, isn't she?" Jennifer asked, sitting back on the couch. "I'm amazed how well she's adjusted to the loss she's suffered."

"Until she met you, she spent most of her days in bed," Bryan said bluntly.

Jennifer's brows drew together in concern. "Was she sick?"

"Not unless you call the tendency to sleep your life away being sick."

"But she seems so...so...normal."

"She opens up when you're around, Jen. Maybe it's because you're a woman, I don't know, but she seems to have come out of her shell more in the past few days than she has in the whole past year."

Jennifer's eyes widened. "Really?"

Bryan grinned. She looked so naively pleased sitting there, this woman who'd given birth while still a child herself. "Yeah. Really. Listen, I promised Nicki a trip to the beach as soon as Calvin got caught up on things. Why don't you come with us? We could take a couple of days, leave the day after tomorrow. What do you say?"

"To the beach?"

"Yeah. You can even pick the beach, as long as it's on this coast."

"I haven't been to the beach since I was about ten."

"Then it's high time you went, wouldn't you agree?"

"Just the three of us?" she asked, looking excited and scared out of her wits at the same time.

"Just the three of us. It'll give us a chance to see if we've got something good going here or not." It was time to make some decisions.

"I'm not sure I want to know if it's the 'or not,'" she said.

He didn't want to know that, either. But it was time he found out one way or the other. And if, as he suspected, Jennifer was fine with Nicki once she allowed herself to relax, *then* he'd have to find out if Jennifer cared enough for him to understand when he told her who he really was, or rather, who Nicki really was.

"Don't you want to find out now if we're kidding ourselves here?" he asked.

"I guess." She took a deep breath. "Okay. I'll go. Just give me a couple of days to clear things up at the office."

"You got 'em," Bryan said, telling himself he was doing the right thing. He wasn't going to finally meet a woman who didn't make him feel like her sheets were a straitjacket only to lose her before he ever really had her. He simply wasn't going to let that happen.

NICKI WAS LOOKING FORWARD to the trip to the beach now that Ms. Teal was going with them. Uncle Bryan wouldn't get bored with his pretty girlfriend along. They were going to some private beach Uncle Bryan knew about off the Florida Keys. It only had one hotel, and Uncle Bryan had gotten a three-bedroom suite for them. Nicki spent the next two days packing, and promising Lucy that she'd have a good time next door with Mrs. Baker and that she'd only be gone a few days.

Nicki really liked Ms. Teal. She didn't talk much, but her voice was soft when she did say stuff and she always paid attention when she, Nicki, talked. And she smiled at her like her mom used to do sometimes when she came home from school. It made Nicki feel special, even if she really wasn't.

Nicki looked at the three swimsuits spread out on her bed, wondering which one to pack. They were all one-pieces. When she'd gone to Shallowbrook for her birthday, her friends had all been talking about their new two-piece swimsuits. Knowing her uncle would never go for that, especially after he'd refused to buy her the baby T she'd wanted, Nicki looked back at the suits she had. She liked the plain green one the best, but the top was a little tight, and it made her feel kind of funny wearing it, like everyone could see that she was getting breasts. But the other one-pieces had flowers all over them and made her look like a little girl. She finally threw all three of them in. Maybe she wouldn't go swimming at all.

She'd bet Ms. Teal looked like one of the ladies on TV in her swimsuit. It probably didn't have any flowers. And she'd bet that Ms. Teal wouldn't feel funny if her top fit tight, either. Ms. Teal probably never felt funny about anything. She was just about the most perfect person Nicki had ever met. Nicki'd sure love it if her other mother turned out to be someone like that.

But she wouldn't. Someone like Ms. Teal would never have given her baby away. She'd have found a way to keep it, no matter what.

They were only going to be gone for three days, but Nicki packed all her new summer stuff. She didn't want Ms. Teal to think she dressed like a dope.

She froze as a thought suddenly occurred to her. What if her real mother dressed like a dope? What if she didn't understand about how some colors were good on some people but looked awful on others? What if she didn't know how to wear her makeup or style her hair? Omigosh! What if she didn't have any teeth?

Nicki giggled as she folded up one of her new shirts, picturing an old witch with no teeth knocking on the door, and Uncle Bryan telling her she had the wrong house when she asked for Nicki. But she stopped laughing when she thought about her other mother really showing up. Maybe she should tell Uncle Bryan she didn't want to find her other mother—now, before it was too late.

She'd been worried a lot about why her first mother had given her away, about meeting a lady who'd allowed complete strangers to take her own baby. She'd been worried about the lady still not wanting her.

And besides, if Uncle Bryan was falling in love, if Ms. Teal was going to bring peace to his wandering soul, which surely she would since Nicki had never known her grandma to be wrong, then he'd be settling down, anyway, which meant Nicki didn't need to worry about him feeling cramped and leaving her.

And Nicki hadn't been feeling so crazy these past few days, either. She even felt a little happy about going to the beach and didn't just want to stay in bed all the time. So maybe she didn't need to worry about having something wrong with her from her other mother. Maybe she didn't need her other mother at all anymore. And if she didn't need her it wouldn't matter, then, whether her other mother wanted her or not.

Ms. Teal would surely want her. Nicki could tell she liked her, 'cause she smiled at her so nice. And she'd wanted to come to the beach with them, too. Besides, she loved Lucy. It had been her idea to get down on the floor to play tug-of-war with Lucy's stuffed turtle, and she didn't even say anything when Lucy's hair had gotten all over her pretty white dress. She'd even laughed when Lucy had jumped up in her lap and kissed her. And if she loved Lucy she had to be someone who wouldn't mind having a kid around.

Yeah, maybe if things went as good as she hoped at the beach, Nicki would just tell Uncle Bryan she didn't want to find her other mother, after all.

THEY LEFT ATLANTA early Sunday morning. Bryan and Nicki picked Jennifer up at the penthouse before breakfast and drove straight to the airport. Nicki and Jennifer had breakfast there while Bryan got the plane ready to go. He said he'd grab a couple of doughnuts to take with him out to the hangar.

Jennifer stood with Nicki at the counter while they waited for the food they'd ordered, and then followed her to an empty booth, sliding in across from her.

Nicki smeared catsup on her hash browns, then handed the dispenser to Jennifer. "I liked your place, Ms. Teal. It's really neat having your own key to the elevator and everything."

"Call me Jennifer, please. Ms. Teal makes me feel so old. And the elevator is actually a pain a lot of the time," Jennifer said, reminding herself to pretend she was talking to a miniature version of Bryan or Tanya as she, too, covered her potatoes with catsup. "It takes forever to carry things up from the car after I've been shopping all day. And if you have to go to the bathroom, forget it."

Nicki giggled. "What do you do then?" she asked.

"Tap my foot a lot."

Nicki laughed again. Jennifer started to relax.

"You know, you're pretty when you do that," Jennifer said.

"Do what?" Nicki looked down at her plate, her face flushed.

"Smile," Jennifer said, losing confidence. She'd bungled things already. She'd never have told Tanya she looked pretty when she smiled. And now she'd gone and embarrassed the child.

Nicki looked up, her eyes serious. "Thank you," she said.

Jennifer's fork hung suspended in midair. "For what?"

The child shrugged. "For saying that. My mom used to tell me I was pretty sometimes, but Uncle

Bryan...well, you know, he's a man. He mostly doesn't like to see I'm growing up."

"He's giving you a hard time about it?"

"No. He just doesn't want boys to notice me, which is okay, 'cause I don't, either, but that doesn't mean I wanna look dumb."

"You don't look dumb! But I think I understand," Jennifer said, trying not to smile. "Your uncle still sees you as a little girl, huh?"

"Yeah." Nicki smiled and took a bite of toast.

"That's not all bad," Jennifer said, remembering her own youth. "At least he notices—and cares." Maybe things wouldn't have turned out as they had if someone had guided *her* a little more carefully.

"That's what I thought, too," Nicki said.

Bryan came in to get them just as they were finishing. He charged their meal to his account and led them out to the waiting plane.

"Jennifer, you climb up first," he said, helping her up the steps. "Nicki's riding in front with me."

"I am?" Nicki asked, clearly surprised.

"Of course. When have you ever flown with me and not been my copilot?"

"Never. But I thought—"

"Wrong," Bryan said. "God forbid something should happen to me, but if it did, you'd know what to do with the plane. Jennifer's only been up once."

"Besides, I'm happier back here, Nicki," Jennifer said, just as she'd have done to make one of her customers or employees more comfortable. "All those dials make me a little dizzy."

"They're nothing once you get used to them." Nicki smiled, climbed into her seat and put on her headset.

Bryan glanced at Jennifer in the back, his eyes thanking her even as they glowed with a more heated emotion. Jennifer smiled and stuck out her tongue at him.

The scenery below them was beautiful as they reached cruising altitude, but Jennifer found her eyes straying to the pilot more often than not. She was in love with him. She guessed she'd known it deep inside for a while now. She'd finally admitted it to herself when she'd picked up some birth control the day before. The last time she'd made love, it hadn't been love at all, and it hadn't been because *she* wanted to. And the consequences had been devastating. This time she was prepared all the way around.

He said something into his headset, apparently to Nicki because she grinned over at him and said something back. She really was a pretty child. And a nice one, too.

So far being with Nicki wasn't as bad as she'd thought it was going to be. The pain was still there, the regrets, but they'd always been there, even if she'd tried not to acknowledge them. Being with Nicki just made them impossible to ignore.

But somehow, being around Nicki also made the pain a little sweeter, almost consoling. On and off over the past twelve years, she'd found herself wondering how her daughter would feel about something, what kind of things she'd be into at the different stages in her life. And watching Nicki, Jennifer finally had answers for some of those questions. At the very least, she had some ground upon which to base those answers.

She still didn't feel any more certain about developing a relationship with Nicki, about her own ability to be the type of person a child would be comfortable with, but she was determined to give it her best shot. She wanted this thing to work.

Bryan had a limousine waiting for them at the airport in the Keys, and he'd arranged for a technician to service his plane, too.

"Jeez, Uncle Bryan, I can't believe it!" Nicki teased as they followed their driver to the car. "You're actually going to let someone else touch your plane. Grandma would've been shocked!"

Bryan grabbed Nicki in a neck hold, rubbing his knuckles against the top of her head. "Don't bug me, sprite. I'm on vacation."

"I'm sorry already," Nicki said.

Jennifer could barely understand her through her giggles. The sound was so infectious she joined in.

She opted to wait with Nicki by the luggage while Bryan checked them into the hotel. And as she stood there, she imagined how the three of them must look to the people around them, like a normal family vacationing in the Florida sun. She hadn't seen herself in a picture like that before, and though it felt odd, it also felt good. Very good.

Maybe someday...

"Did you want to..." She turned to Nicki, only to find that the girl wasn't beside her anymore. She'd been there a couple of seconds ago.

Panicked, Jennifer flew around, scanning the massive hotel lobby. Her stomach settled back where it belonged when she saw Nicki, only a few feet away, gazing into the window of the gift shop. Jennifer looked beyond the girl to the blue plaid two-piece swimsuit hanging there. The top wasn't so much a bra as a crop top. It would look good on Nicki's burgeoning young figure. Nicki turned, and with one last glance over her shoulder, walked back to join Jennifer.

Bryan reached her at the same time.

"You can check in with Dennis as soon as we get to the room if you want to," he told her.

Jennifer hadn't given Teal Automotive a thought all morning. "Don't bug me, Chambers. I'm on vacation," she said, grinning at Nicki. "Besides, it's Sunday. Dennis doesn't work on Sundays."

"Only the chairman of the board does that, huh?" he asked. Jennifer stuck her tongue out at him for the second time that morning.

Nicki laughed. Bryan grinned at his niece and then looked back at Jennifer. "You can catch flies that way, you know."

Jennifer closed her mouth.

Bryan gave the bellboy their room number, arranging to have their luggage brought up, and then led them to the elevator.

"Who's ready to hit the beach?" he asked as they rode up to their suite.

"I could stand a few hours of that," Jennifer said. She couldn't believe how good it sounded to do something so lazy.

Nicki seemed to be way too interested in the advertisement for the hotel dining room that hung on the elevator wall.

"How about you, Nick? You ready to take on the waves?"

Nicki shrugged.

"What's the matter? You were always the one begging to get down to the water," Bryan said, frowning.

"I know." Nicki ran her fingers over the buttons on the control panel.

"You wanted to come to the beach, Nick. What'd you think we'd do once we got here?"

"I don't know."

Bryan looked at Jennifer, obviously perplexed. Jennifer started to panic. If he didn't know how to handle the situation, what were they going to do? *She* certainly had no idea what had changed Nicki's mood so suddenly, and no suggestion for how to make things better.

The elevator stopped and the doors opened on their floor. Jennifer followed Bryan and his niece to the door of their suite, feeling horribly awkward and out of place. She wasn't good with children at the best of times, but dealing with them when there was a problem was simply beyond her.

Still, she had no desire to leave. Nicki was not a surly child. Something was bothering her. Jennifer wished she had a clue as to what it might be. She wished she didn't feel so damned inadequate.

The suite was spacious and open, with a living area large enough to house a family of six comfortably. It even had a kitchenette, complete with a two-burner stove and half-size refrigerator.

Nicki opened the refrigerator. "It's empty," she said, sounding disappointed as she shut it again and then peered into the cupboard.

"We can make a grocery run if you like, and make you the official cook," Bryan offered, grinning at her.

Nicki looked like an angel as she grinned back at him. "Don't bug me, Uncle Bryan. I'm on vacation," she said.

Jennifer started to relax again.

Her room, complete with its own bathroom, was too big for one person, but luxuriously appointed, and as soon as the bellboy delivered their luggage, Jennifer took a couple of minutes to hang her clothes and set out her toiletries.

It was as she put her swimsuit out on the bed that it hit her. Nicki had been looking at that suit in the shop window downstairs. She'd even glanced back at it as she'd walked away. And it had been Bryan's question about going down to the beach that had brought about the sudden mood change. *And just that morning at breakfast, Nicki had told her about Bryan wanting her to dress like a little girl.* Though the suit she'd been looking at in the lobby had been appropriate for a girl Nicki's age, it would definitely not make her look like a little girl. But Jennifer would bet a month's profits that whatever Nicki had brought with her would.

Jennifer remembered herself at that age. She remembered how painfully shy she'd been about the changes taking place in her body, how self-conscious she'd felt about her looks, how desperately eager she'd been for any word of praise. And how hard it had been when none had been forthcoming.

Collecting her wallet, she went back to the living room. Bryan was there, opening curtains to the ocean view.

"I'm going to run downstairs for a second," she said. "I'll be right back."

She hurried out the door before he could ask her where she was going. She had a hunch she could solve Nicki's problem, and she didn't want him stopping her.

The blue plaid suit was still in the window, and the clerk directed Jennifer to a whole rack of identical ones in various sizes. She had to guess at Nicki's size, but with her description and the clerk's help, she was pretty sure she found a suit that would fit. She handed over her credit card and didn't even bother to look at the slip as she signed it. She didn't care how much the suit cost. She could afford it. And even if she hadn't had more money than she knew what to do with, she'd have bought it, anyway. It was that important.

Barely ten minutes after she'd left, she was back in the living room of the suite, bag in hand and nervous as a wet hen. What if she was way off the mark? What made *her* think she knew what Nicki needed?

"Did you find what you went after?" Bryan asked, coming in from his bedroom.

"Yes. Where's Nicki?"

"Still in her room, I guess." Bryan walked over and knocked on his niece's door. "You okay in there, Nick?"

The girl's "yeah" came muffled through the door.

Aware of Bryan's curious scrutiny, Jennifer walked over to Nicki's closed door. "Are you decent, Nicki? Can I come in for a minute?" The bag was slipping from her sweaty fingers and she rolled it up further, tightening her grip.

Nicki opened her door, standing to one side. "Sure," she said. She was still wearing the shorts and T-shirt she'd worn on the plane. She shut the door behind Jennifer.

"I brought you something," Jennifer said, handing Nicki the bag before she chickened out.

Nicki grinned. "Me? What is it?" she asked, looking inside the bag.

"Oh, Ms... I mean, Jennifer," Nicki said, looking from the bag to Jennifer and back again. "How'd you know? Oh, thank you!'' She threw her arms around Jennifer in a hug. Jennifer felt like a starving woman brought to a feast.

Nicki finally pulled back. ''I can't believe you got the one I wanted the most,'' she said, pulling the suit out of the bag.

''Why don't you go try it on?'' Jennifer suggested, smiling at Nicki's eagerness.

Nicki looked up, her eyes alarmed. ''Do you think Uncle Bryan will like it?'' she whispered, as if only now realizing that her uncle was just in the next room.

''I'm sure he will,'' Jennifer said, crossing her fingers behind her back. She had about two minutes to convince Bryan Chambers that he had to like Nicki's new swimsuit. She figured that was about how long it was going to take Nicki to get into it.

He was standing just outside Nicki's bedroom door waiting for her. ''You heard?'' Jennifer asked.

He nodded, seeming not the least bit repentant for his eavesdropping. ''How *did* you know?'' he asked softly.

Jennifer and Bryan moved farther away from Nicki's door and into the middle of the living room. ''I saw her staring at it downstairs. But I wouldn't have figured it out if she hadn't said something to me at breakfast this morning.''

Bryan followed her over to the window, his hands in the pockets of his shorts. ''What was that?''

Jennifer glanced up at him, this man whose biggest strength was his love for the child in his care. ''She says you want her to keep looking like a little girl even though her body's starting to grow up. She thinks it makes her ugly.''

Bryan frowned, looking toward Nicki's door. "She said that?"

"Maybe not in those exact words, but I knew how she felt. My mom was still buying me undershirts when I was fifteen."

"So that's why she didn't want to go down to the water."

Jennifer nodded. "I think so. Please tell her you like it, Bryan, even if you don't. Your opinion means so much to her right now."

Bryan ran his fingers through Jennifer's hair, then cupped her face with his palms. "I think I could get used to having you around, Jennifer Teal," he said, and dipped his head to kiss her.

Jennifer gave herself up to the heady feeling his kisses always brought her, welcoming the thrust of his tongue against hers, wishing he could hold her like that forever.

She pulled away from him at the sound of Nicki's door opening.

"Do you like it?" The girl walked out into the living room, her arms crossed over her chest, her eyes darting everywhere but at her uncle. Her gaze finally landed on Jennifer's smiling face.

"You're going to be the death of me in that thing, you know," Bryan said. Nicki's gaze flew to him, her eyes anxious until she saw the grin on his face.

"I can keep it?" she asked him, dropping her arms.

"You can keep it."

Nicki ran to him, throwing her arms around him with the exuberance of a normal twelve-year-old. "I love you, Uncle Bryan."

"And I love you, sprite."

Jennifer swallowed a lump in her throat as she stood apart from them, knowing that the moment they shared was one forged through years of getting through the good and the bad together, as a family. A family she wanted to be a part of more than she'd ever wanted anything in her life.

THEY SPENT almost every hour at the beach that day and the two succeeding ones, taking turns playing in the waves and lying on towels on the sand. Bryan spent a lot of time with Nicki in the water, swimming out to the buoys with her, dunking her in the waves, until Nicki enlisted Jennifer's help and the two of them together did their best to force Bryan's head underwater a time or two. They were successful, sort of. Not wanting to fail Nicki and seeing failure as imminent, Jennifer finally resorted to dirty pool and grabbed Bryan intimately under the water. He was so shocked he stopped struggling long enough for Nicki to finally succeed in dunking him. Jennifer was well out of reach by the time he resurfaced.

But her body sang with anticipation when his gaze met hers across the water promising retribution. Later.

They went sailing the second afternoon and had dinner at a different restaurant in the hotel every night. Each evening they went back out to the beach after dinner to listen to the band the hotel had hired to play there. They stayed outside until Nicki was ready to turn in, and Bryan was encouraged when he noticed that each night she stayed up a little bit later.

And each night, after his niece went to bed, Bryan played with fire. He pulled Jennifer down to the couch with him, holding her in his arms, touching the body that all day, in the sleek, black one-piece suit, had driven him crazy. And when he'd nearly driven himself crazy with desire, he'd lose himself in her kisses.

All in all, Bryan figured their time at the beach was about as perfect as a vacation could be, with the exception of the constant misery his body was suffering. Holding and kissing Jennifer was not enough. He needed to make love to her. And he couldn't. Not until he told her the truth about her and Nicki.

And he couldn't do that until they were back home, where they wouldn't be forced to stay together if her reaction to his duplicity was as bad as he feared it might be. Where she'd be free to take some time away to assimilate the facts, adjust to them. He just hoped to God that when she calmed down, when she listened rationally to his explanations, she'd have a big enough heart to understand.

He was no longer worried about how Nicki would fare. Jennifer obviously adored her.

CHAPTER THIRTEEN

NICKI WAS INVITED to play volleyball during their last day at the beach, and Bryan was so delighted to see her having a good time with kids her own age that he let her stay out a bit longer than he should have. By dinnertime it appeared she'd had too much sun, and she was complaining of an upset stomach.

Jennifer helped by rubbing aloe cream on Nicki's burned skin and convincing the girl to eat most of a bowl of chicken soup. Nicki finally fell asleep around six-thirty, and knowing that sleep was the best thing for her, Jennifer and Bryan closed her door and left her alone.

Bryan called room service, ordering a bottle of wine to accompany their filets and baked potatoes. He had the waiter set the whole thing up out on their balcony, which faced the beach. He didn't want to take a chance on waking Nicki.

The hotel was having a bonfire on the beach that night, and Jennifer's face glowed from the muted light of the flames as she sat across from him at the small wrought-iron table. She was wearing a white halter dress that looked incredible against her newly acquired tan. Bryan could barely keep his eyes off her.

They ate and talked about Nicki, about places they'd traveled, about the tornado that had taken Bryan's family and the car accident that had taken

Jennifer's. They even talked about some of the people they could see below them on the beach, deciding that one couple were newlyweds and another on their second honeymoon. Bryan, trying to get a rise out of Jennifer, suggested that the second couple was really a married man on an illicit tryst with his secretary, but Jennifer point-blank refused to have any part of his potentially unhappy scenario.

And before he knew it, the food was all gone, and there wasn't a drop of wine left in the bottle. But he wasn't ready for the evening to end.

"I think I saw a bottle of wine in the minibar. Would you like another glass?" he asked Jennifer.

Her slow sensual smile just about brought him to his knees. "I've probably had enough already, but yes, one more glass sounds good. It's so lovely out here. I'm not ready to go in yet."

Bryan opened the bottle and filled their glasses. "I just looked in on Nicki, and she's still sound asleep."

"I know. I looked, too, when I went in before."

Bryan wasn't sure just when their conversation filtered away, or why he was torturing himself by touching her soft silky hand where it lay on the table, but there was no mistaking the invitation in her eyes. Or the way his body was responding to it.

"I think I've had more wine than was wise," he said, his gaze locked on hers in the darkness.

"I *know* I have. But I still want to make love with you, Bryan Chambers. I have for a very long time."

His body throbbed with her words. "It's just the wine talking," he said, trying to hold on to the thin thread of sanity he had left. "It has a tendency to make you think that way."

She smiled and shook her head. "Not me it doesn't. I've tried it a time or two, you know. I've tried to get in the mood, to let myself go, to enjoy a perfectly normal adult experience, but it never worked, no matter how much wine I drank."

"Never?" he asked, his eyes intent. "Are you telling me you haven't . . ."

"Not since I was fifteen," she whispered. Her eyes were moist as she held his gaze, but they were full of such conviction, such pure sweet wanting, that Bryan knew he was a drowning man. And he didn't care. Satisfying the desire in her eyes was worth dying for.

He pulled her up and into the suite, turning off the living-room light as he led her into her bedroom, which was on the opposite side of the suite from his and Nicki's.

Her bare back was a golden lure of femininity as she entered her room in front of him. She took a long look at the huge bed in the center of the room, then looked back at him. He thought he saw fear in her eyes, but it was quickly replaced by the fire that had been glowing from within her all evening.

"Are you sure?" he asked, trailing his fingers down her neck.

"Absolutely sure."

He pulled her against him, letting her feel how ready his body was for her before they'd even begun. "I've never wanted a woman like I want you."

"I think I knew that," she whispered, flicking her tongue along his neck. "I've never wanted a man before, period."

Bryan knew that what she was telling him was important, that he needed to understand certain things about her, but all he could think about right then was making the night ahead everything she'd ever dreamed of. He didn't just want her to want him now, he wanted her to want him afterward, too. Desperately.

And maybe, if he could show her how much he cared for her, she'd be forgiving when he told her what he'd done, why they'd met....

He pulled the pins from her hair one by one, watching as the long auburn curls fell down past her shoulders and over his arm.

"It's a crime to keep this all tucked away," he said, running his hands through the silky strands, imagining it over him, around him, beneath him.

"Long tangly hair doesn't fit my image."

He buried his face against her neck. "It fits the image I have of you perfectly."

"Oh? And how do you see me?" she asked, leaning back to grin at him as she tugged gently at the rubber band on his ponytail.

But Bryan saw the flicker of apprehension in her eyes in spite of the grin. She really needed to know and was afraid of knowing at the same time. Incredible.

He smoothed the hair back from her face, cradling her head between his hands, caressing her cheeks with his thumbs. "I see you as a siren and an innocent, as a strong capable woman and yet one I want to take care of."

Her gaze held his as she reached up to him, running her fingers through the shorter hair on the sides and top of his head, to the longer strands in the back that hung freely past his shoulders. "You are the man of my dreams, Bryan Chambers," she whispered. "I don't know what I've ever done to deserve you, but I can't not love you. I tried, but I just can't."

His heart plummeted, and then sped up, reminding him of his first roller-coaster ride. Adrenaline surged through him. "Then stop trying," he said, and kissed her. *She loves me,* he thought. It was all that mattered in those moments as his lips laid claim to hers. *She loves me.*

Jennifer had no idea where this night might lead. She was afraid to think of the future, to consider the fact that Bryan might want to marry her, that he might even want to have other children someday. She didn't know if she'd be strong enough to turn him down; or was the real strength in accepting him? She didn't have the answers anymore, but she knew, clear to her soul, that the present was right where it should be. She was where she belonged—in Bryan's arms.

He looked like a heathen, a pirate, as he bent over her, his hair creating shadows around him in the dim light of her bedroom. His black cotton pants and T-shirt added to the illusion, and Jennifer shivered with the excitement this man could raise in her.

His lips devoured hers, his kisses different than they'd ever been before, harder, more determined, and the more he asked of her, the more she gave him, the more she took. She couldn't seem to keep her hands off him, filled with a need to touch every part of him. His warm broad shoulders, his strong back, his lean, muscled buttocks.

"Lord, woman, what you do to me," he groaned, pressing her against him.

"The miracle is what you do to me," Jennifer said, giving him more than her body. She was laying her soul on the line for this man, and she hadn't a single regret. "I know all about sex. I know what goes where, how it all works. But never, ever, have I dreamed I could ever feel like this.''

Bryan led her to the bed, unhooking the neck of her halter dress, turning her to face him, watching every inch of her as it slid away. "So what's the 'this' you're feeling, Jen?'' he asked, touching the tip of one bared breast with his finger, gently, reverently.

She gasped. "Like I'm on fire. Like I'm going to die right here and now if you don't stop that and make love to me,'' she said, pulling his hand away from her breast. She was getting the most curious sensation in the pit of her stomach, as if she was going to collapse in a heap before they'd even begun.

Bryan's hand returned to her breast and kneaded it tenderly. "But I am making love to you, Jen, body and soul.''

She sank onto the bed, naked except for her white silk bikini panties, feeling not one moment of embarrassment as she lay before him. He was her man, her love. It was right that he see her.

She didn't think she could get any more turned on for him until he started to strip off his clothes. There was no playacting, no pretense, just a steady removing of material, a gradual revealing of such male perfection that her breath was snatched away. And when he loosened the drawstring at his waist and slid his cotton pants down over his hips, she was just plain shocked.

"You're not wearing any underwear!'' she said, thinking how prudish she must sound.

"It's too constricting,'' he told her, completely comfortable with his nudity as he lay down beside her.

Jennifer was still too rattled from the first unexpected sight of his engorged manhood to belabor the point.

Bryan Chambers was a magnificent lover. His hands were everywhere, caressing her, giving her pleasure. She tensed when he found her scar, the only thing she had left of the baby she'd given birth to so long ago, but even that he touched reverently—as if it was special simply because it was a part of her.

Jennifer had had no idea she had so many erogenous zones, but he showed her every one of them and introduced her to a few of his own, as well. She was a willing, eager, if impatient pupil, but Bryan ignored her impatience, imploring her to trust him, to hold on.

"Let me show you how good this can be," he said when she was once again urging him to complete their union.

"If it gets any better than this, I'm not going to live through it," she murmured, smiling up at him. His face was so precious to her. She'd never loved anyone as she loved this man.

"Yes, you will. You're going to live long enough to do it again and again and again..." His words trailed off as he pushed himself slowly into her.

"Oh, my God," Jennifer groaned as she stretched to accommodate him, feeling finally some measure of completeness.

"Come with me, Jen. Let me take you on the wildest ride of your life."

"Isn't that where we are already?" she gasped as he moved within her.

"We haven't even left the ground yet, lady."

He reached down between them, touching Jennifer intimately and rotating his hips at the same time.

And as he continued to love her, tension built within Jennifer, her body holding him tighter and tighter as she fought to control the sensation.

"Come with me, babe. Come with me," he said.

Jennifer thought she'd break into a million pieces. She could hardly breathe. "I can't!" she cried, wishing he would never stop what he was doing to her, yet knowing she couldn't take much more.

"Yes, you can," he said, kissing her, his tongue entering her in rhythm with his lower body. "Let go, Jen. I'll catch you," he said. His voice sounded as strained as she felt.

She did as he bid, giving herself up to him completely, letting go of the tenuous thread of her control. And as she exploded around him, as she accepted his climax within her, her soul cried out in triumph.

She lay beside him afterward, unable to muster enough strength to speak, let alone get up. She couldn't even work up the effort to wonder what he was thinking about as he lay silently holding her. She'd finally found the peace she'd been searching for. He hadn't "taken" her or "done it" to her. He'd made love with her. And by doing so, he'd given her back a measure of the dignity she'd lost so many years before. Rather than feeling worthless, she felt beautiful.

She thought he might have fallen asleep, until his hand shifted around her, cupping her breast, his finger slowly, almost aimlessly, tantalizing her nipple. She lay still, wondering if he was indeed asleep, if he was even aware of what he was doing. And then he shifted again, his other hand cupping her other breast, his penis nudging her.

Her stomach started fluttering and she felt herself grow moist. "Again?" she asked, giggling in spite of the tension slowly building within her.

"Again and again and again . . ." His voice sent excited chills down her body as he leaned over and took her nipple into his mouth.

BRYAN WAS at his drafting table by noon the next day. He'd barely made it back to his own room that morning in the hotel before the phone had rung. Calvin had the flu and wasn't going to be able to keep his appointment with Wonderly.

They'd planned to sleep in and fly back leisurely that morning, but Bryan had had to wake Jennifer and Nicki and hurry them out of the hotel a few hours earlier than planned. Or at least he'd hurried them after he'd woken Jennifer properly. Lovemaking with her was as good the morning after as it had been the night before.

The Wonderly president and his executives were flying in to sign the papers that would seal a big contract with Innovative Advertising based on the preliminary campaign Bryan had done for the company a few months before. Bryan only had another hour to go over the long-term campaign Calvin had mapped out for him before the group arrived.

He tried to concentrate on the Wonderly account, but moments from the night before and the morning after, with their passion and their promise, continued to play themselves out in his mind. He was impatient to get on with it, to know that things were settled once and for all, to finally introduce Nicki to her mother.

He'd invited Jennifer over for dinner that night and he was going to tell her who Nicki was before he took her home that evening. After the past several days with Nicki, there was no longer any doubt that Jennifer was good with children, or at least with Nicki. Even Jennifer had to be settled on that score. There was no longer any need for secrets.

He was going to ask Jennifer to marry him.

The phone rang on his desk, bringing him back to the business at hand. "It's Nicki, Bryan," Jacci called through the door connecting their offices.

He snatched up the phone. "You feeling okay?" he asked. Nicki had been better that morning, but she hadn't eaten much and her skin had still been extremely sensitive. Jennifer had found a loose-fitting sundress for her to wear down in the gift shop.

Nicki giggled. He still wasn't used to hearing that sound. "Yes, Uncle Bryan, I'm fine. Jennifer's right, you know. You never do say hello."

"Hello doesn't mean anything." Bryan smiled. Jennifer had brought Nicki back to him. He was eager to give them to each other.

"It means hello, but I don't care if you don't say it. I love you just the way you are."

"I love you, too, Nick. The days at the beach were fun, weren't they?"

"Yeah." The way she said it left a huge "but" hanging there.

"So what's up? You sound like you got something on your mind."

"I just need to talk to you, that's all."

Bryan glanced at his watch. Wonderly was due in about twenty minutes. "Shoot."

"I don't know how to say it."

Bryan's gut clenched. Was there trouble in paradise already? "Just like you always have, Nick. Just say it right out."

"Okay. You can quit looking for my other mother. I don't want to find her anymore."

Bryan froze. "What do you mean you don't want to find her? That's all you've talked about for ages. Why don't you want to find her?"

"'Cause I don't need her." His niece's soft words stopped him before he hollered at her. She couldn't mean this. Not now.

"How's that, Nick?"

"I just don't," she said. "Besides, the more I thought about it, the more I didn't ever want to meet her. I mean, she gave me away, you know?"

He felt the blood drain from his face. "Maybe she had a good reason." *Like being sixteen and alone, with parents who were never there for her.*

"I can't think of a good enough one. And anyway, she might not even want to meet me, and if she doesn't, I don't want to know."

"But what if she does, honey? What if she's been missing you all these years and would love to meet you?"

"It's okay, Uncle Bryan. I know what you're trying to do, letting me know it's okay to find her even though you don't want me to, but I'm not just saying this to make you happy. I've really changed my mind. You can call those people and tell them to stop looking. By the way, can I cook dinner again tonight? I wanna make spaghetti. That's easy."

Bryan's heart felt like lead. Food was the last thing he cared about. "Sure. That'd be great, Nick. We'll see you around five-thirty, okay?"

"'Kay."

"I love you, sprite."

"I love you, too, Uncle Bryan. I gotta go now. Lucy's scratching to go out."

Bryan slammed the phone down. So much for paradise. Nicki didn't want to meet her mother. But after what he and Jennifer had shared at the beach, he still had to tell her the truth. His love for her demanded it. But now he was going to have to hurt her more in the telling. He was going to have to tell her that, for some reason, Nicki had changed her mind, that she no longer wanted to meet her birth mother. It might even spell the end to their relationship. Because his first priority was still Nicki. And if she refused to accept Jennifer, then he'd have to honor that decision.

Bryan was almost relieved when the Wonderly president called to say they were going to be a couple of hours later than planned. Their flight had been delayed. Damn. There was no way he was going to be out of here in time to make it home for dinner. He called Jennifer to cancel.

"I haven't told Nicki yet—she's planning to make spaghetti," he said, more tired than he could ever remember being. Though he knew it had very little to do with the near-sleepless night he'd spent.

"Then just tell her to go on ahead with her plans, and we'll have dinner just the two of us. If you're really nice, maybe we'll even save you some," she said, her tone making her words seductive enough to heat his blood.

"You'd better save me some, woman," he growled, foolishly thankful for the reprieve. One more night of loving her before everything blew up in his face.

"You can have it all, Bryan," she returned softly. "You know that."

"I'll call Nicki," he said before ringing off. It couldn't hurt to have Nicki spend some time alone with Jennifer in the real world. If his niece grew fond enough of Jennifer she wouldn't be able to turn her away.

"YOU GOT A MINUTE?" Jennifer pushed open the door to Dennis's office.

He set aside the papers in front of him. "Sure, what's up? Did you have a good time in Florida?"

"The best." Jennifer blushed.

Dennis grinned. "I see."

She sat down on the couch. "No, you don't see. I've got a problem."

"What?" He got up from his desk, coming around to the armchair across from her.

"I just had the best three days of my life, and I'm feeling so guilty I can barely look at myself in the mirror."

Dennis frowned. "Jennifer, if anyone deserves to be happy, it's you."

"It's not that so much. It's Nicki."

"What about her?"

"I think Bryan might ask me to marry him. That would make Nicki mine, too."

"You can handle it, Jen. You'll be a great mother to her."

She smiled sadly. "You know what? I finally believe that I might not be a half-bad mother, but no matter what I tell myself, I can't help feeling like scum for wanting to love Nicki when I abandoned my own child. I made this vow, you know, that night in the hospital when I gave my baby away. And the thing is, if I believe it doesn't mean anything and I don't have to uphold my part of the bargain, then I also have to believe nobody's been watching out for my baby all these years."

She sighed. "In my head I know I was just a child when I made that promise, that it's crazy to live my life based on such a ridiculous thing, but I just can't get beyond the fact that I promised my baby I'd never replace her, as long as she grew up happy." She paused. "As long as she didn't have to grow up with parents like mine."

"That's not very likely, Jen. There aren't many parents as selfish as yours, thank God."

Jennifer frowned. "They weren't selfish. They just didn't know anything about caring for a child."

Dennis swore, shocking Jennifer with the words coming out of his mouth. "No one's born with the knowledge, Jen. It's something you work at, learn as you go. Your parents were too wrapped up in themselves to even try. Maybe it's because you came so late in their lives, or maybe they were just too set in their ways, I don't know, but for whatever reason, they never made any concessions to having a child in their house."

Tears sprang to Jennifer's eyes. "It wasn't like that." *Was it?*

"It was exactly like that. They always came first. Did they ever once take part in anything you did? Girl Scouts, dance recitals, birthday parties, anything where they had to do something just for you? Were you ever even allowed to laugh and make noise when they were home?"

"They were busy. They had the business to run. And when they were home, they were tired. They couldn't help being older than most parents." Her protests sounded weak even to her own ears.

Dennis shook his head in dismay. "When are you going to open your eyes, Jen? They failed you over and over again, and you always blamed yourself. And what about when you really needed them, when you gave birth? Hell, you were doing what they wanted— you were giving away the baby you already loved—and they still wouldn't take the time to help you through. After they signed the papers for you to have the C-section, they didn't even stick around until the baby was born. They went straight back to work. They never came to see you. They sent *me* to pick you up and take you home. It wasn't you who was lacking, honey, it was *them*."

"They left? They didn't stay when I went into surgery?" Jennifer was aghast.

"I thought you knew that," Dennis said, coloring.

"They left before I had the baby?"

"The doctor told them they wouldn't be allowed to see you for a while, and their manager had just walked out on them at the dealership," Dennis said, as if by trying to excuse them he could take away the pain he'd unwittingly caused her. "They left the dealership's phone number at the hospital with orders to call if they were needed."

Her face streaming with tears, Jennifer finally heard the things Dennis had been trying to tell her for years. Her parents had let *her* down, not the other way around.

Dennis crossed to the couch and put his arm around her. "You see?" he said. "It wasn't your fault you'd always been in their way. It was theirs."

"You really think so?" she asked.

"I know so, Jen. I was there, too, remember? I'd been working at Teal for over a year before you ever took up with Billy the Bastard. You were a victim back then, honey. It's time you saw it all like it really happened and forgave yourself for something you couldn't help. You were just a kid looking for love, trying to be happy in the only way you knew how."

Jennifer took the tissue he handed her. "But what about my baby?" she asked, tears still streaming down her face. "I can't love another woman's child or even have another child of my own until I know that my firstborn has all the love she needs."

"She's probably happy as a clam."

"I hope so. I've been counting on it every day for twelve years. But I still don't feel free to love another child until I know for certain. It's crazy, isn't it?"

Dennis squeezed her shoulder. "So what're you going to do?"

"I don't know." She couldn't look at him.

"I think you do, Jen. It's time to quit running."

She turned to face him, sniffling and smiling at the same time. "I'm going to look for her, aren't I?" she asked. "I'm finally going to look for my daughter."

Dennis smiled, standing up and pulling Jennifer with him. "Yes, my friend, you're finally going to do what you've been aching to do since the minute you left the hospital without her."

Jennifer gazed warmly at Dennis. "You've always known, haven't you?"

He nodded.

"The reason I'm not married yet wasn't because I didn't have time. It was because I couldn't go on, I couldn't break that promise, until I was sure she had a happy life," she said, seeing things so clearly now.

"Probably."

Jennifer wiped her tears away and walked toward the door. "I've got some calls to make." She stopped with her hand on the doorknob and looked back. "Thanks, friend."

"Don't thank me, Jen. You figured it out all by yourself."

"I don't just mean now. I mean for always."

"Go make your phone calls," Dennis said, stepping back behind his desk. She'd embarrassed him, but she'd pleased him, too. She could tell by the color in his cheeks. It gave him away every time. But she kept the knowledge to herself as she left to go call her lawyer. *Baby Doe, here I come.*

CHAPTER FOURTEEN

"IS THERE ANYTHING I can do to help?" Jennifer asked as Nicki led her into the kitchen later that afternoon with Lucy underfoot. Bryan's house smelled like an Italian restaurant.

"Nope. We have to eat in here 'cause Uncle Bryan's model stuff is all over the dining-room table."

Jennifer grabbed the plates and silverware Nicki had put out on the counter and placed them at the table. "What kind of models?" she asked, bending down to scratch Lucy behind the ears.

"Toy ones. Radio-controlled airplanes mostly." Nicki pulled a pan of bread sticks out of the oven. "He says it helps him think and he has to do that a lot for his work. Sometimes they get really big. You should see the thing he made when he first started working for you." Her smile was infectious.

"Mammoth, huh?" Jennifer asked with a grin, glad to know she'd been important to him even then.

Nicki nodded. "I'll say. It's in his bedroom and it takes up half the room."

"He keeps it in his bedroom?"

"Yeah, that's when I knew you were different. Usually he flies them a little bit and then gives them away to the children's hospital or to families who don't have enough money at Christmastime or something. But he kept this one. And Uncle Bryan never keeps anything," she said, sounding conspiratorial. "Until he got me he never even owned any furniture."

Nicki tossed the spaghetti noodles with a little butter, put them in a casserole dish and ladled sauce over them, then carried the dish to the table.

"You do that very well," Jennifer said, impressed.

"Thanks. My mom loved pasta. We used to have it almost every night." She took the salad she'd prepared earlier out of the refrigerator. Jennifer looked at the bowl as Nicki set it on the table. It was nothing but lettuce. She hid a smile, glad to see that Nicki still did some things like a kid.

"You must miss your mom a lot," she said as Nicki sat down across from her.

"Yeah, I do. My dad, and my grandma and grandpa, too. But Uncle Bryan's great. I used to wish sometimes I could live with him, you know. He'd come and visit us, and I'd have the best time ever and then miss him like crazy when he left."

"I can understand that. He's not someone who goes unnoticed, is he?"

"Nope. He's the best. But sometimes..." Nicki hesitated, looking down as she wound spaghetti around her fork.

"Sometimes what?" Jennifer asked, smiling, encouraging Nicki to confide in her.

"Well, sometimes it's hard, you know, just living with an uncle. I mean he's a *man*."

Jennifer thought of the little-girl swimsuit Nicki had been embarrassed to wear. "Men don't always catch on to things, honey, but your uncle has a great set of ears. You just need to talk to him."

Nicki looked up at Jennifer, her eyes filled with conviction. "There are some things a girl just can't talk to a man about."

"I think your uncle's pretty open-minded." Jennifer was surprised how important it was to her to defend Bryan.

"It's just that . . ." Nicki hesitated again.

"What?"

She set down her fork. "I'm twelve years old now. My mom started her, you know, monthly stuff, when she was twelve."

Ah. Jennifer felt rather obtuse when she finally realized what Nicki had been trying to tell her. And thrilled that the girl felt comfortable enough to talk to her about it. She just wished she had a single clue about what to say. Her own mother had never talked about such things. Jennifer had learned it all from her friends' somewhat exaggerated accounts, and what they hadn't told her, she'd found out for herself.

"I guess it would be kind of hard to bring up with your uncle," she conceded.

"I'll say." Nicki took a big bite of salad—without dressing.

Jennifer did the same, taking comfort in the fact that she and Bryan's niece had something in common besides Bryan.

"I mean, I can't ask him to pick up stuff for it on his way home from work."

Jennifer smiled as she imagined just that. "Have you been feeling any different lately?" she asked, still not sure how to proceed. Should she offer to buy Nicki her supplies? Should she tell her how to use them?

"Nah. I had a stomachache one day, and I was a little scared . . . but it went away. And it's not like just because my mom had it when she was twelve that *I* will."

"You're right to wonder, though. A lot of times girls do take after their mothers."

"Not me. I guess Uncle Bryan didn't tell you. I was adopted."

Jennifer dropped her fork. *Adopted? This child was adopted?*

"You were?" she asked, picking up her fork, trying to rebalance herself.

"Yep."

Jennifer's mind reeled with questions. There were so many things she wanted to know. "Did you like it? Being adopted, I mean?"

"Yep. It was great. I never had to wonder if my parents really wanted me, you know? They picked me out specially. I have this friend back in Shallowbrook, Sally Sanderson. She was a mistake, and her parents had to get married because of her and everything, and all they did was fight all the time until her dad finally just walked out. And Sally always thought it was her fault and if only she'd never been born her mom would be more happy. *My* mom always used to say that my birthday was the best day of the year because if I'd never been born she'd never have been so happy. We used to have a big party every year, and Mom and Dad would make a toast to the woman who gave me to them, thanking her for our happy family..." Nicki's voice wobbled and she took another bite of spaghetti.

"It's okay to cry, honey. It's okay to miss them," Jennifer said, rubbing Nicki's arm, praying her own daughter had found such a loving family.

Nicki sniffled and nodded. "I try not to because it gets Uncle Bryan mad at me."

"Oh, no, Nicki! Not mad. He doesn't want you to keep everything bottled up inside. Men are just funny about tears. Especially if they're crying inside themselves."

Nicki looked up. "You think Uncle Bryan cries?"

"I'm sure of it, Nicki. He lost his family, too, and he hurts every bit as much as you do."

"But he seems so strong all the time, just goes on making jokes and stuff."

"What else would you have him do? Curl up and die? Your mom and dad and grandparents wouldn't want that, would they?"

"No. I guess not."

"And besides, he's got *you* to think of. He wants to make your life happy."

"Did he say that?" Nicki's fork hung suspended in midair.

"He talks about you all the time, Nicki. You're his life now. He'd do anything for you, don't you know that?"

Nicki shrugged. "I guess. I just don't want to bug him."

"You make him happy, Nicki. Never doubt that."

"I think *you* do, too," Nicki said, taking her empty plate to the sink. "Hey. You wanna see some pictures of my mom and stuff? The albums are in a cupboard in Uncle Bryan's office."

"Sure. Let's just do these dishes first so your uncle doesn't come home to a mess."

"Now you sound just like my mom," the girl grumbled, but she was grinning as she cleared the rest of the table.

Half an hour later they sat on the couch with the photo album open between them. Jennifer was anxious to see Bryan's family, the people who meant so much to him, the people she'd never get to meet. There were pictures of him, too, as a baby, a toddler, a schoolboy, a young man. He looked a lot like his dad.

"Grandpa was a doctor," Nicki said, pointing to a picture of Bryan and his father on the steps of a hospital. "That was taken when they named the new wing at the hospital after him."

Bryan had never told her his father had been such an important man. But then, he wouldn't have. He'd only told her what he'd found significant, the good man, the good father, he'd been.

"Uncle Bryan dated every girl in school," Nicki confided as they looked at yet another picture of Bryan, in blue jeans and tennis shoes, standing next to a beautiful girl all decked out in prom finery.

"It looks that way," Jennifer laughed, telling herself her pang of jealousy was absurd.

"Don't worry. The school was really small. Besides, Grandma said it was just because he liked to date, but he didn't want any of the girls getting any ideas about tying him down, so he never took any of them out more than once or twice. It used to drive her crazy. I wish she could've met you," Nicki said, smiling shyly at Jennifer.

Jennifer put her arm around the girl's shoulders and gave her a squeeze. "I wish I could meet her, too, Nicki, but at least I got to meet you."

"Yeah. Look, here's a picture of the Christmas we got Lucy for Mom and Dad."

"You and your grandparents?"

"Nope." Nicki shook her head, her long auburn hair tickling Jennifer's arm. "Me and Uncle Bryan. He flew me to Atlanta one Saturday when Mom thought he was taking me to the movies in town, and we picked Lucy out together. He had to keep her, though, for a whole week before he came for Christmas. She chewed a hole in the wall of his apartment and he had to pay to have it fixed." Nicki giggled.

"I'll bet he wasn't too pleased with Lucy then."

. "I don't think he minded too much. Uncle Bryan doesn't care about *things* that much. At least he laughed when he told Mom and Dad about it. 'Course, Lucy was theirs then."

Nicki turned the page and was silent for the first time since Jennifer had walked in the door that evening. It was obviously Lori's wedding picture. She'd been a beautiful bride with long hair, dark like Bryan's, and big brown eyes. Her dress looked like something out of a designer shop with its layers of silk and lace and beads. She was also obviously very much in love with her husband, and he with her.

A single tear fell onto the page.

"Oh, sweetie," Jennifer said, her throat thick as she hugged the girl.

"It's my m-m-mom," Nicki said, and started to sob. "I m-m-miss her so much."

"I know, honey, I know," Jennifer said, rocking the child back and forth.

She didn't even try to offer any platitudes to soothe Nicki. There were none.

Nicki's sobs tore at Jennifer's heart. She wished there was something she could do, some way to make it better. She felt so helpless sitting there, allowing the girl to hurt so badly. And all the while Nicki cried, Lucy paced worriedly around the couch.

"Sorry," Nicki finally said, wiping her face with the back of her hands.

"Don't apologize, honey. Anytime you need a shoulder, I'm here."

Nicki set the photo album back on their laps. "It's just that she was always so happy, you know, so bouncy and stuff. I never thought of her not being here." She bent over to pull Lucy up on the couch beside her.

"Of course you didn't, sweetie. No one did. But I meant what I said. Anytime you want a woman to talk to, you can come to me, okay?"

"But you're so busy, being so important with your work and all."

"My business is just that, Nicki, business. It isn't life." And for the first time since she'd taken over her parents' business, Jennifer knew that to be true.

"Okay," Nicki said.

She turned the page and giggled again. "Look, here's a picture of me as a baby. It was taken in the hospital right after I was born. They gave it to my mom when she came to get me . . ."

Nicki continued to talk, but Jennifer couldn't hear her for the roaring in her ears. She felt like she was going to be sick.

She stared at the picture on her lap in total disbelief. How had it gotten there? That wasn't Lori's picture. It was hers. Only hers. She'd cherished that picture for twelve years, carried it with her everywhere she went, every hour of every day.

"Are you okay, Jennifer?" Nicki asked. "You don't look so good."

Jennifer didn't know if it was the concern in the girl's voice or the way Nicki jumped up off the couch that made her realize she wasn't alone. But she needed to be alone. Immediately. She couldn't believe that picture in that album. She had to leave. To breathe. To think.

"I'm sorry, Nicki. I—I'm not feeling well. I think maybe I better go home."

"But you don't have to leave! You can lie down on Uncle Bryan's bed."

Uncle Bryan's bed. Bryan knows. He's probably always known.

"Excuse me..." Jennifer ran for the bathroom and promptly lost her dinner. Her stomach heaved with such spasms she thought she might die, she hoped she might, but when it was finally over, she was left with nothing but numbness. Blessed mind-healing numbness.

When Jennifer finally emerged from the bathroom, Nicki was pacing worriedly outside the door, Lucy right beside her. "You okay? It was the spaghetti. I just know I did something to it."

Jennifer couldn't look at the child. She wasn't prepared. She wasn't ready. God help her, she wasn't strong enough to handle it. But neither was she going to allow the girl to blame herself for something completely out of her control. She'd done enough of that herself.

"It wasn't the dinner, honey, or you'd be sick, too. I wasn't feeling very well this afternoon, but I thought it had passed. I just need a good night's sleep and I'll be fine in the morning." Jennifer grabbed her things and headed for the door.

"Do you really have to go? I know Uncle Bryan would want you to stay," Nicki said, still sounding worried.

Bryan. He had so much to answer for. Had it all been an act, then? And for what? What had driven him to use her like this? To be so cruel. And she'd hoped he *loved* her. Just as she'd hoped Billy had, and Tommy. Oh, God, she couldn't go through it all again.

"I'll call him when I get home, honey. Promise me you'll lock up after me?" She had no idea where she got the composure to answer the child.

"I promise." Nicki was standing just inside the door. "Hope you feel better."

"I will," Jennifer said, all but running to her car.

Two blocks from Bryan's house she stopped to put down the top on her convertible. She needed more air.

The picture was in someone else's photo album. Nicki's photo album. Her picture. Of her baby.

She pulled onto the expressway, pressing the accelerator to the floor. The warm night air hit her skin, numbing her as she drove, going somewhere, anywhere, she didn't care. She didn't care about anything. She couldn't care. She didn't dare.

Until she found herself in the parking lot of Innovative Advertising. Then, suddenly, when she knew she'd be facing Bryan in a few short moments, she cared. Far too much. The pain rose to choke her again as she thought of his duplicity. But only for a second. Then the familiar numbness was back, sealed into place.

The outer door was unlocked and Jennifer pulled it open, welcoming the cool air as she stepped into the deserted lobby. She heard Bryan talking and headed toward the sound of his voice, the only door with a light shining beyond it. She walked into the room, his office, judging by the sketchbooks lying around. He was on the phone. He turned when he heard her, his face lighting up when he saw who was there.

His face lit up for *her*. As if she really mattered to him. She saw his eyes skim over her body, saw his look change from welcoming, to slumberous, to the heated sensuality that had melted her blood. A sudden mind-destroying pain ripped through her. He'd used her.

"She's mine," she said, grasping for the numbness that was going to get her through the next hours, the next years.

Bryan spoke hastily into the phone.

"Nicki's mine." She hardly dared say the words. She approached Bryan's drafting table. "Tell me."

He hung up the phone, his eyes worried as he tried to take her in his arms. But it was the guilt she saw flash across his face that was her undoing. Standing right there, in the middle of his office, she fell apart.

Tears streamed down her face as she lashed out at him, hitting him on the shoulders, the chest. "She's mine, isn't she?" she cried. "Isn't she?" She didn't even recognize the shrill voice that screamed at him.

Bryan grabbed her arms, but she kept hitting him. "Yes."

He spoke softly, yet the word slammed into her with the force of a blast. Burning up with pain, she slapped him and then turned to run back out the way she'd come.

Bryan grabbed her before she made it to the door. He tried to hold her, to soothe her.

"Don't touch me." Her voice was cold, foreign.

He dropped his hands immediately.

It was that more than anything else that finally reached Jennifer, the way he did as she said without question, as if he respected her right to be left alone. She sank onto the only chair in his office, put her head in her hands and sobbed. It just didn't make sense. The world had lost its mind. Nothing went together.

Nicki was hers. That adorable, precious, beautiful girl was hers. Her *daughter*.

And Bryan had betrayed her. He'd used her. In the basest way possible.

He stood in the middle of the room, silently. She sensed him there, but she couldn't reach him. He was outside her personal storm. He'd caused it.

"She has my hair," Jennifer finally said. She looked out the window behind his drafting table.

"And your eyes." His voice was thick, hoarse.

Jennifer's gaze flew to him, her heart aching when she saw the raw emotion he wasn't bothering to hide. But he'd betrayed her.

"Why?" she finally whispered.

"She wanted to find you, *had* to find you. She was losing her grip and no one could reach her. I had her to doctors, to counselors—nothing helped. I was afraid of suicide. She wasn't interested in anything— except finding you."

Jennifer swallowed as a fresh flood of tears trickled down her face. Her poor baby. She'd suffered so much. And she was so young.

"So you found me."

"It wasn't easy, but yes, after six weeks of professional searching, I found you."

Six weeks of professional searching. He'd been mighty determined. But then, so would she have been in his position.

"That night at the gallery..."

He nodded. "I knew."

"And the campaign..."

"My 'in' with you."

At least he wasn't trying to worm his way out of any of it. Jennifer remembered how easily she'd fallen in with his plan, how easily she'd fallen, period. She felt sick again.

"Why?" she asked.

She saw by the look on his face that he knew exactly what she was asking.

"A rejection would very probably have been the last straw for her. I saw how you avoided kids. Listened when you told me you weren't any good with them. I didn't have a choice but to wait until something changed."

"You could've told me."

"What, and have you go to her? Have you explain who you were, let her know it was nothing against her, it was just you, but that you didn't want her? Hell, as conscientious as you are, I could see you setting up some bank account for her, providing generously for her, while withholding the one thing she really wanted—you. And all because you didn't believe in yourself. You'd have thought you were doing her a favor. But she wouldn't have seen it that way at all."

Jennifer felt the blood drain from her face as she realized the truth of his words. He knew her well. And a month or two ago, she really might have done what he'd just said. Because she hadn't believed in herself, not outside Teal Automotive. Until their trip to the beach, she probably *would* have thought she didn't have anything to offer Nicki but her money.

He took a step toward her, but stopped when she drew farther back in the chair.

"Think about it, Jen. If I'd told you from the beginning who I was, what I wanted, would you have agreed to meet Nicki and get to know her?"

His hands clenched inside his pockets. She stared at the bulge of his knuckles, focusing on them, as if seeing only them could make the rest go away.

"I don't know," she finally whispered. But she had a feeling she did know. As much as she'd have wanted to be there for Nicki, she wouldn't have believed herself capable of helping any child, let alone an emotionally disturbed one. But she'd have insisted on providing for Nicki, just as he'd predicted.

"I wasn't sure, either, and I couldn't take that chance. You didn't know her then, Jen. She did nothing but sleep and cry and have nightmares. She couldn't have handled another blow. I could've lost her. She was putting everything on the hope of finding her birth mother."

And Jennifer had believed herself to be anything but mother material.

"I guess I should thank you for hanging in there long enough to show me that I could be for her what she needed me to be."

"It's what you needed, too."

Jennifer conceded the point with a bowed head.

Bryan knelt in front of her, close, but not touching her. "I intended to tell you, Jen, tonight when I picked you up for dinner. I want to marry you. I want for the three of us to be a family."

Jennifer couldn't bear to hear the words. They were a mockery of all she'd been foolishly hoping for such a short time before. "That would be convenient, wouldn't it?" she asked.

Bryan looked taken aback. "What do you mean?"

"If you really loved me, *me,* not Nicki's mother, how could you make love to me without truth between us? The rest I can understand, but not that."

"I didn't intend for that to happen."

Rather than soothing her, his words only deepened her wound. *She'd* intended so much for *that* to happen that she'd cold-bloodedly walked into a store and purchased the birth control that would allow it to happen. He hadn't intended it at all.

"What was it—the wine?" she asked. "No, don't answer that. It's bad enough that our relationship had so little significance that you were willing to risk it like this. You know me well, Bryan, very well. Did you honestly think I wouldn't care about having sex when there were still lies between us?"

"No."

"But you made love to me, anyway, making a mockery of what we were sharing." She stood up, brushing by him. "Damn you!" She turned, her look strong enough to kill. "I gave you everything..." She was horrified when she started to cry again. The man didn't deserve her tears.

He had no words to defend himself. He stood before her, proud, tall—and guilty as hell.

"It's all so clear to me, you know," she said, her voice soft now, sad. *He can't help what he is.*

"Then maybe you'll explain it to me, because I can't think of a single way to help you understand that what I feel for you is completely separate from the fact that you're Nicki's mother."

He almost got her with that. Almost, but not quite. Even then, even when everything was resting on it, he hadn't told her what, exactly, he *did* feel. He still hadn't told her he loved her.

"You're a rebel, Bryan, a wanderer. You need your freedom like the rest of us need air to breathe. When you got Nicki you lost that, didn't you? You were cramped beyond your imagination by having the sole responsibility for an emotionally distressed child. So you meet me, you find me attractive and, bingo, you have your solution. Marry me, and you've got an instant mother for Nicki, someone who'd obviously feel bound to take on that responsibility since she's partly mine, and in the process relieve you of some of the responsibility that's choking you."

"It wasn't like that."

"Then how was it?" She wished she could believe it was anything else.

"I don't know," he said.

Bryan racked his brain for something, anything, that would prove the lie to her words, but he couldn't find it. He was ashamed to wonder if maybe there was an iota of truth in Jennifer's words. Maybe the reason he'd never felt claustrophobic with their relationship was because, subconsciously, he had seen it as a means to an end all along. He didn't believe he was capable of such a course of action, but she'd hit a raw spot. His track record gave too much truth to her words.

"Answer me this," Jennifer said. "If you didn't have Nicki, would you still be asking me to marry you?"

He could tell her yes. He might even be able to convince her. But could he live with her, could he live with *himself*, if he wasn't sure? His life had changed so much in the past year he wasn't sure of anything anymore.

"I don't know," he answered honestly. She deserved the truth. She always had.

She didn't say a word.

Weary, and feeling more alone than he'd ever felt in his life, he cleared up his office, wondering as he did if he'd ever see her there again, or if this was it, the one and only time she'd be there, standing silently, hating him. He didn't know how it had gotten so out of hand. He only knew that he felt it all slipping away.

CHAPTER FIFTEEN

"SO NOW WHAT?" Bryan looked at Jennifer in the darkness of the parking lot. She'd been silent the entire time he'd closed up his office and they'd walked down to their cars.

"I want to meet my daughter."

Bryan nodded. "I'll tell her tonight. Why don't you come by first thing in the morning?"

"I'm coming tonight."

He watched her open the door of the Mustang. Not only was it unlocked, she'd even left the top down. Damn! He'd never wanted to hurt her.

And he might not be done yet. "I'm not so sure that's a good idea, Jen. You're upset. She's bound to be upset. Let me talk to her first, and I'll give you a call tonight, no matter how late it is."

"She's my daughter. I'm coming with you."

I don't need her anymore, Uncle Bryan.

"Children don't take these kind of surprises well, honey. It threatens their security to have any major changes in their lives. They say things they don't mean—"

"And they have a million questions," Jennifer said, smiling bitterly. "See? I'm learning already. But in this case, Nicki has a right to her questions, and I'm the only one with the answers. It's not me I'm thinking of Bryan, it's Nicki. I'm coming with you."

"Okay. I'll follow you," Bryan said, unlocking the Jeep.

He pounded his hand on the steering wheel as he watched her pull out of the parking lot. He cursed the Fates that had brought him to this point, that had brought the two people he cared for to this point. His sense of foreboding was so strong it was strangling him, and there wasn't a damn thing he could do about it. He was following the woman he wanted to marry into hell, and he couldn't stop her.

Nicki met them at the front door. "Oh, Jennifer, I'm so glad you're back. Are you feeling better?"

"A little." Jennifer smiled weakly in Nicki's direction. She still looked sick and worried and scared out of her wits.

Banking on the fact that she wouldn't make a scene in front of Nicki, Bryan put his arm around her and led her into the living room. She needed someone to lean on whether she wanted to admit it or not, and at the moment, he was it.

"Come in here, Nick. We need to talk to you," Bryan said after settling Jennifer on the couch.

"What?" Nicki came in. That damn look was back in her eyes, the "frightened fawn with nowhere to run" look. "What's the matter with her? Is she going to be okay, Uncle Bryan?" Nicki's voice wobbled with tears.

"She's going to be just fine, honey." Leaving Jennifer, he crossed to Nicki, gave her a quick hug and led her to the couch. He sat her next to Jennifer. *Please, God, if you never hear another word I utter, hear these. Don't let this be the end. They need each other. And I need them.* Nicki looked from Bryan to Jennifer's bent head and back again. "What's wrong?" she asked, her fear evident.

And now that the moment was upon him, Bryan didn't have any idea what to say. How did you tell a twelve-year-old child that the woman she thought was her friend was really the mother she no longer wanted to meet?

"Well, Nick, it's like this. Remember when you asked me to—"

"I'm your mother."

The bald words fell into the room, leaving a deafening silence in their wake.

Bryan watched Nicki, ready to grab her up and take her away from a situation she wasn't ready to handle. He wanted to take her to a place where only good things happened and children were always happy. She sat frozen, staring at Jennifer, a look of disbelief on her face. Jennifer's head was bowed, as if she couldn't bear to see the shock on her daughter's face. Nobody moved. Nobody said a word.

As if sensing that something was horribly wrong, Lucy ambled over to Nicki, nudged the girl's limp hand, then raised her paws to Nicki's knees.

Slowly, almost unconsciously, Nicki started to stroke the dog. Her movements grew faster, harder, until she buried her face in Lucy's fur and started to laugh.

What the hell?

Bryan's gaze met Jennifer's, their eyes identical pools of worry.

"I thought you said you were my mother," she said, speaking to Jennifer, but looking at the dog.

"I did." Jennifer's words were as gentle as a spring breeze.

But they didn't have a gentling effect on Nicki. "No!" the girl cried, jumping up. "You're not! You're wrong!" She burst into tears.

Bryan pulled the distraught child into his arms, rubbing her back, soothing her with the meaningless platitudes he'd spoken over and over to her during all the nightmares of the past year.

She looked up at him, her face streaming with tears. "Please, Uncle Bryan. I don't want her to be my mother. Please make her go away."

"Shh. It's okay, Nick. Calm down. It's okay." His gaze sought Jennifer's over Nicki's head. He'd never seen such raw pain. Dry-eyed, Jennifer was dying right before his eyes, and there was nothing he could do to help her.

"Come on, Nick, calm down," he said, his voice low.

"Make her go away, Uncle Bryan! I thought she was my friend. Make her leave. I don't ever want to see her again." Her words cut into Bryan. He could only imagine what they were doing to Jennifer.

"Shh. You don't mean that, honey. I think you half love her already."

"I don't. I hate her!"

"Nicki! Don't talk like that." His tone was rough now, reprimanding. No matter how upset she was, he couldn't allow her to go that far.

She jerked away from him. "Why not? It's true. And I hate you, too!" She turned and ran from the room. Bryan stood there in shock until he heard her bedroom door slam.

He looked over at Jennifer. She was staring at the hallway where Nicki had fled.

"I'm sorry," he said. "She's never acted like that before."

"It's not her fault." Jennifer's eyes were dead. "I don't blame her for hating me. It's what I expected."

Bryan sat down beside her, warming her cold hands between his own warmer ones. "She doesn't hate you, Jen. She loves you. She just needs some time."

Jennifer looked straight at him. "I gave her away." Her words, delivered in a lifeless monotone, cut him to the quick.

"You were barely sixteen!"

Jennifer shrugged off his defense of her and got to her feet. "She deserves to know the truth. If it's the only thing I can give her, at least there's that. I'll leave as soon as I'm finished."

"Jen, wait," Bryan said, but she'd left the room.

Dread filled his heart as he followed her down the hall.

"Go away." Nicki's muffled voice reached Bryan as he watched Jennifer enter her room.

"As soon as I've told you a few things." Jennifer's voice was firm, strong. He had a feeling it was the only thing about her that was.

Nicki was lying on her bed, her head buried under her pillow when he entered the room.

Jennifer was sitting on the bed beside her. She reached out, her hand hovering over Nicki's back before it slowly descended. Nicki flinched as Jennifer touched her. Jennifer's hand stilled, but she didn't remove it from Nicki's back. After a couple of seconds, she started to move it again, rubbing it slowly up and down the child's spine. Just as slowly, she started to speak.

"I made some major mistakes when I was growing up, Nicki, but none that I regretted as much as I did giving you up. But I was little more than a child myself when I had you. And a pretty mixed-up child at that."

Nicki lay as still as a statue, obviously listening to every word. Bryan swallowed, his throat thick as he watched mother and child, as he listened to the woman he loved lay herself open to the child who had just rejected her.

"You see, I didn't have the same kind of childhood you did. My parents didn't love me like yours loved you. I never felt special—just in the way. I was a mistake, like your friend Sally. My parents were already in their mid-forties when I came along, and I grew up as little more than an intrusion in their lives. I spent the first fifteen years of my life trying to please them, but what I didn't realize was that my mere presence was displeasing to them, no matter what I did." Jennifer's voice wavered, and she stopped speaking for a moment, but she didn't stop touching her daughter.

Bryan watched that contact, suspecting that they both needed it more than either of them would be willing to admit.

"My parents forgot my fifteenth birthday. There was no celebration waiting when I got home from school, not even a card propped on the counter. So I waited for them to come home from work, thinking they were planning to take me out to dinner. I hoped it would be to one of those places where they bring you a little cake and sing 'Happy Birthday.' I really wanted that little cake."

She smiled ruefully. "They didn't come. But Billy Wilson did. He was one of the most popular boys in school and we'd gone out a few times. I could hardly believe it when he said he actually wanted me to be his girlfriend. I had no idea what he saw in me. My clothes weren't fashionable, my face was plain, my mother was constantly telling me I was too tall—I kept growing out of my pants. But here was Billy, on my birthday, with a bouquet of flowers just for me.

"He told me he loved me, and I was so starved to hear the words that I believed him."

Jennifer stopped, tears brimming in her eyes, but she blinked them away. Bryan stood by the wall, his hands clenched behind him. He didn't want to hear any more.

"He told me that if I loved him back, I'd do whatever he wanted me to do..."

Bryan ground his teeth together.

"Two weeks later he was spreading it around school what I'd done. The boys all looked at me differently, made nasty remarks. The girls shied away from me. What little bit of faith I'd had in myself was gone. I felt completely worthless."

Nicki turned over, her eyes accusing. "So that was my *father?*" she asked. "A stupid selfish boy who wasn't even very nice?"

Bryan could cheerfully have gagged his niece. Jennifer had been through enough just in retelling the story. She'd obviously already judged herself a million times and come up wanting. She didn't need her daughter's condemnation on top of that.

"No."

What? Bryan straightened in the doorway.

"Then who was?" Nicki asked, still accusing.

"His name was Tommy Mason. He worked for my father. He was Billy's best friend. Or at least he was until Billy turned on me. Tommy came to my rescue. He told me how beautiful I was, how sweet to have cared so much for Billy, to have trusted him so much. After a while we started dating. Tommy had a lot of money for a boy his age, and he spent most of it on me. He was always doing little things to make me feel special. It was only later that I learned he was just like Billy, except that he'd invested more into getting what he was after because he had more at stake."

Jennifer stared into space, and Bryan knew that he and Nicki had lost her to a time before either of them had been a part of her life. Her face was twisted in a grimace of self-loathing so strong it was hard for Bryan to believe she was the same woman he'd known all these months.

Nicki just sat silently, a one-child jury who'd already convicted the defendant.

"They had a—" Jennifer stopped as a single tear slid down her cheek. She closed her eyes. "A bet. If I'd *do it* with Tommy, Billy would give him ten dollars. If not, Tommy owed Billy."

Bryan's dinner was about to come up on him.

"Why'd he spend all that money on you if he was only gonna win ten dollars?" Nicki asked. Her eyes were softer, not forgiving, exactly, but more like the Nicki he knew.

"It wasn't the money that was at stake, it was his ego. He had to win to prove to his buddies that he was as much a man as Billy was."

"So what'd he do when you told him, you know, about me?"

Jennifer smoothed the hair away from her daughter's brow. "He said he wasn't your father. He told my parents that he hadn't been the first boy I'd been with, and that he was sure he hadn't been the last. He claimed that there was no way even *I* could know who your father was."

"What did they say?"

"They believed him."

Bryan left the room. The anger surging through him frightened him. He didn't want to do something he'd regret, especially in front of Nicki. His fists ached to smash into something, preferably this Tommy Mason's face.

Pacing out in the hall, he heard his niece ask, "Was it the truth?"

"No," Jennifer said firmly. "After Billy, there was only Tommy, and only that one time."

Bryan had to stop himself from putting his fist through the wall.

"That still doesn't explain why *you* couldn't keep me." Nicki wasn't ready to forgive her for that. Bryan wasn't sure she ever would be. In her eyes, Jennifer had abandoned her, regardless of how happy Nicki had ultimately been.

He couldn't stand by and let her torture Jennifer anymore. "Let's give it a rest, eh, Nick?" he said, coming back into the room.

Jennifer shook her head at him. "It's okay. She has to know the truth if she's ever going to understand."

Bryan didn't like it, but he leaned against the doorjamb and let her continue.

"I gave you away because I loved you, Nicki."

"How can you say that?" Nicki's look was hard again.

"Because it's true." The peace that settled across Jennifer's face surprised Bryan almost as much as her next words did. "I nearly changed my mind, you know."

"You did?"

She did?

"Uh-huh." Jennifer smiled sadly. "I'd given in to my parents early on in my pregnancy, agreeing to give you up before you were more than a speck in my belly. They wouldn't give me a second's peace, telling me they wouldn't have any part of my baby—"

Bryan could just imagine the terms they'd probably used to describe the child Jennifer had been carrying.

"—and they weren't going to have any part of me, either, if I didn't do what they said. I was scared. I was young. I wasn't even old enough to get a work permit or drive a car. I didn't see how I could take care of myself, let alone a baby. So I did just what I'd always done. I gave in to them and agreed to give you up for adoption.

"But a funny thing happened during those months I carried you. You became the light of my life, the best thing that had ever happened to me. You taught me what love was all about for the very first time. Every time you kicked me, I'd feel like smiling, and when you moved in the middle of the night, waking me up, I'd sit up and play with you, trying to get you to move some more. You were mine. And I wanted to take care of you and protect you for the rest of my life."

"So why didn't you?" Nicki asked.

"I did," Jennifer said softly. "I had to have you by cesarean, and so I was unconscious when you were born, but that night, the night before I was due to leave the hospital, I talked a young nurse into bringing you in to me. I hadn't signed the papers yet that would release you to someone else, and I didn't intend to ever do so. But when I held you in my arms—" tears filled Jennifer's eyes, but she was still smiling at Nicki "—you were so small, so defenseless, so precious, I knew I couldn't take you home to that unhappy house. You deserved so much more. I couldn't bear to think of you growing up the way I had, with my parents frowning their disapproval upon you. And secretly I was afraid that maybe I'd be like them. I didn't know any more about raising a baby than they did, and I might be just as awful at it. After all, I'd failed at everything else I'd ever tried. It was then I knew I couldn't keep you. So I made a promise, instead."

"A promise?"

"I promised God that if He'd give you a happy loving family, I'd let you go. I wouldn't look for you, or bother you, and I wouldn't ever replace you, either."

Bryan finally understood. More than just a fear of being a bad parent had kept Jennifer from registering to find Nicki. She'd made a pact with God, and if she broke her half, He might not uphold His. Bryan had never felt such a surge of love for the woman he wanted to make his wife.

Nicki looked at Jennifer, as if not quite sure how she felt anymore. "So when did you get rich?"

"After I got out of college. I took over my parents' business and for the first time in my life I did something right."

Nicki nodded. She still didn't look at Bryan—she hadn't since she'd run out of the living room—but she'd certainly calmed down.

"Can I ask you something?"

Jennifer brushed her fingers along Nicki's arm as if she couldn't get enough of touching her. "Sure."

"How long have you known who I was?"

"I just found out tonight."

"You did? You mean you didn't know when you were nice to me at the beach, when you bought me that swimsuit? You did that just because you liked me?"

"Just because I like you, sweetie. You're a pretty special young lady."

Nicki shrugged off Jennifer's praise, as if not quite sure how much weight it carried. "So Uncle Bryan just told you tonight?"

Bryan suddenly wondered how she *had* found out. He'd been so concerned about her reaction to the news that it hadn't dawned on him to wonder how she'd come by it.

"No. This did." Jennifer pulled a picture out of the pocket of her dress and handed it to Nicki.

"It's me!" Nicki said, gazing in awe at the battered photo. "It's the same picture we have in the album."

Jennifer nodded, tears in her eyes again.

"You mean you didn't know until I turned that page and you saw this picture?"

"That's right."

"Omigosh," Nicki said, looking at the picture again. "How come it's so beat-up?"

"It's been through twelve years of my life with me, honey, every hour of every day."

"Always?" Nicki asked, her expression defenseless all of a sudden.

"Always."

Nicki's gaze was glued to Jennifer's; Bryan had a feeling they didn't even know he was still there. "You must have loved me an awful lot."

Jennifer smiled. "With all my heart, Nick."

"Is it okay if I hug you?" Nicki asked, suddenly awkward as she finally looked at Jennifer in a new light.

"I thought you'd never ask," Jennifer said, gathering her daughter into her arms for the first time in twelve years.

Bryan slipped from the room.

THE DINING-ROOM TABLE was strewn with the makings of a miniature double-winged biplane, similar to the one the Wright brothers flew. Bryan had always admired them, not only because their early experimentation had opened up the skies, but because of their quest to have their freedom no matter what the cost.

Freedom had always meant that much to him, as well. More than a home, more than a wife or children, more than possessions. He left Nicki in with Jennifer, left them to forge a relationship that didn't include him, and went out to work on his plane. It was ridiculous for him to feel left out. He had no reason to feel threatened. And lonely wasn't a feeling he'd ever had time for. There was always that unknown something beckoning him from just over the next hill. So why couldn't he hear its call now?

He split a piece of balsa with his razor-blade knife. He could finish the plane with just a few more hours' work. He was anxious to see how it flew. Maybe he and Nicki could take it to the coast over the weekend and send it up over the ocean. A day alone with Nicki sounded good to him. He had a plan. With renewed purpose, he set to work.

NICKI FOUND HIM in the dining room after spending an incredible hour getting to know her birth mother. He was so intent on the little piece of wood he was shaping he didn't even notice her. Figured.

She moved closer to the table and picked up a packet of glue.

His head shot up. The wood in his fingers cracked into two pieces. Nicki held her breath. She'd heard him swear before when that happened. And this time she'd caused it.

"Where's Jennifer?" he asked.

Nicki felt funny having him refer to her mother by her given name, and yet, she didn't know what else to call her. She couldn't call her Mom. Not ever. She already had a Mom. She felt guilty even thinking about it, like she was hurting Mom by even *knowing* Jennifer.

"Nicki? Did Jen leave?" he asked, getting up from the table.

"No. She's still in my bedroom. She said I had to come talk to you." Nicki hadn't wanted to, she'd just wanted to leave, but Jennifer hadn't budged.

"I'm sorry this was all such a shock to you, honey. I wouldn't upset you for the world, you know that, don't you?"

Nicki shrugged. She didn't know what to think.

He came around the table and put his arm around her. It felt so good to have him hold her, but something made her shrug his arm away.

"Hey!" He knelt down in front of her. "What's going on here, Nick? We're a team, you and me, remember?"

"If we're a team, then why didn't you tell me the truth about her?"

He hesitated, and Nicki knew he was trying to think up something to tell her. Which meant he wasn't going to tell her the truth.

"I was going to tell you, honey. I just wanted to make sure you liked her first. I planned to tell both of you tonight, except that I had to work late."

He'd known she was her birth mother for months. Even back when all that mattered had been finding her other mother, he'd already known who she was. And he'd told Nicki he was still looking. Even on her birthday he'd said that.

He'd lied to her. And that hurt so bad she didn't even want to look at him.

"I want to go stay with her."

"What? Why?" He jumped up, clutching her shoulders as if he could keep her with him by sheer force. "You don't need to leave here. We live close enough for you to visit her every day if you want to."

"You're hurting me!" Nicki said, trying to pull away.

"Sorry." He loosened his hold, but he didn't let go of her. He rubbed her shoulders softly with his fingers until they felt better. But *she* didn't. He'd lied to her.

"I don't want to *visit* her, I want to *stay* with her, find out what she's like."

"You can spend a couple of nights with her, I guess, if that's what you want. It's summer and you wouldn't be missing any school." He went back to the table, picking up a new piece of balsa wood and his littlest pair of scissors.

He'd given in so easily Nicki almost started to cry. But she wasn't going to do that. Not in front of him. She'd promised herself she wouldn't. It wasn't like she hadn't known, anyway. Uncle Bryan was a free spirit; he was used to being on his own. She'd thought maybe he'd changed, that with Jennifer around he'd want to settle down, but her birth mother had just told Nicki that she and Uncle Bryan weren't going to be seeing each other anymore. She hadn't said why, but Nicki figured it was because Uncle Bryan wanted it that way. He was always the one who broke things off.

Nicki figured she'd better go before he broke things off with her, too. She couldn't stand to stay, worrying about when he'd do it. She'd been worried for months about cramping him. And now she had Lucy, too. But she also, finally, had someplace else she could go.

"I don't want to just visit her," she said again. "I want to move in with her. Lucy, too."

He didn't even look up. "You can't do that, Nick. You belong with me." His voice sounded strange. Faraway. Was he paying attention to her at all?

"No, I don't. I'm not really a Chambers. Or a Hubbard, either. I'm a Teal. I want to go live with my *real* mother." It killed Nicki even to say the words. She held her breath, waiting for Uncle Bryan to tell her she was wrong, to take her in his big strong arms and tell her he'd never let her go.

He was quiet for so long Nicki wondered if he'd forgotten her. He worked on his little piece of wood until he got it just right and then glued it to the front of the model he was building. It was another airplane—an open one with two wings on each side. It would probably be fun to fly. They could put a little man in the cockpit and then they'd have to fly it almost perfect or the man would fall out.

"Is it okay with Jennifer?"

She jumped when he finally spoke. He'd never used that voice with her before, like she was someone he didn't know very well. Was he already that glad to be rid of her?

"Yes." At least she hoped it was. She'd only asked her birth mother if she could spend the night with her.

"Then I won't stop you."

CHAPTER SIXTEEN

I WON'T STOP YOU... I won't stop you... I won't stop you...

The edge of the razor slid into Bryan's finger. "Damn it to hell!" he said, sucking on his finger as he went into the bathroom. He swore out loud the entire time it took him to stop the flow of blood and get a bandage on his finger. It didn't matter what he said or how loud he said it. There was no one around to hear him.

I won't stop you. What an incredibly asinine thing to tell her. What in hell had he been thinking? He could have at least tried to stop her. What did he have to lose by trying?

So why hadn't he?

Turning off the bathroom light, Nicki's bathroom light, he wandered into her bedroom. It was surprising how much stuff she'd been able to pack up in the half hour it had taken her to leave him. The room looked so vacant. Sure, her magazines were still stacked on the shelf. Her little jewelry box was still on the dresser. He opened her closet. Her winter clothes still hung there, and some dresses. There were even a couple of pairs of shoes.

He glanced back at the bed. But there was no Nicki. The room mocked him with its emptiness. Hell, the whole house mocked him. He'd bought it for her.

But if she didn't want to be with him . . .

Bryan went back to his airplane.

He could have tried to stop her, but what good would it have done? He couldn't make her want to stay. And deep down, he wondered who had more right to her, he or Jennifer. If he fought them, if they fought him back, if Nicki went to court and testified that she wanted to live with her biological mother, how much chance did an adoptive uncle stand?

Or was there another reason he hadn't fought any harder to keep her? Deep down, had he welcomed the chance to hand over the mammoth responsibility of looking after Nicki, of dealing with her ups and downs? Had he, per chance, wanted his freedom, as Jennifer had accused earlier that evening?

He looked at his watch. It had only been four hours ago that Jennifer had appeared in his office, but it seemed like days. Then again, Nicki had become his in the space of five minutes, the time it took a tornado to destroy half a town. Why shouldn't he lose her just as quickly?

He'd become a father overnight. The question was, could he resume his old life just as rapidly? Did he want to?

He finished the model at three o'clock in the morning. He'd have gone outside to try it out, but he didn't want to wake the neighbors. So instead, he wandered around the house again, thinking of the things he'd been planning to do, the dark paneling he wanted to rip out in the den, the tile he wanted to lay in place of the outdoor carpet on the covered porch, the wall of windows he wanted to put in in his bedroom. He'd promised Nicki a pool for the backyard, and he'd figured he'd throw in a Jacuzzi for himself, as well.

He'd planned to landscape the whole backyard around the pool, building a fountain made out of rocks that would empty into the deep end of the pool. And he'd wanted fruit trees, too, and lots of lush green grass so Nicki could run around barefoot.

But what did he know? A pool was probably a pain to take care of. And grass had to be cut. Maybe he'd just sell the house.

He was behind his drafting table at Innovative Advertising two hours later, chased out of the house by something he didn't understand. He'd showered and changed his jeans for a pair of shorts, his polo shirt for a bright red tank top, and he'd left his hair loose over his shoulders. He was going to go to the batting cages as soon as they opened at ten o'clock, and then maybe he'd try to catch a Braves game. And surely there was someone he could call for a date that night, even at this late notice...

Anything was better than going home to that house again. He couldn't stand another evening there.

JENNIFER BARELY SLEPT all night. She missed Bryan.

And her daughter was asleep in bed right on the other side of the wall. Jennifer shivered with disbelief just thinking about it. She got up out of bed three times to make sure Nicki was really there. And she watched the clock until she knew Tanya and Dennis would be up. Maybe when she told her friends about Nicki it would begin to seem real.

Damn him. Damn him for using her, for making her believe in love again, for showing her how wonderful love could be. Damn him for not being there to share Nicki with her, to share her excitement—and her fear that it was all just an incredible dream. To hold her until she believed.

Damn him for not loving her.

But he'd given her Nicki. He'd given her back her daughter. So try as she might, she couldn't hate him.

Nicki was still sleeping soundly at seven o'clock. Jennifer stood in the doorway of her guest room, Nicki's room as of last night, and watched the covers rise and fall with her daughter's breathing. Nicki's hair was tangled and spread all over her pillow. Lucy was curled up to her chest, almost as if Nicki had been cuddling her before she'd fallen asleep.

Tears filled Jennifer's eyes and slid slowly down her face as she stood there watching, trying not to think of the years she'd lost, thankful beyond comprehension for the years she'd just gained.

She'd been through so much, this poor baby of hers, but Jennifer was set to shower Nicki with enough love to ease the pain that had taken over the child's life. She was going to do whatever it took to help Nicki be happy again.

It wasn't going to be easy, Jennifer knew. Nicki had barely said a word since they'd left Bryan's house the night before, in spite of the fact that she'd insisted she wanted to come live with Jennifer more than anything else in the world. And even though Jennifer had already suspected Bryan had planned all along to ease his own responsibility to Nicki by bringing her, Jennifer, into the picture, she was still surprised by how easily he'd capitulated to Nicki's request. Surprised, and hurt.

And Nicki must have been hurt by it, too. No matter how much she thought she wanted to live with her birth mother, she still loved her uncle—and she'd already lost so much.

Leaving Nicki's door open a crack, Jennifer went out to the kitchen and phoned Tanya.

"Are you free for lunch?" she asked her friend as soon as they'd said hello.

"I think so." Tanya sounded sleepy.

Jennifer wrapped the cord around her finger. "I have something to show you. How about meeting me at Max's?" She named one of their favorite restaurants.

"Sure. What time?"

"Noon."

"Fine. Now what're you not telling me?" Her friend was definitely awake now.

"Why does there have to be something I'm not telling you?"

"Because I've never heard you sound so, I don't know, excited, maybe."

"I'll see you at lunch," Jennifer said, intending to hang up before Tanya could worm her surprise out of her. She wanted to see Tanya's face when she walked in and saw Nicki sitting there with her. She wanted to see if Tanya noticed the resemblance between them, or if she was only imagining it.

"It's Bryan, isn't it? He's asked you to marry him."

"No. As a matter of fact, I don't think I'm going to be seeing him as much."

"You're not... But Dennis said your trip to the beach was a miraculous success. He said you and Bryan even, you know..."

"I never told him that!"

"I know. He just said he could tell."

Jennifer felt stupid, blushing on the telephone. "Well, it doesn't matter now. It's over."

"Oh."

"Don't sound so disappointed in me. I didn't do it this time. *He* did."

"Oh. Oh-h-h." Now the word was filled with sympathy.

"Yeah," Jennifer said, promising herself she wouldn't cry again. She'd been a fool to think she could have it all. And at least Bryan hadn't left her all alone. He'd given her the one thing she'd wanted more than anything else in life—a second chance with her daughter.

And she wasn't going to ruin it by wanting his love, too. She just wasn't.

"What happened?" Tanya finally asked.

"Wait until after lunch, and then I'll answer any questions you have left."

"It's not nice to drive a pregnant woman crazy, Jen."

"Lunch, Tanya. Oh, and tell Dennis I won't be in today, okay?"

"You sure you're all right?" Tanya asked, sounding concerned again.

"I've never been better," Jennifer said, though it was only partly true. She yearned for Bryan. As much as he yearned for freedom.

"HAS UNCLE BRYAN ever met your friend?" Nicki asked Jennifer as they sat at their table at Max's later that morning waiting for Tanya to arrive. It was the fourth time she'd mentioned her uncle that morning.

"He met her once at one of her art shows. But he knows her husband pretty well. Dennis works for me."

"So she's the artist Uncle Bryan told me about you being friends with?"

"She must be, 'cause she's the only artist friend I have."

Nicki was wearing the same flowered culotte dress she'd worn the first night Jennifer had met her. She looked beautiful. Jennifer felt like everyone in the restaurant was looking at them, recognizing them as mother and daughter. She wanted to introduce Nicki to every last one of them.

"Do they...know about me?"

Jennifer covered her daughter's hand with her own. She hated that frightened-doe look in Nicki's eyes, and wondered what it was going to take to help Nicki feel secure again.

"They don't know yet that I found you, if that's what you mean."

"But they know you had me? Had a baby, I mean?"

"Dennis brought me home from the hospital after I had you."

"Where was your mom?"

"At work."

"But you said you had stitches and stuff."

"Uh-huh."

"Jeez," Nicki said. Jennifer nodded. That just about summed it up.

"Tanya spent your first birthday with me."

"She did?" Nicki brightened. "You mean you celebrated it, too?"

Jennifer wasn't sure how much to tell Nicki, how much the child needed to hear or should hear, about that time in her life. "Sort of," she said.

"You remembered at least," Nicki said, making the words sound more like a question, an important question.

"I never forgot, Nicki. Not for a second. That night I cried almost the whole night. I'd just lost the first year of your life and I knew I was never going to get it back," she said, listening to her instincts.

Her stomach tightened when tears sprang to Nicki's eyes. She'd made her daughter cry. "I'm glad," Nicki said. "I mean, I'm not glad you were sad, but I'm glad you remembered, like you really cared and all."

"I always cared, Nick. Always."

"Jennifer?"

Jennifer turned at the sound of her friend's voice. Tanya was coming toward them like the building was on fire.

"You found her? Why didn't you tell me?" Tanya asked, staring at Nicki. "I can't believe you didn't tell me!"

Nicki looked as if she was ready to bolt.

"Sit down, Tanya," Jennifer said, concerned for Nicki, but so full of pride she thought she'd burst.

"Where did you find her?" Tanya was still looking at Nicki as she slid into her chair. "I can't believe how much she looks like you."

Nicki stared at her plate.

"You'll have to excuse Tanya, Nick. She never did have any manners, but she's nice enough once you get to know her, I promise," Jennifer said lightly.

Nicki glanced at Jennifer, an uncertain smile flickering across her face.

"Tanya Bradford, meet Nicki Hubbard. Nicki, this blabbermouth is my friend, Tanya."

"Hi," Nicki said.

"Hello yourself, sweetie," Tanya said, embracing Nicki with her smile. "I've been waiting a long time to meet you, and you're even more beautiful than I imagined."

Nicki blushed.

Their waitress came over, having seen Tanya arrive, and they were soon taken up with the business of ordering lunch, all three of them deciding on turkey croissants. Nicki was having hers with french fries.

Tanya looked from Nicki to Jennifer again as soon as their waitress walked away. "Boy, your lawyer sure works fast."

Jennifer put down the water glass she'd been sipping from. "My lawyer?"

Tanya frowned. "Isn't that how you two found each other?"

Jennifer shook her head. "I haven't heard back from him yet."

"You were looking for me?" Nicki gazed at Jennifer with glowing eyes.

Jennifer nodded. "I had to find you before I could love your uncle and the child I thought was just his niece."

"You did?"

"I couldn't give my heart to you until I knew for sure that my own child was happy."

"Oh." Her daughter was smiling the biggest smile Jennifer had ever seen. "I thought you didn't want to find me. Uncle Bryan told me you hadn't registered," her daughter explained.

Jennifer covered Nicki's hand with her own, afraid to tell Nicki the truth—but more afraid not to. There had already been too many lies in their relationship. "I didn't until just a week ago. I didn't want to interfere in your life, honey." That part was easy. "And I was afraid to know where you were, knowing I couldn't be a part of your life, afraid of how badly it would hurt."

Nicki pulled her hand away. "But I needed you."

"I'm sorry, Nicki. So sorry. But the truth is, until very recently, I believed that even if you needed me, I'd just fail you again, like I had when I was sixteen. That's why I didn't register to find you sooner. Not because I didn't love you."

"Wait just a minute here," Tanya said, looking from one to the other of them. "Are you saying that *she's* Bryan Chambers's niece? The one you went to the beach with?"

Jennifer and Nicki looked at each other and nodded.

"And you didn't know... He didn't... Oh, my G— Oh. But why?"

"He wanted to make sure we got along before he introduced us. He didn't want Nicki to be hurt any more than she already had been."

Nicki's gaze flew to Jennifer. "He didn't?"

"Didn't he tell you that?"

Nicki shook her head.

"That's why he didn't let you know who I was, Nicki. He was trying to protect you the best way he knew how."

"Well, if she's his niece and your daughter," Tanya asked, confused, "then what's the matter with you and him?"

"It wasn't me he wanted so much as a mother for Nicki," Jennifer said, choosing her words carefully in front of Nicki.

"You don't know my uncle," Nicki said, sounding far more mature than her twelve years. "He's always taking off for places, and you can't do that when you have a kid around. I guess you can't do it with a girlfriend around, either, only he didn't show it with Jennifer because of who she was.''

Tanya looked at Jennifer. "This is true?"

"Maybe. A little," Jennifer said.

"Well, what happens now?"

Jennifer took her daughter's hand, gave it a squeeze and held on to it. "We live happily ever after...."

"How is she?" His voice jolted Jennifer out a sleep-induced haze.

"Bryan?"

"Of course. Is everything okay?"

She pushed herself up in bed, willing her heartbeat to settle back to its normal pace. He was calling about Nicki.

"Fine. We're fine. She's fine. She's asleep."

"I figured she would be. That's why I waited so late to call. I don't want her to think I'm checking up on her or anything."

"Then why are you calling?" His voice sounded so good to her, too good.

"To check up on her, of course. I... Oh, never mind. I'll call you tomorrow." He made it sound like a chore.

"You don't have to do that, you know. We're doing fine. I'd call you if we weren't."

"You're telling me not to call you anymore?"

Did he have to make it sound so final?

"I'm telling you it's not necessary."

"Have you been reminding her to brush her teeth? She just got her braces off six months ago."

"She's brushing her teeth, Bryan, and eating, and she even took a shower today." *You're free to get on with your life. Now let me get on with mine.*

"Lucy's not getting in your way, is she?"

What did it take to ease this man's conscience? If he needed to be free, they weren't going to hold him back. She and Nicki had discussed it over dinner.

"Lucy's fine, though she's missing her yard, of course. I'm thinking about looking around for a house someplace. Right after I look into schools."

"It sounds like you're taking to motherhood just fine."

She was. It was the womanhood she was still struggling with. He'd been her lover for one night, and she felt like she'd lost a limb.

"I guess I'm better at it than I thought."

"Good. Good." Was that relief she heard in his voice? Was he now going to take off into the sunset? She'd told herself that she wouldn't hold him back, that she didn't want a man who couldn't be happy by her side, a man she'd constantly have to worry about leaving her. And yet she'd never thought saying goodbye would hurt so much.

"I never meant to hurt you, Jen."

"I know." But that didn't stop the tears from springing to her eyes. Again.

"Maybe we could—"

"I don't think so, Bryan." She cut him off before he talked her into settling for less than she really wanted. She'd been doing that all her life, believing that she wasn't worthy of more, that she was weak-willed, and she wasn't going to do it ever again. She wasn't looking at herself through her parents' eyes anymore.

"I'll call you tomorrow night." He hung up before she could beg him to leave her alone, and she didn't trust herself to call him back. She lay down, but the sleep she needed so badly eluded her. She was counting the hours until she heard his voice again. And torturing herself with images of just what he might be doing with his newfound freedom.

"UNCLE BRYAN called me today," Nicki said over dinner almost a week later. She and Jennifer were still living in the penthouse, much to Lucy's disgust, but Jennifer had seen a couple of homes she liked and was thinking about making an offer on one.

"He did?" she asked now, more disappointed than she should have been. Did that mean, then, that she wouldn't be talking to him that night as she had every night since Nicki had come to live with her? She waited all day for those nightly calls.

"Uh-huh." Jennifer's throat caught at the sight of her daughter's happy smile. Nicki missed her uncle more than she was letting on.

"So what did he have to say?"

"He went to the ocean over the weekend to fly his new model plane. He says he might keep it, too, if he doesn't sell his house."

He's thinking about selling his house? "Sounds like he had a good time."

Nicki shrugged. "I guess."

"You know, honey, if you need to move back with him, or even just go visit him, it's fine with me."

The frightened-doe look was back in Nicki's eyes. "You don't want me here?"

"Yes! Of course I want you. You can live with me until you're old and gray if you'd like. But it's more important that you be happy, Nick, and Bryan is all the family you have left. It's natural you'd need to see him. I just don't want you to feel like you'd be disloyal to me or hurt my feelings by going back."

Nicki shrugged. "It doesn't matter. Like we said my first night here, he can't help how he is. He can't help it if I get in his way over there. But it was still fun to talk to him."

Jennifer let the subject drop, but she was troubled by the unhappy look in Nicki's eyes. Whether Bryan's blood flowed in Nicki's veins or not, he was her family and she needed him.

"Can I ask you something?" Nicki asked later that evening as she sat with Jennifer in the living room. Lucy was curled up on the floor by Nicki's feet.

Jennifer looked up from the work she'd had Dennis drop by for her that afternoon. "Of course, honey. What's up?"

"Remember that talk we had that night at dinner at my... at Uncle Bryan's house? The one about it not mattering about my mom being twelve and all when she... you know."

"Uh-huh," Jennifer said, suddenly nervous.

Nicki dog-eared the pages of her magazine. "Well, I was wondering... how old were you?"

"I was twelve, too, so you probably are right to think you might be getting close. Why don't we stop off at the drugstore tomorrow on our way to Phipp's Plaza and get you stocked up on stuff so you're ready when the time comes?" It wasn't nearly as hard as she'd thought it would be. It actually felt right to be talking to her daughter about such things.

Apparently Nicki felt so, too. "Okay." She grinned. "But I really don't know what I'll need for sure."

"I think between the two of us, we can figure it out..."

"YOU KNOW, NICK, it's okay if you leave some of your stuff lying around if you want to," Jennifer said the next evening. She'd been signing some letters while Nicki watched her favorite sitcom on TV. But her attention had wandered again and again to her daughter, to the wonder of actually having her there in the same room with her.

Nicki laid her head back against the couch, her legs curled up beneath her. "Uncle Bryan said the same thing when I came to live with him, but I just like to put things away. I don't really even think about it. Uncle Bryan says it's my dad's fault. The first game he taught me was one where we raced to pick up my toys."

Jennifer smiled at the contented look on her daughter's face. "Who won?" she asked.

"Him mostly, but that was okay 'cause that meant he picked up the most toys."

"Aha, so you were a conniver even as a little tike, huh?"

Nicki laughed. "Not really. It was just fun watching him crawl real fast all over the floor. He'd do tricks and hide toys and stuff and then I'd find them in my toy box. He was really good at magic stuff."

They spent the rest of the evening as they'd spent most of the previous ones, talking. Jennifer wanted to hear every last detail of Nicki's first twelve years. She was getting to know the entire Chambers family through Nicki, and the more she heard, the more she grew to love them. They'd given Nicki a wonderful childhood, raised her in a safe, secure, but most important, *loving* environment. They'd shaped her into a beautiful young woman, inside where it counted. The only thing to which Jennifer could lay claim was the outside.

"HEY, THERE, you want some company?"

Bryan squinted up through his sunglasses at the scantily clad, dark-skinned Bahamian beauty who was dripping water all over his beach towel.

Hell, yes, he wanted company. Badly. "Not today, but thanks for the offer."

His gaze followed her all the way down the beach. Had he lost his mind? The woman was gorgeous, her walk so sensual, her bottom so tempting, he should be drooling into his umbrellaed drink.

But she wasn't Jennifer.

He finished his drink in one gulp, jumped up with his towel in hand and headed back to the hotel lobby. Maybe he'd take a course in skin diving. It was something he'd always wanted to do, and he had all the time in the world at his disposal.

Back at the hotel he was halfway to the concierge desk to sign up for skin diving when he turned around and headed for the elevators. Once in his room, he packed his duffel and called down for a ride to the airport. There were lots of skin diving classes offered in Atlanta. He'd check into it as soon as he got home.

He called Nicki from the airport before he left the Bahamas. The conversation was the same as it had been every other day over the past week. She sounded happy to hear from him, but when he asked her how she was doing, when he tried to get her to talk to him, her voice cooled, like he was some friend of the family, rather than family itself.

He'd blown it, plain and simple. Like an idiot, he'd tried to play God. And he'd lied to Nicki. By omission, he'd lied to her mother, too. He'd betrayed their trust. Oh, he'd told himself he'd been doing it for Nicki, that he'd had no other choice, but as he flew above the clouds, more alone than he'd ever been in life, he wasn't sure Nicki had been the only one he'd been thinking about. As much as he loved her, having the sole responsibility for a fragile twelve-year-old was an incredible burden, especially for a confirmed bachelor like himself. So had he, as Jennifer had accused, been biding his time, wooing her, simply as a means to an end? Had his desperate need to show her that she could love a child, love Nicki, been not solely for Nicki's sake as he'd thought, but for himself, as well?

He wished to God he knew.

CHAPTER SEVENTEEN

SCHOOLS. SHE'D SAID she was going to look into schools before she bought a house. But she couldn't register Nicki for school. Only *he* could do that. He'd already *done* that. Because Nicki was his. *His.*

The front two legs of Bryan's chair slammed back down to the floor. Damn it. What in the hell was he doing sitting here in his office missing her?

He cleared off his desk. "Jacci!"

"Yeah?" His secretary's head popped inside the door.

"Clear my calendar for the afternoon. I'm leaving for the day." Checking his back pocket for his wallet, he put his sunglasses on and grabbed his keys out of his in tray.

"You finally going after her?"

Bryan looked back at his secretary. "Yeah, you wanna make something of it?"

"Nope. But you might want to comb your hair—it's a mess," she called after him.

Bryan grabbed a comb from the dash of his Jeep, pulled it through his hair and found a rubber band to secure it into a ponytail. For the first time in two weeks he had a reason to look responsible.

He called Jennifer's apartment from his cellular phone as he pulled out onto Peachtree. Nicki was home alone, but Jennifer was on her way home for lunch. That was fine with him. He wanted to see her, too. He rang off without telling Nicki he was coming.

The doorman recognized Bryan and let him upstairs when Bryan explained why he was there, wishing him luck as the elevator closed behind him. Bryan didn't stop to think about needing a little luck. He was on a mission.

Jennifer pulled the door open when he knocked. "Bryan!"

He walked past her and into the apartment, with Lucy jumping at his heels. "Where's Nicki?"

"She's—"

"I'm right here," Nicki said, coming into the living room. She approached him slowly, watching him strangely. But he wasn't going to be deterred. Not anymore. He strode across the room and grabbed her up into a hug that lifted her right off the floor.

"I've missed you, sprite," he whispered as he kissed her on the neck.

Nicki looked at him, nose to nose. "You have?"

How could she doubt it? "I have." He remembered his mission. "I've come to take you home." He set her down, raising his hand to forestall her reply. "Don't bother arguing with me. You're legally still mine, and I'm taking you back where you belong. You're a Chambers whether you want to believe it or not. We raised you, we taught you everything you know, we loved you. *I* love you. Now go get your things. You're coming home." He paused. "Okay?"

Bryan had no idea how much her acquiescence meant to him until she nodded and scampered off. He told himself he'd have taken her even if she'd argued, but it sure eased some of the loneliness of the past two weeks to have her agree to come back to him almost as easily as he'd agreed to let her go in the first place.

He bent down to calm Lucy. "How about you, girl? You ready to come home?" He was surprised how good those words sounded to him. His family was coming home. All of it, he hoped.

He felt Jennifer's gaze on him and he turned, knowing he had yet to fight the toughest part of this battle. Her eyes were dry, but filled with anguish.

"I'm not taking her away from you, Jen. I want you to come with us." She looked so good to him, like a glass of cool water in the middle of the desert.

"I can't."

He should have expected the words, but he hadn't. He'd hoped she'd been as miserable as he had, hoped she'd be as eager as he was for them to be a couple again.

"I want to marry you. I want us to be a family. All three of us."

He couldn't believe it when she shook her head, her eyes flooded with tears. He could have sworn when she'd opened the door to him that her eyes had flashed with relief—and longing.

He strode over to her and pulled her into his arms. It was what he should have done to begin with. What he'd been wanting to do since she'd walked out of his house two weeks before.

She leaned into him, shuddering as she laid her head against his shoulder. Her arms wrapped around his neck, squeezing him against her. Finally. His world was righting itself after spinning out of control for two long weeks.

But then she pushed him away. "I can't go with you, not until I know why you were interested in me in the first place, not until you can tell me that your feelings for me don't have anything to do with my being Nicki's mother."

"You're asking the impossible, Jen. You *are* Nicki's mother. Giving her up, loving her all these years, has made you the woman you are today."

"I asked you this two weeks ago, Bryan," she said, "and I'm going to ask you again. If you didn't have Nicki, would you still be asking me to marry you?"

Bryan's answer was still the same. He honestly didn't know. Now he looked in her eyes, her loyal, trusting, anguished eyes, and said nothing.

She turned away from him. "There's your answer." Her shoulders shook. He knew she was crying.

He reached out and turned her to face him. He had to make her understand. "I'd still care this much, honey. Having Nicki doesn't change the way I feel. It just changes what I do with it. Before Nicki I simply would never have thought to ask you to marry me, at least not right away. But I would've been everything to you a husband should be. I would've been faithful to you."

"But for how long?" she whispered. "Don't you see, Bryan? Marrying you would be like playing the lottery. I may win it all, but chances are, after all the hoopla dies down, after Nicki grows up and doesn't need us anymore, after *you* don't need me anymore, I'll be left empty-handed. You aren't the marrying kind, and I can't get married knowing in the back of my mind that the day may come when you won't be walking in the door at night. Or that someday the phone may ring and it'll be you telling me you're in Fiji or climbing a mountain somewhere. Or just plain on the other side of town, needing your freedom."

She couldn't do this. He'd had it all in the palm of his hand. "Life doesn't have the kind of guarantees you're looking for," he said, swallowing the emotion threatening to choke him.

"I'm not looking for guarantees, Bryan. I only want a fighting chance. I've made enough foolish choices in my life. I can't make another one."

So taking a chance on him was a foolish choice. There didn't seem to be much more to be said. He nodded, shoving his hands into the pockets of his shorts before they could betray him and take her with him against her will.

"You're welcome to Nicki any time you want her," he said.

"Thank you." Her eyes filled with tears. "You'll call me, won't you, if she needs anything? If you, uh, need a woman's advice?"

"Of course. We can work out some kind of visitation, too, where you'll have her on a regular basis. If you want to, that is."

"I'll take her any time. If you feel crowded and need to take off for a day or two, you call me. I'll keep her for you."

"If I take off I'll take her with me, but I mean it about the visits, Jen. You're a part of her life now."

He couldn't believe how civilized they sounded, like some couple after an amicable divorce.

Nicki came back into the living room, carrying the suitcases she'd taken with her. "I left some things here for when I come visit," she said, looking at Bryan. She wouldn't look at Jennifer.

"We were just talking about that. We're going to set up a regular schedule for you to spend time with Jennifer, every other weekend or something, and other times in between, too, if you want."

Nicki nodded, still not looking at her mother.

Jennifer walked over to the girl, pulling her into her arms. "It's okay, Nicki, honey. You belong with your uncle. I've known that all along. I'm just glad I had this time with you, and we'll have lots more time together in the future, too, I promise."

"But I said I wanted to live with you. You were going to buy a house and everything." Nicki's voice was loaded with guilt.

"I know, sweetie, but I also know how much you missed your uncle. And he's right. You *are* a Chambers, through and through, and that's the way it should be."

Nicki pulled away to study her mother's face. "You're not mad at me?"

Jennifer shook her head, smiling through her tears. "Not even the tiniest bit, sweetie. Now, take Lucy back to her yard where she belongs, okay?"

Nicki nodded, smiling through her tears. "Can I call you?" she asked.

"You better."

"Every day?"

"Twice a day if you'd like."

Nicki stared at Jennifer for a long moment, as if weighing her thoughts. "I love you," she finally said, so softly Bryan could hardly hear her.

"I love you, too, Nicki. With all my heart."

And with one last hug between mother and daughter, Nicki was Bryan's again. But he left a vital part of himself behind when he walked away.

Jennifer stood in the doorway, holding back her sobs until she saw the elevator doors close behind them. If only he'd said, even once, that he loved her...

DENNIS CALLED BRYAN at home two days later. "There's been an accident. Jennifer was broadsided—"

"When? Where? How is she?" Bryan asked, his skin cold with dread. She wasn't going to leave him. Not like this.

"They took her to Oldike Memorial, but nobody'll tell me how she's doing. The cop that called just said her car was totaled. I'm on my way to get Tanya and head over to Oldike now."

Her car was totaled. "I'll meet you there," Bryan said, hanging up the phone and grabbing his keys.

"Nicki?" he called, his stomach a sick knot of fear. He had to tell her. As much as he wanted to leave her in blissful ignorance, he couldn't do that to her ever again.

"Yeah?" She was wearing her daisy outfit, and her smile as she came into the room was like a ray of sunshine, warming him.

He took her into his arms, needing to shelter her even as he needed her comfort. "Jennifer's been in a car accident, honey. We don't know how badly she's hurt yet, maybe not badly at all, but I have to go to the hospital where they've taken her. Do you want to come?" he asked.

Nicki's body went limp against him as she absorbed the words. He waited for the sobs he knew were to follow. Damn the Fates that hurt this child so unfairly. She was everything that was good and right.

Why in the hell did she have to keep getting stomped on?

Hold on, Jen. I'm coming.

Thirty seconds passed before he realized Nicki wasn't crying. "Nicki?" he asked. Had she passed out? "Nick, you okay?"

She pulled out of his arms and straightened her shoulders. "I guess." She *was* crying, just not hysterically.

"Do you want me to call Mrs. Baker to come over and stay with you while I go?"

Nicki shook her head and wiped her eyes with the back of her hand. "No. I want to come. And we better hurry so she knows we're there," she said, charging ahead like the Nicki of old.

Bryan wasn't going to question the miracle that had just happened, wasn't going to wonder how or when Nicki's inner strength had returned to her. He was only going to hope there were two miracles in store for him that day.

"Let's go," he said. Jennifer was going to be okay. She had to be okay. Because he finally had her answers. He finally knew why she had to marry him.

HER HEAD HURT. She wished someone would turn off that bright light. And turn down the noise, as well. Couldn't they see she was trying to sleep?

"Shh," she finally said, pushing aside the hand that had just touched her eye. Couldn't a person get any rest around here?

"She's come to!"

The speaker obviously hadn't heard Jennifer's command for silence. "Can't you guys be a little quieter?" she mumbled, trying not to wake herself up.

Her head still hurt too much. She needed to sleep a while longer.

"Ms. Teal? Can you hear me?"

Who was that? Bobby? The mechanic at the Ford store whose son had been hit by a car? "Of course I can hear you," she said, trying not to bite his head off. She tried to open her eyes, as well, but they were too heavy. She'd apologize to him later. If he'd just turn off that damn light ...

He could fix the car later. Couldn't he see she was sleeping?

The voice came again. "Ms. Teal? I'm going to look in your eyes now." Look in her eyes? What on earth for? And why, come to think of it, was she sleeping in a mechanic's bay?

"My head hurts," she said, hoping he could shed some light on the situation for her or at least leave her in peace.

"I imagine it does, ma'am. You've been in an accident and you have quite a shiner where you hit the windshield."

"An accident?" Her mouth felt as cottony as her brain, as she finally forced her eyes open.

She recognized the stethoscope around the doctor's neck immediately, and the IV-drip tube. Fear engulfed her, threatening to put her under again as she tried to sit up.

"Is everyone okay? Nicki? Was she with me?" No. Of course not. Bryan had taken her away two days before.

"Calm down, ma'am." The doctor's hands pushed her gently back down. "You were alone in the car, and you weren't hurt, other than that bump on your head.

You're going to have a doozy of a headache tomorrow, I'm afraid.''

"I have a doozy of a headache now," Jennifer said, wishing she could just go back to sleep. Except that there was a terrible ruckus on the other side of the curtain surrounding her.

"Where is she? This is her daughter here. We have a right to see her."

"Bryan?" she called. This time she succeeded in sitting up. She didn't know why he was there, how he'd known to come, but she'd never wanted to see anyone more in her life.

"Jennifer?" The curtain around her moved, and then he was there, standing beside her bed looking as if he'd been the one in the car accident, not her.

"Your hair's a mess," she said, reaching up to smooth back a loose strand.

"I tried to tell him he should comb it before we came in, but he wouldn't listen."

Jennifer's head swiveled, stars filling her eyes for a second at the sudden movement. "Nicki?"

"Yeah." The girl's voice was a balm for Jennifer's sore head. Nicki came forward and took Jennifer's free hand. The one that Bryan wasn't clutching.

"You should've seen Uncle Bryan. They told us you were okay, but they wouldn't let us see you, so he just pushed past the nurse and came, anyway. It was really cool even if we do get in trouble," Nicki said, smiling.

"You really shouldn't be in here, sir." The doctor spoke for the first time.

"How is she, Doctor? How soon can I take her home?" Bryan asked.

The doctor shrugged. "Now seems like as good a time as any. Just give me a few minutes to get a nurse in here to remove the IV and help her dress."

"You mean she's really all right? There's nothing the matter with her?" Bryan asked, his sharp tone making Jennifer's head hurt all the more.

"Nothing that a couple days' rest won't cure. She's pretty bruised up and she's bound to be sore for a few days. She also suffered a slight concussion, but other than that, she's just fine."

"My car..." Jennifer only just remembered. She'd been driving the Mustang that morning.

Bryan leaned over her again, trailing his finger across her lips. "...is just a car, honey. You've got the real thing now."

SHE'S JUST FINE. She's just fine. Bryan kept repeating the doctor's words to himself while he watched Jennifer sleep later that night. She was lying in his bed, in spite of her protests, and he was keeping an eagle eye on her, waking her every half hour just as the doctor had instructed. Her long amber hair was a riot of tangles around her, a hint of the fire he knew she harbored inside. He didn't know what he would've done if he'd lost her. But he knew what he was going to do now. He was going to marry her. He wasn't going to waste any more time.

"Bryan?"

He jumped up from the chair he'd pulled next to the bed when he heard her voice. "I'm right here, honey," he said, sitting down on the bed beside her. He gently smoothed back the hair matted against her forehead. She had one hell of a bruise there, but no cuts. She'd gotten lucky.

"I'm thirsty," she said, licking her lips, her eyes still closed.

Bryan poured some water from the pitcher on his nightstand and lifted her up as he held it to her lips. She drank half a glass before lying back down with a sigh. "Thanks."

"How's your head?" Bryan had a lot to tell her, but he wanted her coherent when he did so.

"Still hurts," she said, drifting off again. When he was certain she was sleeping soundly, he went back to doze in the chair by the bed.

Bryan kept up his vigil through the night, undressing sometime just before dawn and climbing in beside her. The next time he woke up, she was snuggled against him. He willed his starved body to behave.

She moved, her hip brushing against his groin, and he lost his battle. His body filled with wanting. He was going to have to get up.

"Feels a little dangerous down there," she said.

Bryan froze. Was that laughter he heard in her voice? "Depends on what you consider dangerous," he said, not daring to move.

She lay still against him. "Loving someone who doesn't love you back." She'd spoken so softly he almost missed it.

Very gently, careful of her tender body, he rolled over, holding his weight on his arms as he lay above her, gazing into her troubled eyes. "Then there's no danger here at all, lady, because I love you more than life itself."

She closed her eyes. "You don't have to lie to me, Bryan. I'm ready to give in, anyway. The past two days have been hell."

"You don't have to give in. I do love you. I have for a long time. It just took me a while to trust myself with the feeling. But when Dennis called, when I thought I might never see you again, I was filled with such panic I knew for certain that this feeling I have for you wasn't something that was going to go away in the morning."

Her beautiful hazel eyes widened. "You've loved me for a long time?"

"Probably since the first time I kissed you. You were different, Jen. Instead of looking for ways to escape you, I just kept coming back for more. But you hit a sore spot when you started talking about forever. I didn't know if I could promise it or not. Not because I didn't want to, but because I'd never been able to before."

She smiled, reaching up to brush her fingers against his neck. "So what changed?"

"When faced with the fact that I might never see you again, I realized it didn't matter *why* I'd fallen in love with you, only that I had. I don't know if, in the beginning, I pursued you as a means to relieve some of my responsibility to Nicki. Maybe I did. But there's nothing wrong with that. Being a parent isn't easy. Being a single parent is damn near impossible sometimes. Wanting a partner to share the load is only natural."

"But what about your freedom? How do you know you won't be choking to death on your wedding vows a year from now?"

"I had my freedom, honey, for two whole weeks, and it damned near killed me. Life changes people. It changed me when it took away my family in one swoop of a wind cloud. I suddenly had a whole new perspective, a whole new set of needs that aren't any less valid because they're new. What's around the bend doesn't matter to me anymore. It's what's right here that counts.'' He lowered his head to kiss her, tenderly, reverently.

He could wait until she felt better to make love with her; he was going to have her in his bed for a lifetime. Now was the time for giving her his love with his heart, not his body.

As SHE WAITED for Jennifer and Uncle Bryan to get home, Nicki hummed a tune her mother used to sing to her when she was a little girl. She'd just come in from school and found Jennifer's note. They were due home any minute.

She couldn't believe how happy she was. Jennifer and Uncle Bryan had been married for just over three months, and Nicki didn't feel the least bit disloyal about loving Jennifer anymore. Her mother would be so happy to see Uncle Bryan married she'd be friends with Jennifer just because of that. And she'd be mad at Nicki if she wasn't friends with her, too. Besides, the way Nicki figured it, lots of people had two moms. Like when you got married and got your husband's mom, as well as your own.

"Nick? You home, honey?" she heard Jennifer call as the front door opened.

"I'm in here," she said, plopping down on the living-room couch. Jennifer came in, frowning like she was worried about something.

Uncle Bryan came in behind her. He was grinning from ear to ear.

"Are we?" Nicki asked, holding her breath. She wanted it so bad it hurt to even think about it.

"Yep!" Uncle Bryan said, giving a silly whoop.

Jennifer frowned at him, then crossed to Nicki and sat down beside her. She took one of Nicki's hands in hers, rubbing it gently like she'd done a couple of months before when Nicki had gotten her period for the first time and had such terrible cramps.

"Are you sure you're all right with this, Nicki? I don't want you to feel like we're pushing you out of your place here. You're still our first, and you always will be."

Nicki giggled and hugged Jennifer. "If you knew how badly I've wanted a brother or sister, you wouldn't ask me that," she said. She could hardly believe it. She wasn't going to be an only child anymore. "Besides, the way I figure it, this is just about perfect."

"How's that?" Uncle Bryan asked, coming over to sit with them.

"Well, it'll be my half brother or sister biologically, right?"

"Right."

"And it'll be yours biologically, too, right?" She looked at her uncle.

"Right."

"So that means our blood's finally connected."

Uncle Bryan's face got all tight for a second, like he was going to cry or something, but then he grinned at her just like he had when she'd finally beat him at one of his arcade games. "You're absolutely right, Nick. Our blood's finally connected."

A FEW HOURS LATER Nicki waited for Jennifer to come in to kiss her good-night, butterflies wrestling themselves in her stomach. There was only one thing bothering her about the new baby, and she needed to get it settled.

"Can I ask you something?" she said to Jennifer when she'd straightened from kissing Nicki's cheek.

"Of course, sweetie."

Nicki wasn't sure how to say it without sounding jealous or something. "Well, it's just that, even though I had Mom, you're still my mother, too, right?"

Jennifer sat down on the bed. "Yes."

"Just as much as you'll be the new baby's mother."

"I thought you were okay with that, honey." Jennifer stroked Nicki's cheek with a finger.

"I am. It's just that it doesn't seem right that he or she will get to call you Mom when I just call you Jennifer—like you aren't really related to me or anything."

Jennifer's finger stilled. "I guess we can teach him or her to call me Jennifer, too," she said. But she didn't sound very happy about it.

"Or...I could, maybe, call you Mom—to make it easier," Nicki said, holding her breath.

Jennifer's eyes shimmered with tears as she gathered her daughter into her arms, against her heart where she belonged—and so did Bryan's as he watched from the doorway. Lori's baby had finally made it home again.

NICKI'S NEW BABY SISTER came home from the hospital on Nicki's thirteenth birthday. Bryan didn't know who was the happier of his women as he walked behind them out of the hospital. Nicki was fairly bouncing as she pushed Jennifer's wheelchair, craning her head so as not to lose sight, even for a second, of the baby in Jennifer's arms.

Jennifer's face was radiant as she glanced back at him. Bryan could only imagine the emotions surging through her as she finally left the hospital with her babies—her new one, and her firstborn.

"Do you have it?" she asked him.

"I thought we'd wait until we got home." His arms were full of flowers.

"No. It has to be here. Nick, stop a minute, would you, honey?"

Nicki rolled her eyes at Bryan, a grin on her face. "I thought she was supposed to quit being weird after the baby was born."

Bryan grinned back, then glanced at his wife. Her lovely eyes were filled with sudden tension.

He set the pots of flowers down and reached into his pocket for the jeweler's box Jennifer had given him before she'd gone into labor. "It's right here, honey."

Jennifer took the box, handing him the baby, and pulled Nicki onto her lap.

"This is for you, love." She gave Nicki the box.

Nicki looked at the box and then up at Bryan.

"Go ahead, sprite."

Slowly Nicki opened the box, her hands shaking when she saw the tiny gold baby ring nestled there on a shiny gold chain. It wasn't identical to the one she'd lost, but it was close. Jennifer had spent months looking for just the right one.

Bryan put his free hand on her shoulder. "It's beautiful, Nick."

Nicki picked up the ring and turned it over, reading the inscription engraved on the inside as tears dripped down her cheeks.

"Thanks, Mom," she said, throwing her arms around Jennifer.

Jennifer squeezed her daughter close and then took the chain and fastened it around Nicki's neck. "Don't take this one off even to swim," she said through her tears.

The ring settled against Nicki's throat, back where it belonged, and when Nicki smiled, Bryan knew that his family, wherever they were, were smiling with her.

The inscription read "Nicki and Lori, forever."

**UNLOCK THE DOOR TO GREAT ROMANCE
AT BRIDE'S BAY RESORT**

Join Harlequin's new across-the-lines series, set
in an exclusive hotel on an island off the coast of
South Carolina.

Seven of your favorite authors will bring you exciting stories
about fascinating heroes and heroines discovering love at
Bride's Bay Resort.

Look for these fabulous stories coming to a store near you
beginning in January 1996.

Harlequin American Romance #613 in January
Matchmaking Baby by Cathy Gillen Thacker

Harlequin Presents #1794 in February
Indiscretions by Robyn Donald

Harlequin Intrigue #362 in March
Love and Lies by Dawn Stewardson

Harlequin Romance #3404 in April
Make Believe Engagement by Day Leclaire

Harlequin Temptation #588 in May
Stranger in the Night by Roseanne Williams

Harlequin Superromance #695 in June
Married to a Stranger by Connie Bennett

Harlequin Historicals #324 in July
Dulcie's Gift by Ruth Langan

Visit Bride's Bay Resort each month wherever
Harlequin books are sold.

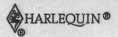

HARLEQUIN SUPERROMANCE®

If you've always felt there's something special about a
man raising a family on his own...
You won't want to miss Harlequin Superromance's
touching series

**FAMILY
MAN**

He's sexy, he's single...and he's a father!
Can any woman resist?

HIS RUNAWAY SON
by Dee Holmes

Detective Burke Wheeler's son is in trouble.
Now he's run away, and Burke and his ex-wife,
Abby, have to work together to find him. Join the
search in this exciting, emotional love story.
Available in July.

Be sure to watch for upcoming FAMILY MAN titles.
Fall in love with our sexy fathers, each determined to do
the best he can for his kids.

Look for them wherever Harlequin books are sold.

HARLEQUIN SUPERROMANCE®

Come West with us!

In Superromance's series of Western romances you can visit a ranch—and fall in love with a rancher!

In July watch for

She Caught the Sheriff by Anne Marie Duquette

Let us take you to the Silver Dollar Ranch, near Tombstone, Arizona.

Rancher Wyatt Bodine is also the town sheriff. But he's never had a case like this before! Someone's left a hundred-year-old skeleton in Boot Hill Cemetery— practically at the feet of visiting forensic investigator Caro Hartlan. Needless to say, Caro offers to help the handsome sheriff find out "who done it"—and why!

Look for upcoming HOME ON THE RANCH titles wherever Harlequin books are sold.

HOTR-7